MILKING WITH THE MINOTAUR

A MINNETAUR DAIRY PREQUEL

CASSANDRA MEDCALF

LOVE OUT LOUD PRESS, LLC

DEDICATION

For everyone who's supported my weird, kinky monster romances:
stay milky

And a special thank you to everyone who donated on Kickstarter to
make this book a possibility, but especially:
B. Cyrus Young
Ari the Wandering Bard
Jess T
Melissa
Angeles Sanchez
Kaiidth
Amanda
Chelsie Meade
Jess Chandler

Hey, you. Thanks for picking up this minotaur romance. I bet you saw the cover and you were like, "Aw! Look at that adorable little human/minotaur family. They have a baby! I bet this is going to be a sweet, cozy little book about farming and love that will give me the warm fuzzies and distract me from all the horrors of the world!"

And you know what? You're about 90% right. This *is* a cozy little book. It *is* about found family, and it totally will give you the warm fuzzies! I'm all about that life.

But in addition to that, there's some content that might not be for all readers. Please remember as you read that this is a work of fiction. Art and stories are safe spaces where humanity can explore their deepest, darkest, weirdest fantasies. But that might mean that a few of the topics included in this book might turn you off. So I've provided this handy list of included content to peruse at your discretion.

<u>Triggers and Tropes:</u>
    Pregnancy/Childbirth
    Childhood trauma, including SA (mentioned/implied)
    Family separation
    Adoption
    The foster care system
    Single motherhood
    Termination of pregnancy (mention)
    Death during childbirth (mention)
    Breastfeeding & related struggles
    Tractor abuse
    Light bondage
    Roleplay
    Tails
    Horns
    Big ol' flared dicks
    Internalized minotaurphobia
    Cum that tastes like milk
    Knotting
    Hucow kink
    ANR/Breastfeeding kink
    Discussion around consent
    Pegging (mention)
    Bestiality (mention? And also, like, the MMC is a minotaur, so…)
    Class struggles
    Unconventional family structures
    Creative carpentry
    Zeus's misogynistic ass
    Gods that really couldn't give a shit
    Gods that give maybe like, a little bit of a shit (implied)
    90's Girl Power vibes, and
    Glitter bombs

I'd also like to mention as a disclaimer: in general, I believe that people who foster orphaned children are some of the best examples of humanity. Betsy's experiences are *fictional*, and are not an accurate representation or indicative of my feelings toward foster parents, social workers, or government assistance programs.

If you read through this book and discover something that should be on this list, please reach out to me at cassandra@cassandramedcalf.com.

Godspeed!

CHAPTER 1

BETSY

The look on Petra's face was indignant.

"That good-for-nothing, no-good, dirty cheating basta–... assh–... *scoundrel!*"

Despite everything: the swollen ankles, the lack of sleep, the never-ending morning sickness, and the fact that my boyfriend up and abandoned me with his unborn child, I couldn't help but laugh.

Petra was my foster sister, my best friend in the whole world, and Minnesota nice through and through. We'd both been through the wringer growing up, but she'd never let it get her down. And to her credit, her positive attitude and manners had gotten her farther than me in life. Whereas I was twenty-three, single, and pregnant, she was working her way through school to become a teacher. And while I *loved* a good cuss word, I had never once in our nineteen-year friendship heard her curse.

Although I had to admit: if she were ever going to, today would be a great day for it.

I slumped in my vinyl seat, stuffing a french fry into my mouth. The plastic farted beneath me. "You know, you can say bastard, Petra. Or asshole, even. Shoot, why not throw in manwhore while we're at it? Every man in my life is a son-of-a-bitch."

"Betsy! We're at a *Wendy's.*"

She said the name of the fast-food chain as if it were the sacred resting place of Mary, mother of Jesus, herself. I braced myself for a lightning strike, but alas: we were both still here.

"Forgive me, Wendy's. I have sinned." I bowed my head, rubbing my eyes with my fingers.

Six months ago, I'd hopped on the train to Chicago for my first ever true vacation. I'd bought tickets to Lollapalooza and was determined to enjoy every second of it. A much-needed break from seven years of pinching pennies and double-shifts at the sex shop.

Maybe I'd indulged a little more than I should have. But could you blame me? I'd needed a break.

I'd been hustling since I was sixteen when I'd been emancipated. I'd escaped from my fourth and worst home, with nothing but the clothes on my back and a hundred dollars I stole out of my sleazy foster dad's underwear drawer. Waited on the steps of the courthouse in the early morning 'til the doors opened.

The first thing I did after the judge set me free was find Petra.

Thankfully, she'd been placed in a better home than me, albeit a pretty crowded one. They didn't have any extra room, but I'd been able to couch surf with a guy from her high school. Found my job working as a cashier at an adult toy store in downtown Minneapolis. Hopped from couch to bed for a couple months until I saved up enough to put a deposit on my own shitty apartment.

Two weeks was about the longest any of my relationships lasted in those days. The job, though, I'd managed to keep for over seven years. Until today. According to my boss, my baby bump was now big enough that it was "turning off the customers.".

Yep. A bunch of sons of bitches.

I was gonna miss the steady gig at the sex shop. As frustrating and weird as it could be at times, there'd been plenty of overtime available. I'd learned a lot about the world. Plus, combined with Petra's income from the convenience store, the two of us were able to earn enough to split a two-bedroom apartment within biking distance of the important stuff.

But it was a constant grind. Living with Petra was by far the best situation I'd ever had, don't get me wrong. But after a few years, I'd gotten an itch for something more than just getting by. Something to look forward to, you know?

So I'd saved up enough cash to take a trip. Somewhere for *me*, where I could truly enjoy myself. And I had. Going to Lollapalooza had been a literal dream.

Until the consequences caught up with me.

I crossed my arms over my big belly.

"You deserve better than him, anyway." Petra reached awkwardly over the two Biggie-sized fries and Frosties on the table to pat my elbow. "I knew he was trouble the day you brought him home. *Never* trust a man you meet at a music festival."

Oh, but I'd wanted to.

We'd met in the line for the porta potties. He'd given me a hit of his joint, and then we'd returned to the mainstage high out of our minds to rock out to Beck and the Old 97's. He'd invited me back to his tent after that, and he'd blown my fucking mind.

Not just because he had an incredibly talented tongue—though that was certainly part of it.

No. What had really changed my life that night was when

he let his glamour fall as we'd climaxed together, and I'd realized that I had just had sex with an honest-to-god *god.*

And not just any god. Zeus.

Yeah. *That* Zeus.

I hadn't told Petra that tasty little tidbit. Probably because, deep down, I always knew that he'd never stick around. I might have dropped out of high school, but I remembered enough from ninth grade English class to remember the stories about him. Not even the myths painted Zeus as the loyal type.

But what can I say?

When you're swept off your feet by a hunky, lightning-wielding deity, it makes you start to engage in a little magical thinking. Thinking like: maybe this is karma for all the shit I've endured. Maybe I was meant for something greater all along.

Maybe this time, the king of Olympus—the one who's famous for cheating on his immortally beautiful, powerful goddess wife and knocking up mortals whenever the fancy strikes him—might actually stick around and help me raise his little Hercules.

I guess you could say I was lucky that he even stuck around as long as he did. Even if it had given me false hope.

"Hello? He-*llooooo?* Earth to Betsy!"

A light slap on my forehead alerted me to the fact that Petra had clearly been trying to talk to me for a few minutes while I'd been zoning out in my own little world.

"Sorry," I said, straightening in my seat. "Spaced out again, huh?"

"Even worse than usual," she agreed, nodding as she swiped a floppy french fry through her chocolate shake. "Do you think it's the hormones?"

"Nah. I think I'm just broken," I said, grabbing my own fry to enjoy my sweet-and-salty craving.

Some women craved pickles and ice cream, some egg rolls and chow mein, but me?

It'd been milkshakes and french fries since day one with this baby.

Thankfully, Petra had the day off today, from work *and* school. When I'd called her in tears after I'd been fired, and all of my attempts to reach Zeus had failed, she ran right over.

Which was good. Because today of all days, I really needed my best friend.

"Petra. What am I going to do?"

If I wasn't so far along, I'd have options. But twenty weeks was in the rearview now.

And adoption was out of the question. After everything I'd been through as a kid? Dropped on the courthouse's stoop when my junkie parents decided they didn't want me? Abandoned to the system?

There was no way I'd ever put any kid, but especially not *my* kid, through what I'd been through.

Nope. This baby wasn't going into the system. He was stuck with me.

And we were totally, 100% screwed because of it.

I sighed. "I've got no money coming in, no boyfriend or husband, and a baby on the way."

"You've got me."

I looked up, blinking back the tears that were finally threatening to spill over, now that Zeus's betrayal was sinking in. Staring into my eyes with so much genuine love and kindness it physically hurt, Petra gave me a watery smile.

She squeezed my arm. "It's the 90's, girlfriend! You're a smart, beautiful, modern woman with a healthy baby boy on the way. We've got girl power on our side. You don't need a man to have it all."

I sniffed. "I'd like one, though."

"Well, sure, yeah, who wouldn't? That's not the point. The point is," she leaned in and ripped my hand from my face, lacing her fingers with mine and squeezing hard, "you're gonna be okay. You're baby's going to be okay. Because *we're* going to make it okay. We've come this far, haven't we?"

Maybe she had a point. Against all odds, she and I had managed to get ourselves a better life. We'd paid our rent and our bills. Leaned on each other through break-ups and bad days. Pulled ourselves up by our bootstraps.

She was even studying to be a teacher, for Wendy's sake.

And if she believed in me, then I could try to believe her.

I grabbed her hand and squeezed back. "You're right, Petra. We can do this. We can give this little guy a better chance than you or me ever had."

"Darn right!"

For a while, I thought maybe that was enough. That maybe we *would* be okay.

Until three months later when my water broke and I gave birth to an honest-to-gods *minotaur* baby.

CHAPTER 2

FELIX

I loved spring.

The loamy scent of the soil waking up. The calm that filtered through the chickens when they finally emerged from their heated coop to stretch their wings out in the sunlight and peck at the emerging worms. Even the snow melt that made the grounds of my modest farmstead a soupy mess was a welcome sight after the long, cold winter.

This morning, the damp chill from a lingering rainstorm had finally lifted, and as I embarked out onto the property to get to my many chores, a rainbow arced proudly across the wide, blue sky.

What a start to the day!

I was riding my tractor down the rows of my field, spreading fertilizer into the freshly plowed dirt when the engine made a terrifying *pop*. My calm instantly evaporated, and I shifted my foot off the accelerator and let out the clutch of the antique machine, letting it stall to a stop as I hopped down to check to see what's wrong.

My hooves sank into the freshly turned earth as I walked

around the giant metal frame, only to be greeted not by a smoking engine, but–

"Felix. Long time, no see."

A slender woman with curly strawberry-blonde hair stood before me, golden wings settling behind her as she found her balance on the loose ground. I scowled at her strappy sandals and loose-fitting chiton wrapped with gold and turquoise ribbons.

My snout wrinkled with a huffy snort. "Iris."

"You seem to be taking well to your exile."

"I like my privacy."

"Then this little plot in the middle of nowhere seems perfect for you." Her eyes squinted with a patronizing smile. A smile which I didn't return.

"I was having a good day, Iris."

"Was? What happened?"

"*You.*" I shook my head and crossed my flannel-covered arms over my chest, glaring down my nose. If it weren't for her wings, I'd have towered over her. She was always a little on the short side for a god. "What are you doing here? Haven't I suffered enough at the hands of the court of Olympus?"

"Felix," she began with a cluck of her tongue. "Come now. We went over this. The terms of your exile were very clear. You get to keep your life on earth, *far away from humans,* to serve out your sentence, provided you answer the call of the gods when needed."

"What could the gods possibly need from me? I thought, after millennia in Hades, they were done serving me more punishments. I grow their grain. What more do they need?"

"Felix, you killed Hephaestus's daughter. Surely you didn't think they'd just let you dilly dally in corn fields all day?"

"I thought I'd paid my penance." Between the guilt I felt every day, and the centuries I'd toiled in Tartarus.

"Hera feels differently." The goddess waved her hands, and a clipboard appeared in her pale arms.

I knew if I continued to argue with her, it would only make me angrier. These gods and their ever-changing rules. They played with the lives of demigods and mortals as if it was nothing to them, discounting the feelings of everyone but themselves.

Iris's cold eyes scanned the barren field around her, wrinkling her nose at the scent of fertilizer as it warmed in the sun.

"What do they want?" I grunted at last, ready for her to leave so I could get on with my chores.

"There is a woman not far from here. A consort of Zeus. She is in need of assistance."

"A woman?" Of all the things for her to say, that was the furthest from my mind. The whole reason I was exiled to begin with was because I was fraternizing with a woman I was not supposed to. The most explicit term of my sentence was to stay far away from any humanoid woman, no matter how disconnected from the gods she may seem. "You're sending me to assist a woman?"

A consort of Zeus, no less. Surely this was some kind of cruel joke? A test of some sort?

"I know. But there's a complication, and unfortunately it demands someone of your particular… skillset."

I looked around us, searching for whatever she could mean. "A farmer?"

"A minotaur."

I narrowed my eyes. "I swear to Hades, if this is a running with the bulls joke–"

"The woman had a baby. A… half-bull baby. A baby like you."

I gaped at her. For a long moment, neither of us spoke. Eventually, she broke eye contact, shifting uncomfortably and pulling at her tunic, before shuffling the papers on her pointless clipboard.

When I felt like my brain cells were working again, I broke the silence.

"Let me get this straight. Zeus comes to earth and impregnates a human woman, and nine months later, she births a minotaur?"

She pursed her lips. "It appears so."

I barked out a laugh, tears stinging the backs of my eyes. "Oh, that is rich! The high king's swimmers getting a little rusty there from the cage Hera keeps on his thunderous balls?"

Iris glanced around nervously, as if afraid someone might overhear. "You stop that! Don't you dare say such things about the king and queen!"

"They deserve it," I quipped through clenched teeth—my amusement flicking to vengeance-fueled rage in a heartbeat. "I hope Zeus feels the fool. He deserves to. He's spread nothing but pain and chaos with his seed on this forsaken planet. Why should I care if his son is an abomination? What, is he embarrassed? Or is this one too difficult to explain away to Hera?"

"Hera's the reason I'm here, actually."

I rolled my eyes. "Of course she is. Heaven forbid she learn–"

"She *knows*." The goddess scowled at me, and I frowned in confusion. "This isn't about Zeus, or Hera. This is about the woman."

"The woman," I deadpanned. "Since when do the gods care about mortal women who aren't their own spawn?"

Iris sighed. "It was not an easy birth. Were it not for Hera's interference, the human and the baby would have died."

My frown deepened. "I'm sorry to hear that."

And I was. I always thought it cruel how much mortal women suffered to bring life into this world. Why was something so miraculous, so necessary to the survival of the species, so painful? So deadly?

But deeper, another emotion stirred. One I was too ashamed to even acknowledge.

Stupid. Do not seek to understand why the gods behave as they do. It will only make you angrier.

"That's not all," Iris continued, cutting into my thoughts. "The human's body is not recovering from the pregnancy as it should, even with Hera's influence. She's healed by mortal standards, but the child... he requires more from her than she can provide. He is needy. She needs help."

"How could I possibly help her?"

"First of all, she needs a place to stay. Somewhere far from prying eyes."

My hackles raised. I crossed my arms emphatically, shaking my head. "No. No! Absolutely not. This is *my* farm, my *oasis.* You can't possibly–"

"This is your *punishment.* I'll remind you, Felix, the gods granted you this farm as a mercy. They could have simply ended your life and called it a day!"

I threw up my hands. "But then who would help them with their minotaur bastards?"

"Glad you agree!" Before I could respond, Iris spun the clipboard in her hands and shoved it into my chest, hard enough to push the air from my lungs. "Here's your instructions. She will be arriving later today, so make sure you have a room made up for her and a crib for the baby. I trust you have everything you need!"

Still gasping to catch my breath, I couldn't even form my lips around a protest before her wings flapped once, twice, and she launched into the sky. The rainbow disappeared with her ascent. Behind me, the tractor jolted back to life, tutt-tutting happily as if nothing had ever happened.

But something did happen. Something with the power to cast my peaceful exile into a living Hades.

Fuck the gods.

CHAPTER 3

BETSY

I rubbed my eyes, red and itchy from too little sleep. Then I peeked out the curtains on our second-story window to watch the road again.

I had my baby in my arms. My adorable, *impossible* baby.

And that baby was the reason I was waiting for a mysterious car to come take me away.

"No. *No.* Absolutely not, Bets. You *just* gave birth. I'm not letting you do this!" Petra stomped her foot to emphasize her cries as a modest, unmarked car pulled up to the curb. I reached for the small suitcase I'd packed this morning.

I was gonna miss this place. Petra and I shared the second floor of a little two-apartment craftsman house on a fairly quiet street in Minneapolis—two blocks from the main road of the neighborhood with our favorite pizza shop, record store, and late-night video rental place. How many times had I stopped by after second shift to rent a cheesy horror flick? How many nights had Petra and I stayed up late eating a vegetarian pie and listening to bargain-bin cassettes while we flicked through outdated magazines?

"What choice do I have, Petra?" I gestured with the strategically-wrapped baby in my arms.

Since he was technically the son of Zeus, I'd decided to name him Apollo. A knit cap covered the nubs of his horns on his head, a wide-rimmed pacifier obscured his definitely-not-human snout, and the blanket he was swaddled in thankfully hid his furry backside and hooves.

Hooves!

Every time I looked at him, I was reminded of how much of a miracle he was. And not in the way that every new mother thought her child was a miracle. Apollo was something wholly magical and impossible, and somehow, he'd come out of *me*.

She was still in denial. "The nurses at the hospital can help–"

"The nurses at the hospital had their memories wiped by the literal goddess of rainbows, Petra!"

She couldn't meet my eyes as she fidgeted through her response.

"I don't know what you're talking about. He's just a little… hairy, that's all."

Her entire face, neck, and chest flushed a guilty red as she stuttered out the lie. Truth be told, I wasn't entirely convinced that the goddess hadn't messed a little bit with our memories, too. Neither of us were entirely clear on what had gone down in the hospital five days ago.

I remembered my water breaking, and the lancing pain that felt like it was going to split me in half when things started moving. Petra and I had taken the bus to the hospital when my contractions were twenty minutes apart. But something was wrong. There were complications. The doctor and nurses had started whispering after Apollo crowned, hiding behind their curtain.

That was when the goddess appeared.

Everything was fuzzy after that. All I knew was when I came to, the doctors were gone, I had a minotaur baby in my arms, and Petra was blinking between me and the goddess in disbelief.

Apparently, Hera herself had shown up during labor. She'd wiped the hospital staff's memories, kicked them all out of the room, and gotten me through childbirth. Then she'd done some crazy healing magic on me, handed me my baby, and disappeared. She left Iris, the goddess of rainbows, to handle the lingering details.

I'd been dreading six weeks of diapers and hemorrhoid pillows, but Hera had patched my pussy up as good as new. The fact that I could go to the bathroom without pain and I didn't have to worry about infection down there after everything I'd gone through was a blessing, to be sure. But despite the goddess of childbirth herself healing me, my body hadn't completely adjusted to being a new mom.

There was one thing in particular that I was struggling with. And it broke my heart every time I looked at Apollo's chubby little face.

I shook my head. "Trust me, girl. I hate this as much as you do. The last thing I want to do is get dragged to another home. But what choice do I have? The goddess said he could help."

"Please, Betsy, I'm begging you. There has to be another way." Her eyes were wide, the whites stark against her dark skin. It broke my heart to see how much pain I was causing. I knew this was bringing up all sorts of memories for her, just like it was for me. Being split up again, one of us getting picked up by some mysterious car to take us away to a new home while the other was left behind. "You can't just climb into the back of a stranger's car because some toga-wearing supermodel told you it would fix your boobs!"

Apollo squirmed and I shushed at him, in what I hoped was a soothing manner.

But who was I trying to fool? I was a wreck: completely ill-equipped to *sooth* anyone. Not my son. Not Petra.

And yet here I was, trying to assure my best friend that I would be fine while I was freaking out on the inside. Apollo was bound to start wailing any minute.

He was hungry. I knew he was—he was *always* hungry.

And I couldn't make enough milk to feed him.

We'd tried cow's milk, but he'd stuck up his nose at that, crying and crying and crying for hours until I gave up trying to force it. We'd tried to give him formula, too, but he refused to drink any. He literally batted the bottle away whenever we brought it to his lips, before squirming and kicking and nuzzling against me.

If I doubted his holy heritage before, there was no denying it now. He was strong enough to rip his arms out of his swaddle and smack a bottle clear across the room whenever it came near him.

My nipples ached, my breasts were sore as hell, and I'd only managed to squeeze about four ounces worth of milk out since last night. Maybe for a human baby, it would be enough, but for my little minotaur?

He was insatiable.

"Even if I *could* produce enough for a regular baby, no nurse is going to be able to help me with Apollo. I don't need a goddess to tell me that. I'm pretty sure they don't cover 'how to raise your new minotaur baby' in medical school." I sighed, holding back tears. I didn't like this any more than Petra did, but I didn't feel like I had a choice. "He's got *horns*, Petra. He's covered in *fur*. I can't just bring him along to a lactation clinic. I need to get out of the city—somewhere remote, safe, where no one's going to be poking around and figuring out what he is."

"But... but what about you?" Tears shone in her eyes as Petra grabbed my shoulders. "Betsy, you don't *know* anyone where they're taking you. You don't even know if it's safe. You won't have anyone there for you."

I knew what she was saying, without saying it.

You won't have me.

Her eyes shone. "Girl, the last time I let you out of my sight, you got knocked up by *Zeus.* What'll happen if I let you get in that car with your baby, and they take you somewhere where I can't look out for you?"

And that was when the dam broke. Her voice broke on a sob, and neither of us could hold it in any longer.

I WAS LOSING SO MUCH ALREADY. I really didn't want to lose her, too.

Tears flowed in wet paths down my cheeks unhindered, and I couldn't wipe them away without jostling Apollo. I didn't want him to start crying again, not when this was the last conversation I'd have with Petra for a long time.

I wasn't ready for any of this. I hadn't slept since before I went into labor. I was so tired I could barely think straight, and now the tears were blurring my vision and blocking my view of the one person who'd always been there for me.

Outside, a horn blared.

"I'm so sorry, Petra," I blubbered. She was crying, too. We were a complete mess. "But I have to do something. I'm the only person he has."

"I'm the only person *you* have," she whispered. "I feel like *I* have to do something, too."

"You could write to me?" It was the only thing I could think to say. Whenever the two of us had been placed in separate homes, we'd write each other letters. We couldn't always mail them—stamps weren't always in great supply—

but we'd exchange them the next time we were reunited. "And I'll write to you?"

I attempted a smile.

She sniffled, brushing me off—but then she seemed to remember something. Her fingers squeezed my shoulder. "Hold that thought!"

She sprinted to her bedroom. Meanwhile, the driver in the car outside honked again.

"Petra, I need to–"

"Just wait a few more seconds! I swear it's around here somewhere... ah ha!"

A moment later, she bounded back into the front hall, carrying a box in her hands. I didn't get a good look at it before she snuck behind me and stuffed it into my backpack.

"What are you doing?" I asked, loudly at first before decrescendoing into a hiss as I remembered the half-sleeping baby in my arms.

"It's a stationary set. And a whole book of stamps. So you *can* actually write to me and let me know if you're not being treated well. And I'll write back! For real this time!" The *zwhip* of the zipper pulled closed behind me, and she reappeared in front of me, cheeks still ruddy from tears. "It'll be like summer camp."

I sniffled. "We never went to summer camp."

"Well, I'm going to think of this as you finally getting your chance to go," she said, attempting a grin. She almost succeeded. "Who knows? Maybe you'll even learn to make lanyards."

Her last word ended in a choke. I tried to respond, but she pulled me into a bone-crushing hug before I could, squishing Apollo between us. She murmured into my ear, "be safe. Please. And if anyone hurts you, get the h-e-double hockeysticks outta there as fast as you can, you hear me? Get to a payphone, call me, and I'm there. I'll find a way to get you home."

We pulled back, and I nodded awkwardly. I was never good at goodbyes. I steeled myself. "If I'm gone for longer than a few weeks... you should get another roommate."

"And replace you?" She looked at me like I was nuts. "Never!"

"But rent–"

She waved me off. "I've got enough saved up for a month or two. Don't worry about me. You worry about *you*. And send me your address. Don't forget."

"Okay," I whispered, and despite everything, I smiled, too. She was trying so hard to look on the bright side; matching her energy was the least I could do.

The car honked a third time, and leaned on it. We were out of time. I hoisted Apollo and my backpack into more comfortable positions before bending down to pick up the suitcase.

I took in my best friend's face, eyes darting between hers. Memorizing her. "I love you, Petra."

"I love you too, Betsy. You're gonna be okay. *Both* of you." For the first time, she bent down and gave my little monster a kiss on the head. Then she leaned her forehead against him. "And you, little man. You be good to your mama. She's giving up a whole lot to keep you fed and watered. Understand?"

He didn't respond, but he also didn't cry. I was going to take that as a win. She met my eyes, squeezed my shoulder again, and I nodded.

"Bye, babe. Take care of this place, ya hear?" I crooked up the corner of my lips.

She gave a thumbs up, her answering grin just barely reaching her eyes. "You got it, dude."

And with that, I took my few belongings and my baby, and walked out the door.

CHAPTER 4

FELIX

The day my new human arrived, I couldn't bring myself to wait at the house for her. Iris obviously didn't care that May was one of my busiest months on the farm, but I still did. I had chores to do and fields to plant, and I wasn't going to let the arrival of some dumb human mess with my schedule.

It wasn't my fault that she let herself get knocked up by Zeus. Why should I have to give up my lifestyle to care for the consequences? It made no sense.

I dressed in my overalls and kerchief like I would any other day, grabbing my wide-brimmed straw hat on the way out the door to protect my ears and snout from the bright sun. It was a beautiful day, and the ground was now dry enough to run the equipment. The large burlap bags of seed sat ready in the corner of the big red barn, and I carried them over to the tractor, slitting the top of the bag with my knife before hauling it over my shoulder.

I poured the dried corn kernels into the seed drill attachment, preparing to get to planting as soon as I could. But before I could climb into the seat, another blasted rainbow appeared just outside the wide barn doors.

"Felix! What are you doing?" Iris asked, slipping down the fractaled beam of light like a playground slide. "Betsy's going to be here any minute."

"Don't you know how to knock?"

She looked even more ridiculous in here than she did outside, dressed in her white flowy chiton amidst the rusted antique tools and broken straw covering the ground. The farm I now called home had been abandoned decades ago during the Great Depression, and it only functioned now because of the long hours of manual labor I'd poured into rebuilding it.

It was modest by all standards. The house was barely large enough for me, with one bedroom and one bathroom, a small kitchen and a living room that barely fit a couch and an old, boxy television I'd rescued from a junkyard. I kept it clean, but that didn't mean I was up for entertaining guests. The very notion that my property could tolerate any more bodies was laughable at best. It barely fit mine. I still didn't believe this wasn't some ill-plotted prank.

Yet, Iris was still here. Glaring at me and tapping her nails at that godsforsaken clipboard of hers—the one I *thought* I'd thrown away after getting two sentences into her mission description. "Stop your grumbling and meet her at the end of the driveway like a gentleman."

My chest rumbled, and I had to consciously take a deep breath to keep my temper from flaring. My hands gripped the rim of the feed-box so tight I could feel the metal bending beneath them, but I didn't care.

Don't let them see you sweat.

"In case you haven't noticed, Iris, I'm not a gentleman. I'm a monster." I bared my teeth, letting my flat molars grind together and my nostrils flare as I grimaced at her.

"Oh, please. You're a teddy bear with horns. You don't even have fangs." She smirked, eyeing my body up and down as if she were assessing me. "You don't even eat *meat*."

"I didn't realize I had to be a cannibal to be dangerous."

She rolled her eyes. "Regardless, it's time to meet your ward. Now wash up and—Felix? Felix! You listen to me! I'm not going to ask twi-"

But the rest of her sentence was drowned out with the roar of diesel as I fired up the tractor and drove away.

It was a coincidence that the car arrived at the edge of the driveway just as I was seeding that corner of the field. It came to a halt at the mailbox, and one of the gods' minion automatons climbed out of the drivers' seat. It opened the back door of the vehicle, then bumbled away to get inside the trunk.

I tried to accelerate down the row before the human could see me, but then her legs swung out from the seat.

My hoof slipped off the pedal the second my eyes traveled up from her faded canvas sneakers to the bare ankle peeking from the ripped cuffs of her jeans. The tractor stalled. I cursed, jamming in the clutch and turning at the key, but the engine only sputtered before kicking off into silence.

Silence that only served to highlight the way my breath hitched as the rest of her body appeared.

She was not, as I'd expected, a pale blonde waif of a woman I imagined to be Zeus's type. No, this was a sturdier human—still pale by their standards, but with pink cheeks that bloomed red as she took in the dusty horizon. Her thick waist was cinched with a wide belt, half-hidden beneath a loose flannel shirt she wore unbuttoned over a dark tank top that scooped low, showing off a line of cleavage between her amble bosoms. Thick, dark hair that matched her strong brows tumbled over her shoulders, with broken wisps that curled about her ears.

I was struck dumb.

She was *beautiful*.

But my stupor was broken immediately by the cries of a babe as the automaton reached into the other side of the car and unloosed the child from his carseat. He was large for a baby, too large to be merely a few days of age, and I realized in that moment just how devastating its birth could have been to this woman, had Hera not intervened.

I was suddenly very grateful she had.

An expression of pure exhaustion flitted over the woman's face at the sound of his cries, but was quickly replaced by careworn determination as she stood and reached for the babe from the automaton's arms. It was then that I saw the babe's face, darker in complexion than the woman, due to the short coat of reddish-brown peach fuzz that covered its body, with a large snout that instantly identified it as more monster than man.

She cradled the creature against her breast, wincing at the volume of its cries—which were lower in pitch than a human baby's would be. The sound tugged at my heartstrings, as an emotion completely unexpected rose within my chest.

The need to protect.

Damn you, Iris. Damn Hera. Damn all those meddling Olympians.

"You've arrived," I announced, wholly unnecessarily. Her eyes darted to me, and I cleared my throat. "Do you have luggage?"

"I–" she began, only to be cut off by her driver dropping a small suitcase and a backpack beside her feet without a word. It then strode back around the car, got in, and took off, leaving her alone in the dirt with her meager belongings. She turned back to me, shading her eyes in the bright sunlight. "Just these."

She shifted the babe to her other hip. It continued to wail.

"Just that?"

I blinked at her in disbelief. This woman was truly the furthest thing from whatever expectations I had of a lover of Zeus. It was almost enough to make me believe I may have something in common with the god.

Almost.

She nodded, bouncing the babe in an attempt to ease its cries, but I suspected it was a futile gesture. He was hungry and, according to Iris's clipboard, this young mother wasn't able to produce enough to feed him from her breast.

The thought made me blush, as my eyes darted quickly to her chest before I schooled them back to the ground. They were large enough, certainly, so that was not the issue. Perhaps better nutrition would be the answer?

I felt wholly unqualified to help her with her predicament. Aside from sharing a species with her son, who was technically my cousin, once or twice removed, I had no advantage over this woman to provide for him. Why was I being tasked with this, again?

And why didn't it seem to matter to me anymore, now that I'd seen her?

I jumped down from the tractor and began unhooking the seed drill. The whole time, the woman eyed me curiously, shifting her head to make out my face below the sunhat. Despite my explicit assessment of her appearance, she'd yet to truly observe mine—the sun shone bright behind me, and the brim of my hat cast my face in shadow.

That changed when I walked past her to grab her suitcase and strap it to the fender above the massive tires.

"Are you–"

I know she tried to hide it. Gods know, she came close. But when I turned to face her as she spoke, the fear that widened her eyes and stopped her breath short stabbed my chest like a knife. She instantly averted her gaze, refocusing on the babe, and I watched as her expression morphed to understanding when she glanced between the two of us.

"You're like him," she whispered. "You're…"

"A minotaur. Yes."

She scanned me then, and I almost appreciated the way she didn't hide her fascination as she took in every detail. I towered over her, and the size difference alone would have been enough to terrify a lesser woman. But aside from that initial glimpse, I didn't sense any terror from her. Anxiety, perhaps. But mostly… curiosity?

Her eyes crept slowly from my hooves up my furry legs to the cuffs of my self-tailored overalls, pausing only briefly at the apex of the gusseted inseam before travelling up my broad chest and landing resolvedly at my face.

I wondered what she saw there. Who was this woman, who could look a creature like *me* in the eye with such… determination?

My gaze locked with hers for a solid five seconds. All the while, her child cried. With each passing moment, the furrow between her brows grew deeper, and at last I placed the emotion on her face.

She wasn't resolved. She was *resigned.* Her baby was in trouble, and the gods had told her I was her only hope. She couldn't afford to be afraid.

She had nowhere else to go.

I lowered my eyes to her luggage and jerked my thumb back toward the tractor.

"Hop on the seat. There should be barely enough room for the two of us. I'll drive you to the house."

CHAPTER 5

BETSY

The ride to the minotaur's house was… bumpy.

Bumpy and silent.

Well, that's not entirely true. I doubted my life would ever be truly silent again. Below us, the roar of the puttering antique engine was substantial; it was almost loud enough to drown out Apollo's cries, which were never ending.

Not that I could blame him. He was hungry. Had to be. He hadn't eaten since we'd left the apartment in Minneapolis, and the car ride had easily been close to four hours. My breasts were tender, but dry—a word I couldn't use to describe the rest of me, of course, as I'd been on the brink of tears for the past two days.

As for the driver of the tractor, he was an enigma. He hadn't so much as glanced my way since he'd had to assist me onto this far-too-tiny seat atop his massive tractor. The tires alone were taller than I was, and he'd needed to lift me a clear three feet into the air in order for me to land my foot onto the half-rusted piece of metal that served as a step. The entire time, Apollo cried and cried and cried, as if complaining to our new landlord just how inadequate his mother was.

I muttered my thanks, but he didn't seem to hear it. Instead, he turned hide and clopped off to the other side of the vehicle, hoisting himself up in one smooth motion as he swung his muscular, furry legs onto the seat beside mine before starting up the engine without so much as a nod.

He stared straight ahead, eyes pointed at the small one-story farmhouse on the horizon line.

His upper body was incredible. Big and muscly and wide: so much so that I had to lean to the right to avoid pressing into his massive arms, which he was holding tight to his sides as he gripped the steering wheel with both hands. I ended up weaving my left arm around the metal back of the bench, the hard edges digging into my fingers as I held on for dear life. My other arm wrapped vise-like about Apollo's squishy body as his head flung back with his cries.

It was no surprise when the first tears that clung to my lashes finally gathered enough mass to fall. By the time we arrived at the house, the streaks of water down my cheeks had merged with the trails of snot dripping out of my nose, and *I* was more of a mess than my baby was.

The massive farmer cut the engine and climbed down off the seat without speaking to or looking at me. The only glimpse I got into his psyche was the slight wince he made when he looked up to help me down from the bench and saw my mess of a face.

Great. I'm making an awesome first impression.

I looked away as his large hands gripped my waist, his thumbs almost touching together at my belt. He made me feel *small*. Dainty. I pulled my baby closer.

My breath hitched as he slid me down his wide torso, Apollo smushed between us, and I could feel the tension coiled in every rock-hard muscle of his body.

He was so *big*. When he placed me onto the ground, my head barely came up to his chest. My eyes were level with the central pocket of his overalls, which had clearly been altered to fit him. Strips of denim widened the seams across his legs and waist.

But nowhere were the enhancements to his uniform more obvious than the crotch, which had been let out a *significant* amount to make room for...

There was no way around it. This guy had a truly *massive* wang. The phrase "hung like a bull" chimed like a gong in my head every time I glanced down, which had me desperately seeking any other place to look.

But I couldn't help it. My eyes kept getting drawn there, like a magnet. It was almost an itch, or an annoying ache. The sensation swirled with the butterflies that erupted in my stomach when he lifted me off the tractor seat and set me down on the ground like I weighed less than a sack of flour.

It couldn't help but consume my focus.

I was no stranger to dicks. Between my fractured housing situation in my teens and my job at the adult toy store, I'd seen quite the variety, too. Before Zeus, none of them were anything I'd have described as "impressive."

But one look at my new roommate in his faded denim was enough to wipe all memories of the god king from my mind.

The minotaur in question had gathered my suitcase and backpack from the back of the tractor while I was still getting my bearings, and was now walking away from me toward the house. I scrambled after him, doing my best not to admire his chiseled backside as he climbed the wooden porch steps.

Somehow, Apollo had cried himself out, and he was currently passed out against my shoulder. My heart ached for the little guy, which only made my own sobbing worse. I wiped the back of my left hand across my nose, sniffling as I tried (and failed) to remove the evidence of my breakdown.

What's wrong with me? My baby was literally starving, and I was thinking about a minotaur's dick.

I wiped my hand on my jeans, then hoisted the sleeping bundle higher on my hip before stepping up onto the porch.

When he got to the threshold, he paused with his back to me, his hand hovering over the doorknob. His shoulders rose and fell as he took a deep breath.

"It isn't much," he rumbled. "I... wasn't told you were coming until yesterday. I'm sorry. I didn't have any time to prepare."

"I'm not picky," I blurted, then added more calmly, "I mean, I'm not used to much. Please, don't apologize. I'm grateful for your help."

I forced a smile, the training from my childhood coming back without even having to try. *Be grateful. Be friendly.* Despite the fact that he wasn't looking at me, I hoped he could hear it in my voice.

"Alright, well." He swung the door inward, and I got my first glimpse of my new home. "Here we are."

CHAPTER 6

FELIX

I stared with bated breath as the beautiful human carried Zeus's son into my house.

That face. That *body*. Everything about her completely took me off guard when she stepped out of that car, so much that I had to avoid looking at her just to make it down the long driveway back to the house. I knew that if I'd so much as glanced at her, I'd get lost in the shine of her sad, green eyes; the curl of her deep brown hair brushing against her full, rosy cheeks.

Gods, she was *breathtaking*.

Tension gripped my body the whole time she took in the living room around her, gaze darting from the faded green-and-brown plaid couch by the fireplace to the braided rug covering the dark wooden floor. She lifted her gaze to the archway leading to the kitchen, then to the single door that led to the bedroom and only bathroom, before hitching the sleeping babe higher up on her hip.

'It's so cozy." Her eyes were wide, her mouth slack, and she seemed like she was struggling to find words.

Translation: it's small.

I stomped past her, shoving the bedroom door open with my shoulder and tossing her belongings onto the bed. Thank Hera I bothered to make it this morning, with freshly laundered sheets. I despised doing laundry, but hated the possibility of getting scolded by Iris for having dirty linens even more.

"You'll sleep here," I grunted. She'd followed me through the narrow doorway. The room seemed impossibly small now with the three of us hovering between the dresser and the bed. "Washroom is there."

I pointed to the final room of the house. Past a porcelain threshold, tiny hexagonal tiles stretched beneath the large enameled iron sink, clawfoot tub, and the antique toilet with the pull cord for flushing. Despite being fairly large for a bathroom, everything in it was too small for me. I typically bathed with the hose at the back of the house.

Yet, I'd scrubbed the entire domicile within an inch of its life when I was abandoned here for my exile. Until the white walls shone and the walnut beams gleamed in the late afternoon light that shone through the south-facing windows. When the house was clean, I got to work on repairing the barn. Then fixing the implements. Then farming the fields.

I'd scrubbed it all again last night. So even though it was merely *cozy*, it was clean.

"Thank you." The human nodded. I nodded back, then turned to leave her be and return to my work. But before I could, I felt something grab my wrist.

A hand. Soft, gentle, and so small the fingers couldn't even span its circumference.

I paused. "What?"

"What's your name?"

I looked over my shoulder, taking in her face fully for the first time since I sat her on the tractor. Her skin was red and ruddy with tears, her eyes puffy. My chest squeezed as unfamiliar emotions gripped it, making my breath feel shallow and inefficient.

She'd been crying. I'd felt her shoulders shaking beside me on the tractor, and yet I'd avoided looking over at her. Afraid of what I'd see in those eyes.

But it wasn't anger, sadness, or hate there now, not like I'd expected. They were shining with something I couldn't name. Something... *kind?*

No. Don't do it.

I'd seen what she thought of me when she first laid eyes on my monstrous form. I wouldn't let her pretty face convince me of something when I knew it was an act.

She was just being polite. Just trying to make the most of her situation.

But even in that... there was something admirable.

"Felix," I answered, before letting my gaze fall back to the floor.

"Betsy," she sighed, the name falling from her lips like a prayer as she gestured to herself. Then she bounced her son. "And this is Apollo."

I snorted. Of course. Just another reminder of those hateful Olympians and their control over us. My heart kicked up its pace as even the thought of my half-uncle, or whatever the fuck he was, sent my anger rising. I needed to get out of here. Before I lost my temper on this undeserving beauty.

Betsy.

"Well... make yourselves at home," I muttered through clenched teeth, before storming out of the room and slamming the door behind me.

And who was waiting for me on the porch, but Iris?

"What kind of a welcome was that?" the goddess demanded, following me even as I edged past her to return to planting. I was in no mood for her nonsense. "Hello? Felix! She needs you to help her feed her kid!"

"There's food in the kitchen. She can help herself."

"Felix!"

Faster than I could run away, she flew to the side of my tractor and slammed the heel of her hand onto the hood. The metal dented, and I knew without even looking that she'd just damaged something beneath.

"Dammit, Iris!" I fumed. "You said she needed a place to stay! You didn't say you'd keep me from doing my job so I could play babysitter!"

"I said she needed help feeding her child. Help that only *you* could provide."

"And how in Hades am I supposed to do that?" I spun on her, towering over her slight frame so that her body was cast in the shadow of mine. "You Olympians sure love to make demands of us that we have no capability of fulfilling! In case you haven't noticed, I am not a cow. I do not produce milk from udders. That human in there—that *Betsy* —she has udders that look more than capable of handling that task."

I looked away as I realized what I'd said, heat rising from my chest to my cheeks. It was obscene to say such a thing about a human woman, and yet...

The comparison made me picture things I had no business picturing.

Iris seemed to deduce the reason for my embarrassment. Her lips tilted up in a smirk. "You find her attractive, don't you?"

I refused to meet her eyes, to play her game. "She is not what I would have expected for a consort of Zeus."

"She isn't Zeus's consort anymore. If she were, this wouldn't be an issue."

"What wouldn't?"

"Her supply," the goddess said simply, as if that explained everything.

It explained nothing. I gave an exasperated snort. "That doesn't answer my question!"

"Didn't you read the print-out I gave you?"

I shrugged guiltily, pushing away the thought of the crumpled-up packet of papers she'd given me rotting at the bottom of the burn barrel. Iris pinched the bridge of her nose.

"Felix, a human woman isn't capable of producing enough milk to feed a minotaur baby. Even if you *didn't* read the memo, I explained this to you yesterday."

"But what does that have to do with *me?*" My voice was rising now; I couldn't help it. I glanced toward the window of the farmhouse, but thankfully, Betsy wasn't peeking out at us. The curtain was drawn, and I assumed she and her babe were resting. "Other than sharing a species with her spawn, I see no connection I may be able to provide to solve her problem. The child will die. Zeus will have ruined yet another family. Surprise, surprise, the earth spins on."

Iris adopted a scowl as she folded her arms. "You idiot. Do I really need to spell it out for you?" I stared at her expectantly. She sighed. "Look, a human body usually wouldn't be able to handle any of this. Nursing a demigod? Birthing a minotaur? That would normally be impossible for a human. But mortal bodies change to accommodate their Olympian lovers when given the life essence of a god. Or, in your case, mythical immortal."

I blinked. Then I waved my hand in a circle, gesturing for her to continue her explanation.

"So, give her your life essence."

I raised an eyebrow.

She huffed. "Your semen, cow-brains!"

I froze.

Yeah, I absolutely hadn't gotten to *that* page of the memo.

The goddess ran her fingers through her curls, rolling her eyes as she continued to mutter something, but I didn't hear a word of it. I was still processing the absolute insanity that she'd just spewed out of her blasphemous mouth.

"You… expect me to—to *breed* her?"

I hardly recognized the sound of my own voice as it rumbled from my chest. It was dangerously low, low enough that I knew I needed to contain my rage before I ended up strangling her. Killing one of the most powerful Olympian's daughters had gotten me exiled for millennia, and though Iris was technically a child of the Titans, Hera viewed her as her own. I'd be sent to the worst circle of the afterlife until the end of time if I were to touch a single hair on her pretty blonde head.

Still, the *audacity* of her request was enough to have me at the brink.

"Oh, you won't breed her. She can't have any more children. Not for a while, anyway. Hera's put her womb out of commission."

"She *WHAT?*"

Red.

My fields, my house, my tractor, Iris—everything disappeared in a haze of red as my rage finally overflowed to its breaking point.

How dare they. How *dare* they?!

They couldn't be satisfied ruining the lives of me and countless other immortals who didn't live up to their expectations. No, they had to interfere the lives of *humans*, too. Innocent, beautiful humans who did nothing but fall in love with someone who could never, *ever*, truly love them back.

Fuck these monsters.

No, not monsters. There wasn't a word detestable enough to encompass their cruelty.

"Felix—Felix! Put me down! You're—cho–king–"

"Hera, Zeus, they're all the SAME!" I bellowed, teeth grinding as flesh molded and squeezed below my clenching fingers. "Toying with us all like we're *pawns* to them. He used her, almost killed her with his spawn, only for Hera to exert her own will over the poor woman's body? What does Betsy know of this?"

"She—doesn't know–"

"SHE STERILIZED HER, AND DIDN'T EVEN TELL HER?"

I squeezed, and Iris's normally pale complexion darkened to a bruised vermillion.

"Not–*permanently,*" Iris choked. "It's reversible!"

My grip twitched, and I could feel her breath seeping away.

"Do you—want–to–help her—or–not?"

Only two words made it through my haze of anger.

Help her.

My fingers straightened, and the goddess crumpled in a heap at my hooves as she fell from my grasp. Slowly, color returned to the world around me to the soundtrack of her gasps.

"Help her," I repeated, "by forcing myself on her? Like Zeus did? *That* is the world the gods have created?"

"Hey, it was the titans who created this place," she wheezed, voice hoarse from my attack. I didn't feel nearly as much remorse as I should. She'd heal soon enough. "Trust me, no one's too happy about the way they programmed this shit. Fucking perverts."

I closed my eyes, rubbing them with my fingers as I pictured the overwhelmed human I'd left in the bedroom. *My* bedroom.

"She just gave birth, Iris."

"She's all healed up down there. Hera might be vindictive,

but she isn't cruel. Betsy's equipment is as good as new, give or take a few godly enhancements. The way I see it, the *temporary—*" she gave me a pointed look— "birth control Hera installed is more of a buff than a punishment. She's got enough on her hands dealing with one hungry minotaur. If there comes a time when she feels ready to have another child, the magic can be reversed."

The casual way she spoke of Betsy's body was infuriating. This was none of my business. As attractive as I may have found her, this human and her son had been thrust into my life and home by no choice of their own. And while the gods seemed to have no issue playing games with her reproductive system, I lacked their disregard for common decency.

For the rest of us, actions had consequences.

And yet... I couldn't silence all of the intrusive thoughts in my head. Once Iris planted the idea of filling Betsy with my seed, I couldn't help but picture her luscious body yielding to mine, of her own volition.

She was not delicate. I doubted I would hurt her physically, certainly not if I took my time and pleasured her appropriately beforehand. She'd bedded a god, after all. And, as Iris had so crudely put it, her *equipment* had been enhanced to handle mine.

But what of the other ways in which I could hurt her?

I'd seen the way she'd looked at me. Even if she'd tried to hide it. Like I was a...

A monster.

"Well?" Iris demanded, tapping her foot. "What are you waiting for?"

"I won't do it," I abandoned the tractor with its dented hood, turned tail and headed to the barn. "I can't."

"Felix, wait—"

"You can send me to the deepest level of Tartarus, Iris.

Torture me for all eternity if you must. But I will not fuck that woman."

CHAPTER 7

BETSY

*Y*ou can send me to the deepest level of Tartarus. *Torture me for all eternity. But I will not fuck that woman.*

Of all the homes I'd been sent to, and all the men who'd been assigned as my caretakers, and *Felix* had to be the one with a conscience.

This man—*minotaur*—had just had a woman dumped on his doorstep by the gods. And not only was he refusing to take advantage of me, he was also standing up for me. *Fighting* for me.

While also refusing to do the very thing that would actually help.

I huffed out a breath, slumping onto the bed with a muffled thump. As a bigger woman, I was no stranger to rejection. Nor was I a stranger to the concept of tit-for-tat. The men who offered me housing almost always expected something in return, even if they claimed to find me unattractive.

But for some reason, this particular rejection was bringing up all kinds of conflicting feelings in my stomach.

Maybe it was the shock of it all, the lack of sleep, the hormones. Parts of the conversation I'd overheard were still playing on repeat in my head, and I was struggling to make sense of it all. That woman had dumped a whole lot of information just now—way more than I'd gotten.

Sure, I'd known that my vagina and all the surrounding bits had been patched up magically after Apollo's birth, but the "temporary birth control" Hera'd installed? That was a new little tidbit. Did that mean that I didn't need to worry about getting pregnant again? For how long?

I stroked my fingers between Apollo's horns absentmindedly, wondering how different things would be if Zeus had bothered with some supernatural birth control. I cared for my little guy, desperately, but I couldn't deny that I wasn't exactly equipped to give him a good life.

I risked a peek through the curtains and caught Felix's back as he stormed off toward the barn. The blonde he'd been arguing with stood gaping after him, before she skated away on a literal rainbow.

Oh fuck, I realized. *That's the same goddess that saved me at the hospital!*

And despite all of her help, it looked like my baby and I were still in trouble. I cradled Apollo close to my chest, shame burning through me at her final words. *She's got enough on her hands dealing with* one *hungry minotaur.*

Even the gods didn't think I was fit to be a mother.

Regardless, here I was. Struggling to hold onto a squirming half-human infant who was way overdue for a diaper change.

Thankfully, he'd tired himself out crying during the tractor ride.

You and me both, baby.

After I wiped and powdered him and got him changed, he fell fast asleep once again. Unfortunately, though not surprisingly, there was no crib in Felix's room. So instead, I snuggled up with him in the middle of the minotaur's giant bed, pulling him into the crook of my arm so we could both catch up on some much-needed sleep.

I must have been more exhausted than I realized, because I woke to the sound of Apollo's soft coos a few hours later. The late afternoon sun streamed through the crack in the curtains, casting the room in an orange-tinted glow through the heavy linen fabric. Dust particles danced in the singular ray of sunlight that sliced across the bed.

I estimated I had about twenty minutes before the hungry cries began.

Gently, I shifted his little body onto the pillows as close to the center of the bed as I could. I sat up slowly, then bent to rummage through my backpack for a moment. At last, my fingers grasped what I was looking for.

Stationary box in hand, I plopped onto my stomach atop the comforter. I pulled out a sheet and an envelope, uncapped my favorite purple sparkly gel pen, and sucked on the end as I wondered just what I should tell Petra about my new digs.

The farmhouse was nice, actually. A little old, certainly dated, but surprisingly clean. The whole place—but especially the bedroom—had a warm, comforting scent about it, reminding me of the old bulldog one of my foster families had growing up. I wondered if Felix kept animals.

The thought made me blush.

He is *an animal, you idiot.*

Or at least, part animal. Or was he more than that?

A magical immortal.

Isn't that what the goddess had said? Right before Felix had strangled her for suggesting that he have sex with me?

Embarrassment seized my heart as I looked down at *my* little demigod, who was sure to start crying any minute now. My breasts ached, the tips swelling as they prepared for feeding time. The pain actually gave me some hope. Maybe my body would adjust to his needs on its own.

If Apollo were human, I would be able to provide for him just fine. I was sure of it. After all, what good were giant boobs if they couldn't make milk, right?

But he wasn't human. He was half god. Half *bull*. And if I was going to be his mama, then I needed to get me some minotaur *life essence* to wake up my underperforming mammaries. According to the goddess of rainbows.

I took a deep breath.

Dear Petra,

Well, we've arrived! I'm writing you from my new bedroom, in an adorable farmhouse out in the middle of nowhere in southern Minnesota. Seriously. This place is straight out of the Great Depression. Antique wooden bed, a couch that looks about a thousand years old... everything reminds me of those fancy China cabinets that the Hendersons had with all those gold-rimmed plates and teacups in them? The ones they only got out for Thanksgiving. I think the newest piece of furniture in here is the TV—but even that is really big and chunky. It probably weighs more than I do!

There are fields all around us. I wonder if I'll learn to do any farming? My roommate's name is Felix, and he's a farmer. Drives a tractor and everything.

I debated whether I should tell her the whole truth. I'd kept Zeus a secret, and I know that had stung. But if I told her that Felix was a minotaur like Apollo, would she be relieved?

Or would she come barreling down here to save me from living with a monster?

It was probably safest to keep his physical nature under wraps for now. I wouldn't keep it secret forever—just long enough so that she knew I was safe. I decided to focus on the positive things I could say.

He's very clean. A hard worker, too. He's actually out in the barn right now, while I'm in the house with Apollo. He seems to be pretty familiar with the gods, too.

I considered blurting out everything I'd overheard. The fight he'd had with the rainbow goddess. The fact that Hera *knew* I wouldn't be capable of taking care of Apollo on my own. That if Zeus hadn't abandoned me, I wouldn't have almost died in labor and my breastmilk would have come in by now. That despite that, there was a solution. One that my roommate seemed completely opposed to.

That, in order to make my body produce enough milk to feed a baby minotaur, I'd need a different kind of milk from a fully-grown minotaur.

Life essence, she'd said.

His *semen.*

I shivered, but it wasn't fear that skittered its way down my spine and settled low in my stomach. My mind replayed the image of the sweat on Felix's broad back glinting in the sunlight as he walked to the barn, the feel of his hands squeezing my waist as he lowered me from the tractor. The tailored inseams of his overalls, where the bulge of his *equipment* stretched the worn denim.

I shook my head. Yeah, there was no *way* I was writing any of that. She'd lectured me for sleeping with what she'd thought had been a regular old human at a music festival. Imagine if I told her I was fantasizing about doing the same thing with an immortal minotaur?

I pictured her reaction. The exasperation, the way she'd put her hands on her hips and shake her head.

"Girl, get your head out of the sex shop! Sleeping with immortals is what got you into *his mess!"*

Despite myself, I chuckled. Even in my head, Petra was wise beyond her years.

I missed her so much. But I didn't want my letter to scare her. I was the one who'd gotten mixed up with the gods, and there wasn't anything she could do to help me wrestle with the consequences.

So why worry her?

> *I wanted to let you know that Apollo and I are safe here. I know that you're nervous about this whole situation, but you don't need to be. Like you said before, we can handle this. You and me? We're strong stock. Survivors. Always have been, always will be.*

I wiped my eyes.

> *I miss you already. Love you so much. Say hi to Mrs. Jenkins for me!*
>
> *Love,*
> *Betsy*

I folded the letter and stuffed it into the envelope, sealing it with a quick flick of my tongue before writing Petra's name and our address on the front. Suddenly super grateful she'd been smart enough to include a book of stamps, I stuck one onto the top right, then paused when I glanced at the other corner.

I still didn't know the address of this place, I realized.

But that worry was quickly pushed from my mind as Apollo began to wail. I put the letter down and reached for him.

"Well, little guy, let's see if we can do better this time."

CHAPTER 8

FELIX

$\mathcal{I}$ was deep into replacing the parts Iris had damaged on my tractor when I heard Apollo cry.

The sound shocked me; so much so that I banged my head into the hood of the tractor when I jumped in surprise.

"Argh!" I rubbed the back of my head, where I could already feel a new horn growing. "Fuck…"

Loud enough to carry from inside the house all the way into the barn, the little minotaur's cries stabbed into my heart. *Oh, Apollo…*

I'd already started thinking of him and Betsy as people, instead of a punishment from the gods. I wondered why that was.

I'd only had one conversation with the woman, and the babe had only cried or slept the entirety of our time together. Then again, her beauty was enough to endear me to her.

Maybe I misjudged Zeus, after all. If it was already difficult for *me* to shake the image of her round, pleasing body and sad, green eyes, it shouldn't surprise me that she'd also caught the attention of the king of gods.

The wailing continued, enough that it interfered with my

concentration. My gut twisted. Like it was something instinctual, listening to this tiny creature cry made it next to impossible to focus on anything else. Like it was imperative I do anything I can to stop it.

"So, give her your life essence."

Almost anything.

Iris's words echoed in my head, and I clenched my teeth. There was no way in Hades I was going to force myself on a poor, human woman because the titans created an unjust world. It wasn't fair that the gods had brought about her affliction, and then refused to grant her the cure she needed on a whim.

Not that that was anything new where Zeus was concerned.

When a particularly egregious cry threatened to split my brain from my skull, I threw my wrench and oily rag down on the work bench by the tractor. I couldn't take it anymore.

I stormed out of the barn, hoofing it back to the farmhouse, where I entered through the back door and into the kitchen. I may not be willing to give his mother my semen, but I could at least offer the babe some milk from the fridge.

Only, when I stepped inside, my path to the fridge was blocked.

Blocked by a topless Betsy, who was trying and failing to get her son to latch on her breast.

She didn't see me right away, as her focus was entirely centered on the tiny, distressed minotaur in her arms. She was sitting at the kitchen table, her screaming child half-prone in her arms. Her brow was furrowed, eyes burning with frustration and disappointment as she held him, bouncing and rocking and doing everything she could to calm him enough to get the poor thing to suckle at her breast.

Her bare, swollen, leaking breast.

I licked my lips involuntarily as my gaze honed in imme-diately on her chest. How could the gods possibly believe that this woman's body was incapable of providing for her son?

I couldn't tear my eyes away from the heavy globes as they jiggled with every bounce of her arms. My gods, they were mesmerizing.

"Please, *please,* baby, I know you're hungry. Just drink! I know it isn't enough, but it's something, right?"

I shook myself as the desperation in her voice brought me back to the situation at hand. She'd had to practically shout to be heard over Apollo's continuous racket, and her voice was hoarse from the strain.

"He won't drink like that, it's not natural for him." I approached, grabbing the hand towel that hung from the oven and folding it lengthwise to lay on the ground before her. "Here, kneel."

"What?" she shouted at me, expression switching from exasperation to accusation in a heartbeat. She glared at me. "What the hell are you talking about?"

Fuck. I'd just asked a topless woman to get on her knees.

I bit the inside of my cheek, instantly furious for myself for even entertaining the double entendre at a time like this. I closed my eyes a moment, took a deep breath, then met her gaze.

"He won't drink if he's laying in your arms like that. You need to set him down so he can stand."

"What are you talking about? He was literally born two days ago, He's an *infant.* Infants don't stand!" She practically shook with anger as she rolled her eyes. Then she sighed and added in a more exasperated tone, "Sorry. It's just—what do you mean, 'it's not natural'?"

I shook my head. "He isn't a human baby. He's a minotaur. How many calves have you seen being cradled as they sip from their mother's teats?"

She blinked at me. I held out my arms for the babe. Her gaze darted from my arms, to Apollo, then up to my face.

"Fuck it, I'll try anything at this point."

She handed him to me and hiked up her jeans. I averted my gaze, blushing furiously at the way her top half jiggled and swayed as she knelt atop the towel.

I instead focused on Apollo. He'd abruptly stopped crying when his legs were no longer trapped in his mother's hold. He blinked about stupidly, taking in his new vantage point as I adjusted my grip, holding him out in front of me by the armpits.

Once Betsy was settled, I bent at the waist to set young Apollo down on his hooves, doing my very best to ignore the fact that her new position put her head just below the waistband of my overalls.

As I knew he would, the babe wobbled forward, toppling over before catching himself on his mother's lap. Betsy lurched toward him the second he stumbled, but I held her shoulder back with a firm hand.

"Let him figure it out," I mumbled, my muzzle dangerously close to her ear as I knelt beside her. "He's half bull. We're steadier on our feet than baby humans."

His tiny arms straightened, and slowly, he pushed himself up from Betsy's knee, freestanding for a half second before he dragged himself forward, grasping at her chest with his outstretched hand.

"Ah–" she gasped as he used her body to stay upright, gripping her right breast with both tiny hands. Then, as if realizing for the first time that her nipple was exactly at the right height for him to do so, he leaned forward and opened his round muzzle to clamp down.

For a moment, the two of us watched with bated breath

as he maneuvered his mouth around her. Then the soft, rhythmic sound of suckling filled the tense space between us.

Relief filled my chest as I watched him, until I realized I was literally staring at a human woman's tit. I quickly turned my head and went to rise, only to be stopped, once again, by a small hand on my wrist. I lifted my gaze slightly to meet Betsy's eyes, only to see there were tears there. Again.

My heart stopped.

"I'm sor–"

"Thank you," she sobbed, voice hardly louder than a whisper. Her grip squeezed tighter as the tears flowed faster, but no other part of her body moved. It was as if she was afraid even the slightest shift would send Apollo into a fit again. "For over a day, I haven't been able to—he hasn't... I've been so *scared*!"

I had no idea what to say. Gently, I twisted my arm out of her grasp, moving my hand to rest it on her shoulder. It was only then I realized how much tension she was holding in her neck and back—no doubt caused at least in part by the heavy breasts that hung from her chest. But I couldn't help but wonder how much stress she'd been holding there as well. Perhaps the tiny suitcase and backpack were not the only baggage this woman had brought with her.

I squeezed the curve of her neck with my fingers reassuringly, and she closed her eyes on a sigh. She reached her hand forward, and for a moment I tensed in anticipation of her touching me in return.

But instead, she only patted her child's back, stroking gently as he drank his fill from his mother's breast. "That's a good boy, Apollo. That's what you needed, huh?"

It was now all too clear that this was a moment between a mother and her son, and I was absolutely intruding. I removed my hand from her shoulder, chastising myself for thinking that her show of emotion was anything other than relief at finally being able to provide for her child.

I rose back onto my hooves, edging carefully around the pair as they continued his feeding on the floor. Already, the boy's legs were looking more steady, his arms more sure as he supported his weight. I was certain in a few days, he'd likely be tottering all around the house on those hooves of his, getting into all kinds of trouble.

I sighed. Guess I'd need to calf-proof the house before then. It'd been so long since my own childhood, I didn't even remember the kind of mischief my siblings and I caused for my mother.

"I'll wrestle something up for the rest of us for dinner," I announced, opening the fridge and pulling out a basket of mushrooms, carrots, potatoes, and eggs. I didn't eat meat, but kept a dairy cow and a dozen or so chickens to keep the farm stocked with essentials to supplement the produce I grew in the back garden. We were low on fresh greens at the moment, but still had plenty of root vegetables to hold us over until the asparagus and kale came in. "I hope you're alright with hash."

A contented hum was her only response as I got to cooking.

CHAPTER 9

I was doing it.

I was actually breastfeeding my baby.

The entire world faded away as I watched my little monster stand on his own two legs and suckle at my breast. I was fascinated.

Apollo was *amazing*.

Never, in a million years, would I have guessed that my baby would be standing—crawling, even—at three days old. But of course, baby cows and horses stood within minutes of birth. And Apollo wasn't a *normal* baby human or cow, he was a *demigod*. Obviously he'd develop differently.

The steady, relaxing stream of milk slowed from my right breast, and he instinctually pulled off my nipple to switch to the left one. I reached under his arms to shift him to the other side of my lap, where he stood even more certainly than he had at my right, grabbing onto the sides of my boob immediately and latching without hesitation.

Tension I didn't even know I'd been holding onto leeched from my shoulders and back into the floor as I sank into my heels, rubbing a steadying hand over Apollo's back and relishing the sensation of my body just… doing what it was meant to do. It felt so natural—right, even—to have him suckling from me, to feel the letdown and slow release, the heaviness and ache receding minute by minute as the painful swelling went down.

My fingers nestled between my baby's horns, and I gently stroked his curly hair as I took a moment just to appreciate him. I'd been so stressed, so frantic, bouncing from the pain of labor to the fear of discovery to the helplessness of being shuttled from the only real home I'd ever known to the farm of a complete stranger. I had yet to take a moment to just hold my son. My beautiful, amazing son.

Was this what it felt like to be a mother?

A bittersweet pang tugged inside me as I wondered if my mother had ever felt this with me. And if she had, how could she have ever given that up?

How could Zeus?

Memories of my fling with the King of Gods flashed through my head. I'd known he wasn't the type to stick around, and yet, he hadn't left when he found out about the baby. For a few impossible months, he'd stayed by my side. Hanging out with me at work during the day, and testing out all the fun toys he'd discovered at night.

Had I expected him to stay? No. Not really. But I hadn't cared. Our relationship had been completely spontaneous and exciting. And in the beginning, it never felt transactional.

For once in my life, I hadn't felt like the unwanted foster kid. We'd met when I was on my first ever vacation, high on live music and the thrill of being noticed by an honest-to-goodness *god*. After he revealed his identity, I continued sleeping with him with eyes wide open.

But the more pregnant I got, the less easy it was for me to have crazy, wild sex. And in the end, that had really been all he'd wanted. So he left me, just like I knew he would.

But in doing so, he also left *him*. Left *this*.

Our precious little monster.

I'd been struggling to keep it together since he'd left. In less than a month, I'd lost literally everything I'd ever built for myself: my home, my best friend, my independence, and been thrown headfirst into motherhood without even a semblance of a plan. I knew more than anyone how children could fall through the cracks. Who was I to think I could somehow prevent that with my own son?

But kneeling here with him, doing the thing that human women have done for hundreds of thousands of years? The thing I *hadn't* been able to do since he was born?

I was *feeding my baby*.

And it felt so good.

Maybe I wasn't a total fuck-up after all.

I jumped when the sound of a cast iron pan clanking on steel grates jolted me out of my reverie. I was suddenly reminded that Apollo and I weren't the only ones in the kitchen; Felix was here, too, and he was cooking us dinner.

Well, cooking *me* dinner. And himself.

I was taking care of Apollo.

Okay, I know, I was bragging a little. But I couldn't help it! After everything I'd been through, I deserved a win. And this felt like a big one.

The feeling faded a bit, though, when I realized that I was very much in the way of Felix as he tried to carefully step around me every time he added something into the pan. That's when it hit me.

I was kneeling, topless, in the middle of a strange man's kitchen. While he cooked me dinner.

Eep!

"Oh my gods!" I shouted, frantically trying to pull my tank top up over my right boob. This aggravated Apollo, however, who was still sucking hungrily on the left. A tiny growl rumbled from his chest, and for a moment I forgot myself.

"Um, excuse me, Mr. Man, but you will *not* growl at your mother that way! I don't care *who* your father is."

A low chuckle sounded behind me, and I glanced over my shoulder to see a smirk denting the side of Felix's cheek. I felt my own cheeks heat.

Oh my. The big, strong, grumpy minotaur roommate had *dimples.*

To his credit, he hadn't looked at me once since helping me get Apollo to latch. At that moment, I'd been so overwhelmed and helpless I hadn't even realized that I had my boobs out in plain view. I was just so desperate to get my baby to eat.

I had felt how weak he was in my arms, his struggling less energized than it had been the day before, and I was actually terrified the unthinkable would happen if I couldn't get him to latch.

I couldn't even remember getting onto the floor. All I knew was that Felix showed up and held out his hands, claiming he had a solution. By that point, I was so grateful for the help, I didn't even process what he told me to do or what I was wearing.

Or *not* wearing.

And then Apollo was latched, and standing, and the unbearable ache in my chest had eased.

But now that desperation wasn't making me stupid, I was all too aware of the hulking hunk avoiding me as I knelt half-naked on his kitchen floor.

"I'll, uh, I'll just throw something on once he's done, I'm so sorry–"

"There's a robe in the closet."

I couldn't have heard him right. He wasn't a particularly articulate minotaur; his voice was so low and rumbly that it wasn't always easy to hear what he was saying. Whenever he did speak, it was like my whole body shook with the frequency of his voice, it was so deep.

But it sounded like he'd just offered me his *robe*.

"Excuse me?"

"A robe. In the closet. It's a little big, but if it's easier for the first few days while he's feeding…" he trailed off, and was it my imagination, or was the dark reddish-brown of his skin a little redder?

"Are you… *blushing?*" I blurted. *Oh my gods, what is happening right now?*

"No!" He scowled at me, only to realize I was still basically topless and immediately turning away again. "I just mean… look, young minotaurs are hungry, okay? You've got a lot of… layers on." He waved at my plaid button-down and tank top with his spatula, still refusing to look at me. "It might be easier for you while the two of you get your strength up if you're not constantly… you know what? Never mind."

My left nipple pinched, and I let out an *oomph*. I looked down to find Apollo sucking harder, his puffy cheeks hollowed as he attempted to squeeze every last drop out of me by force of his mouth alone.

"Ufda, easy there, buddy. The well's dry for now. Try again in a couple hours, okay?"

I gently tugged him free, hoisting him into my side while trying to wrestle my shirt back up to cover myself so Felix and I could continue our conversation. Of course, this request was *not* welcomed by the little man in my arms, and I could sense another meltdown was imminent.

"WAAAAAAAAAAAAAAHHH!!!!"

I winced.

Yep. So much for the moment of peace.

"I'm sorry, little guy, that's all I got!" I tried lifting him back into my arms to rock him, but he instantly kicked and squirmed, and I had to rear back to avoid getting a hoof in the chin.

What had happened to the adorable little angel I'd been holding mere seconds ago? I pushed him from my chest at arms' length, then whipped my head around to see Felix's muzzle pursed in disapproval.

Ah, fuck. He's judging me, isn't he? First, he has to teach me how to nurse my own son. And now...

I needed to get out of there, before my inadequacy ruined whatever goodwill had been built between us. "I'm sorry, I'll uh… maybe he needs a change."

Yeah. A change of mom.

I held back tears as I climbed back to my feet, rushed Apollo back into the bedroom, and shut the door behind me.

CHAPTER 10

I stood, frozen, two bowls of root vegetable hash and over-easy eggs in my hands, staring at the closed bedroom door.

It took me longer to plate than it normally would—seeing as I had to dig around the drawers of the kitchen to see if I'd kept any of the silverware from the previous tenants. Normally, I just ate from the bowl. Spoons, forks, and table knives were too small and delicate for my large hands, and since I didn't eat meat, there was rarely anything I made that required cutting or maneuvering beyond its initial preparation.

I'd finally found a smaller serving spoon tucked away in a cabinet that I was able to perch in the bowl for Betsy's dinner. Not that it mattered, since she hadn't so much as made a peep since she'd disappeared into the bedroom.

She'd been in there for half an hour. Far longer than it took to change a diaper.

Should I knock? Call out?

The sound of crying had finally stopped just after I'd finished frying the eggs, and the silence was a welcome reprieve I didn't want to fuck up by making too much noise. Then again, I wasn't about to barge in on the woman a second time, considering the first…

I'd seen her perfect, naked chest on display in the middle of my kitchen.

I shook my head. This was nonsense. Completely ridiculous! I was acting like an intruder in my own damn home. If Betsy wanted dinner, she was a grown woman. She could come out and get it herself whenever the fancy struck her. I wasn't keeping her from it.

But she is a guest here. And she didn't exactly seem comfortable when she stormed out of here after you told her to cover herself.

That was stupid. I thought I was being practical, simply offering her something that could make her life a little easier. Breasts were heavy and inconvenient when they were full of milk. Tucking them away in those fabric cages human women were so fond of underneath layers of *even more* clothes seemed like a terrible hassle when nursing a hungry minotaur. She didn't need to keep up the ritual on my account.

I couldn't care less if she walked around naked the entire time she stayed here. Truthfully, I would myself if the Minnesota winters weren't so harsh. Over the years, I'd gotten used to putting on a base layer to keep myself warm through the colder months, and every now and then the thick denim did provide protection against cuts or dirt from my farm equipment. But it was getting to the season when I'd normally work the fields as the creators intended: with nothing but my fur to protect me.

Humans, however, were more delicate than minotaurs, and I'd forgotten that in the tenderness of the moment. Watching her embrace Apollo's minotaur nature as she knelt to feed him had awoken something in me. I wanted to help her more, make her more comfortable. Encourage her a little, reassure her that she wasn't doing anything wrong.

But offering her my *robe*?

Of course she wouldn't feel comfortable wearing a minotaur's winter pajamas in the home of a stranger. She didn't even seem to believe in letting Apollo wander around unclothed!

Although the idea of a calf in diapers was quite ludicrous. I doubted that would be something that would last very long out here in the country. He'd be outside playing and romping about in the fields in his natural state soon enough. Perhaps when he was grown–

Grown?

Did I honestly just think that? That Betsy and her child would be living here until he was well into adolescence?

I turned away from the bedroom door abruptly, dropping the bowls onto the rough hewn wooden table with a clatter. If they made noise, they made noise. Apollo and his sleeping schedule was *not* my concern. None of this was.

Nope.

Absolutely not.

It was one thing for me to grow crops for the gods, working the fields of my prison. That was part of my sentence—a sentence I *deserved* for killing Hephaestus's daughter.

But I was not about to raise another minotaur into exile. I wasn't here to play house. This wasn't a daycare for the gods' unwanted spawn. This was a *punishment*.

It was no place to raise a son of Zeus.

He wanted to gallivant about earth, knocking up beautiful human women and forcing them to bear his young without caring for them, filling up earth with a bunch of demigods that couldn't even integrate into proper human society. But he didn't want to be responsible for the consequences, nor did any of his brothers. I, myself, was a bastard of Poseidon's from long ago. But *my* mother at least had lived on a farm, and knew a thing or two about animal husbandry.

So, where did that leave the rest of the demigod children, born to less fortunate mothers? Mothers like Betsy, who didn't have any of the resources she needed to care for Apollo?

Were we monsters, ourselves mere rejects of the Olympian's own wanton whims, supposed to clean up their messes out of the goodness of our hearts? Supposed to raise the next generation into obedient workers who hadn't even earned their place in exile?

Not a chance.

I wouldn't let them starve, but I wasn't going to let myself be swayed into developing an attachment to these two. No matter how beautiful or helpless they were. If there was one thing I'd learned from my past mistakes, it was *never* to let myself get involved with a god's family.

It would bring only heartbreak in the end.

I pulled the dining chair back and plopped down into it, holding my bowl aloft to my muzzle as I chowed down on my dinner. I had enough to worry about; fixing my tractor being priority number one. There were jobs for me to do around here: corn to plant, vegetable gardens to weed, chickens to tend and cattle to milk. Poor Daisy was probably about ready to burst, due for her evening milking.

I licked up the last of the grease from my bowl and placed it in the sink. I'd wash all the dishes before I went to bed. For now, I had other chores to do.

* * *

I PULLED A CLEAN, enamel-coated milk can from storage and my trusty wooden stool beside Daisy, the one dairy cow I kept here on the farm. I spoiled her, hoisting fresh hay and all of the potato peelings from dinner into her manger, along with one of the last apples I had from the fall harvest as an apology for being later than usual with her evening milking. She gave a grateful moo, and I patted her broad back before squatting down onto the stool to begin milking.

She was well taken care of.

She'd escaped over my fence back when she was only a heifer, one or two years ago now. Turns out, she'd been pregnant with a calf at the time, a young bull I'd kept until he'd run away last fall. I let him leave, knowing he'd likely find a place at one of the neighboring farms that Daisy had escaped from. I had little room for a herd, and I'd no use for a bull. At least not one so closely related to Daisy. When her milk started to run dry, I assumed I'd need to find a way to secure a bull to shore back up her supply, but until then…

I coughed, as the less innocent thoughts around the aspects of animal husbandry made my throat a little dry. Daisy, of course, was a herd animal—no more intelligent than the chickens I kept in the coop behind the house. That, for certain, was something to be grateful for. Given my family's history, I didn't want any magical or sapient animals anywhere near this farm.

My fingers squeezed around her full udders, coaxing the fresh, frothy milk into the can below her teats. I'd allowed myself to get lost in the familiar habit, but now that I was paying closer attention, the movement was inspiring more inappropriate thoughts.

Thoughts of Betsy, and her own full udders.

I swallowed, withdrawing my hands as I centered myself.

Nope, not appropriate in the *least*.

I hurried up, finishing the task at hand as quickly as I dared. I distracted myself by counting backwards from 1,000 by twelves until the uncomfortable swelling in my overalls went down. By then, Daisy was empty and the milk can was full.

After carrying the jug to cold storage, I decided it was best to distract myself with some harder labor. Something to keep my brain occupied. Like the tractor.

Until my gaze landed on the stall beside Daisy's, where an abandoned feeding trough lay on its side.

"Hmm."

Before I knew what I was doing, I'd walked over and started examining the connections of the boards. It was an old-fashioned wooden manger, dusty from its years in the barn but still surprisingly sturdy. A few side boards were loose with rusty nails. And one of the legs was broken—explaining why it was lying on the floor instead of standing upright at the head of the stall like the others.

I had some old 4x4's lying around here somewhere…

I was drilling new holes for fresh screws into the wiped-down wood slats when Iris popped into existence at my shoulder.

I jumped, the drill buzzing angrily in my hand, as the screws on my workbench went flying.

"Be careful with that thing, would you?" She yelped, covering her pale face with her hands.

"Don't sneak up on me when I'm working with power tools!" I snapped at her, waving the business end of the drill in her face. I lifted the safety goggles from my eyes. "It isn't *my* fault you like to butt in where you aren't wanted!"

But she wasn't looking at me anymore. Instead, she was eyeing the project laid out in front of me: the curved wooden boards I'd fashioned into rockers underneath the reinforced legs of the feeding trough, the pile of rusty nails I'd removed from the boards and was in the process of replacing, and the can of wood stain and sealant and the paintbrush perched on the side of the workbench.

She pointed to it, waggling her finger back and forth. "What's all this, Felix?"

I felt my cheeks heat. At the time, I hadn't truly realized what I was doing; I'd simply seen something broken and decided to fix it. But now that I was being asked to explain it, I couldn't deny that this wasn't just a project for the barn.

I was making a bassinet.

A bassinet for Apollo.

"Nothing," I deflected, lowering my goggles back down over my eyes and switching out the drill tip for a screwdriver.

But a knowing smirk had already crept across her thin lips. "I never took you for the paternal type, Felix."

"It isn't what it looks like."

"So this *isn't* a crib for Betsy's son?"

The sound of the drill came to a stop, and I sighed. I disentangled the elastic from my horns and tossed the goggles across the work station. "What do you want, Iris?"

She paused for a moment, chewing on her cheek. When her eyes met mine, there was pity there. "It's a sweet gesture, Felix. But it won't matter if the baby dies."

"He's not going to die. She just fed him earlier. They're going to be fine."

"For how long? A few days? A week? You've seen how fast he's growing. She won't be able to keep up. Not without another blessing."

I snorted. *Blessing?* That's what we were calling it now?

"Aren't there supplements or something she can take to help?"

Iris's gaze sparked with challenge. "That's a good point, Felix. What will you do with Daisy when her supply starts to dwindle? What kinds of *supplements* kickstart her back into production?"

"That's different."

"You take a bull, and you–"

"Stop it!" I slammed my hands onto the bench, then tore off my gloves. I wiped a hand over my face, as if that would somehow erase the blush that I knew was burning there. "I know what you're trying to do!"

"You need to mate with her. It's the only way to stimulate her to produce enough for little Apollo. You *know* this."

"She's not a cow, Iris."

"And *you're* not a bull." She raised an eyebrow, crossing her arms.

Her attitude was driving me to fury. I looked back down at the tools scattered across the bench, deciding that the bassinet was in good enough shape to start staining. I grabbed it, twisting it until the rockers were perched on the ground, and gave it a cursory push.

It rocked. Success.

The goddess watched as I walked back and forth between the tool chest and the workbench, refusing to leave me alone to my work. "I'm not leaving until y–"

"Have you seen me, Iris?" I snapped, throwing my hands up in the air as I rounded on her. "I'm twice her size. My cock would will kill her!"

"No it won't. Hera's blessed this union."

"I don't care if Zeus himself blessed it!" This woman was insufferable. They all were. Didn't the gods remember why this was a bad idea? What happens when I get mixed up in their affairs? The whole reason I was in exile in the first place? "The last time I mated a woman, she—she…"

But I couldn't say it. Even now, thousands of years after the fact, I still couldn't say her name.

Iris sighed. "That was… different. Trust me. The same thing won't happen with Betsy."

I scowled at her. "How could you possibly know that?"

It was then that I realized, for the first time I could ever remember, Iris looked distinctly uncomfortable. And not just because there was nowhere to sit in the workshop.

No, she looked almost… guilty. Like she was hiding something.

"I don't know what to tell you," she said at last, twisting her fingers and refusing to meet my eye. "Only one thing will make that human produce enough milk for her child, and that's your semen."

"Gods dammit, Iris—"

"*I don't make the rules!* Don't shoot me, I'm just the messenger goddess." She planted her hands on her hips. "It's not as if it's an issue of attraction. I've seen how you look at her."

"This has nothing to do with that!" I balked, shaking my head.

I was sick of this. Sick of Iris bursting onto my property and disrupting my peace. Sick of her secrets and deceptions. Sick of the gods and their endless meddling into my affairs, when all I wanted was to be left alone.

"I've had it up to here with your *rules*. What of the rules of *human* society, huh? Or propriety? Or common decency? You expect me to just whip out my penis and stick it in the first woman you drop off on my doorstep after Zeus fucked her over–"

"For Hades' sake, Felix! This baby is important to Hera. I swear to the gods, if you let him die just because you can't get it up–"

And now she was insulting my manhood??

"If I agree, will you finally leave me *alone?*"

At that moment, I watched as Iris's eyes widened at something over my shoulder. And then before I could even blink, she disappeared with a *pop.* A cloud of holographic particles poofed in her absence.

Swiping a hand to clear away the sudden gust of rainbow

glitter, I sneezed as some of it got into my snout. I stumbled a bit, sneezed again, then got turned around as I waved my hands to keep the infernal stuff from infecting my work-bench. If it got into the open can of woodstain, every barn project would sparkle for decades to come.

"Fucking *glitter*, really?? I swear to Olympus, the next time I get my hands on you, Iris, I'm gonna–"

But as I wiped my eyes free of the sparkling dust, I saw the reason for the goddess's sudden disappearance.

Betsy, standing in the open barn doors. Staring, wide-eyed, at me.

Fuck the gods.

CHAPTER 11

BETSY

My knuckles were white from gripping the corrugated metal of the barn door so hard. There was no mistaking it this time—I knew what I'd heard.

So the conversation from before *wasn't* some hallucinogenic side-effect of new mom sleep deprivation. The gods hadn't delivered me here just so Felix could teach me proper nursing technique, or to keep my minotaur baby from being discovered by humans.

I was here because my milk supply would never be enough to keep him alive. And only Felix could change that.

"Is it true?" I breathed, my voice shaky from nerves.

Apollo had finally cried himself to sleep after I'd swaddled him up in my overshirt and laid him down in the middle of Felix's giant bed for a nap. I trusted he'd be safe for the few minutes it would take for me to run to the barn to thank the grumpy minotaur for making me dinner. It was *delicious.* Like, the best food I'd ever had. I hadn't even minded that I'd had to eat it with a ladle.

But I'd gotten distracted when I'd seen him talking with that goddess again.

And she'd said that, in order for me to produce enough milk to keep Apollo alive, I needed Felix's semen. And he'd almost seemed like he was about to give in.

The large, muscly monster towered over his work-bench, gazing down at me with an unreadable expression on his face. He was breathing heavily, reflective particles swirling in every exhale from his wide snout, which was wrinkled in a frown as he and I stared, unblinking, at one another.

"Is…*what* true?" he rumbled, each word sounding like an effort.

I tugged at the loose strings hanging from the rips in my jeans. Every muscle in my body was taught like a bowstring as I contemplated my answer.

That your semen will make my boobs work?

That having sex with you is the only way I can provide for my son?

That your dick won't break me?

At that thought, my eyes darted down to the crotch of his overalls. My breath hitched in my lungs as I noticed that the denim was stretched tight over his bulge, which was most *certainly* bigger than the last time I saw it.

I gulped. "That my milk will run out? Unless you…?"

I'd asked the question to his pants. I couldn't look away. Even as I stared, the damn thing seemed to get even *bigger,* the tent shifting as the bulge straightened and rose, pointing higher and higher until–

"Yes," he ground out, and *gods,* the grit in his voice had my thighs clenching.

What is wrong with me?

On shaky legs, I stepped forward. Once, twice, again and again until I stood less than a foot in front of him. I had no idea where my boldness came from.

All I knew was, my baby was hungry in the other building, and the demigod in front of me had the power I needed to fix it.

If I could just make him *give* it to me.

I turned off my brain. I must have. Because there could be no other explanation for my hands rising to the clasps of his shoulder straps, my thumbs pushing the buttons through the hooks, my fingers flinging the straps up and over his massive, broad shoulders, reaching so high that my elbows were fully straight. It's the only thing that could have allowed me to drag my nails down his velvety pecs, following the fabric bib as it tumbled down, down, over his tuft of chest hair, sliding past his visible abs and wrinkling in a pile at the shelf made by his hard, giant cock.

It clicked back on, though, when my fingers reached his waist.

"Will you please help me?"

What was I doing?

Why was I getting on my knees?

Why was I white-knuckling the folds of denim between my hands and staring up at the monstrous face of my minotaur roommate through my eyelashes, opening my mouth and asking for permission to suck his cock?

I mean, sure. I'd done this kind of thing before when a person let me crash with them. But they'd expected it. They'd *wanted* it. Whereas Felix...

I will not fuck that woman.

His hands folded over mine, halting my movement before I could free him. I winced.

Gods, he was big. His fingers easily wrapped around my entire hand, his thumb reaching down past my wrist as his dark, brown eyes bore into mine. His heavy brow was twitching between emotions, everything from concern to embarrassment to anger to desire telegraphing in the tiny movements of his face.

How could I have ever thought he was stuffy? This man was *full* of feeling, it was just buried.

I wanted to unearth it all. I wanted to know what it took to unravel this enigma of a monster, break through his hard —*hard*—exterior and discover all that he insisted on hiding.

At least, I did if it was what *he* wanted.

My eyes darted behind him, to a bassinet. Carved and unfinished, but unmistakably hand-made. My heart pounded.

"You built him a crib," I whispered, breaking the unbearable silence as he held me in place.

"It's safer than the two of you sharing the bed."

"Where will you sleep?"

"On the couch."

"Will you fit?" I blurted out. Instantly, my face ignited with embarrassment.

GREAT, Betsy. Perfect! Don't THANK the man who made you dinner and gave up his bed and built your SON a CRIB. Instead, just comment on how LARGE he is!

His nostrils flared, and below my fingers, the denim twitched. His eyes flared, black pupils dilating as the double meaning of my words stuttered his breath.

"Betsy, I..." he trailed off, and suddenly I didn't care how silly or desperate I seemed.

A million emotions swirled inside me: attraction, arousal, embarrassment, worry. And I was *here*. I was right here, and Felix was right there. We could do this. It would be so easy.

"Please." Tears sprung to my eyes, and his fingers squeezed around me. My hands started to shake in his grasp, my desperation at its limit.

I needed him. I needed his help. I couldn't take it anymore.

For nine months, I carried Zeus's son in my womb knowing full well his father would leave me. But never, in a million years, could I have predicted just how much my body would betray me even worse than my own poor judgement when I agreed to let Zeus fuck me under the stars.

I almost *died* when Apollo was born. Would have, if the gods themselves hadn't intervened.

I'd worked so hard to be different than my parents. To get out of the system, to carve a place for myself in the world. To rise above my childhood. To be a good friend, a good employee, a good person. A good *mother*.

I'd do anything at this point, just to be *good enough*.

Something broke inside me, and my shoulders heaved. Sobs wrenched their way out of my throat, as the tears flowed in rivers down my face. The watery blur that was Felix shifted immediately, dropping to a knee beside me until my face was level with his pecs. Then his hands let go of my fingers and before I could move, a solid pair of arms was wrapped around me, pressing me into an embrace.

I wish I could say I took advantage of the moment to savor the fine fur of his deep, mahogany-brown chest, to breathe in his scent of sunshine and loam and corn, to take comfort in the way his body encased mine in muscly warmth.

But instead, snot and tears mixed into a gross soup that drenched his body and mine, until my cheeks stuck to his naked pecs and I'd soaked his delightful coat.

Once again, I'd been reduced to a crying, blubbering mess.

"Do you think it's the hormones?"

"No, I think I'm just broken."

He didn't say a word. For minutes, he just held me so tight it was on the verge of uncomfortable—but not quite. The pressure was strangely calming, allowing me to ride out the surge of grief until my chest unclenched and my breathing evened. It took a while.

And through it all, he held strong.

When my sniffling and hiccuping finally subsided, I slid my hand between our bodies so I could wipe my eyes.

"Here," he said, pulling away immediately and digging into the wrinkled pocket of his overalls to pull out an honest-to-gods handkerchief.

"Thank you." I accepted it, wiping my face before swiping at the puddle I'd left on his chest. "I'm sorry, I–"

"Don't."

His hand was back on mine, freezing the motion of my arm as I attempted to clean him up. With his other hand, he poked a finger under my chin and tilted it, until my face was staring straight up into his.

Our eyes locked, and the concern in his gaze stopped my heart cold.

"Don't clean you up?" I scolded myself internally as my voice shook. I had to bite my lip to keep it from quivering. *Gods,* couldn't I do *anything* right?

"Don't apologize," he corrected, shifting his grip on my face so his thumb could wipe away a tear trail I'd missed with his handkerchief. "None of this is your fault. *None* of it. You do *not*. Need. To apologize." Each word was punctuated with a tap of his thumb on my cheek. His brown eyes didn't leave mine as he spoke. "Do you understand?"

Truth be told, I didn't. I'd been trying to play it cool, this whole "you've got a baby minotaur" thing, but realizing that I'd just gotten on my knees to suck off a monster cock because I was having a little trouble with my milk supply?

Let's just say it was making me re-think whether I was actually handling any of this as well as I thought I was.

So I shook my head. "No. I don't understand any of this!"

I choked on a helpless, sardonic giggle. It wasn't actually funny, but the small noise brought a smile to my lips, and it felt good.

So I giggled again. And then again, a little louder, and then my mouth opened wide in a toothy grin as I realized I was *still* on my knees, on a rough-hewn wooden floor, in a big red barn in the middle of nowhere, with a bark of laughter.

A brief look of confusion wrinkled Felix's snout, followed by a sad smile of his own. Then he laughed, too, and the tension between us lifted a little.

We gathered ourselves, and once he seemed satisfied I was done crying, he moved his grip to my elbows and helped me rise to my feet. The movement shifted Felix's pants, which were still unbuckled about his hips, but they didn't fall.

I was confused for a moment, until I saw that his tail had woven around one of the side belt-loops, its tufted end sticking out as he used it to hold the pants in place until he could adjust the bib straps.

I stared at it.

"You have a tail?"

He blinked. "Of course. Doesn't Apollo?"

CHAPTER 12

FELIX

The second Betsy removed her hand from my waistband, took a deep, full breath. She stumbled in front of me, staring at my belt loops and trying to make sense of my anatomy. But *this* bit of anatomy, I could handle. I'd much rather have her focused on my tail than on my cock.

The entire half-hour she'd been crying at my feet, I'd been fighting my body's reaction to her nearness. I hated everything about it, the lust I felt for her warring with the anger and ache that consumed me whenever I saw just how much this whole situation was making her suffer.

And *gods,* did the hits keep coming. She'd finally fed her child, only to hear that it would never be enough. But I couldn't believe that. How could anyone, who saw the lengths to which this woman would go for her son?

I didn't care what Iris said. Until I knew the source of Betsy's heartache, I wouldn't think of touching her in a sexual manner. I may not be at risk of breaking her physically, what with the magic Hera had supposedly cast between her legs, but what about emotionally? What kind of trauma would I inflict if I allowed her to impale herself on my cock as some perverse medicine for her predicament?

Betsy shook her head, laughing, as I pulled my bib back up my chest and buttoned the shoulder straps. She sniffled, but her hazel eyes were clear now. A grin tilted her lips, and I could feel it ignite something in my chest.

"Apollo's tail is just a tuft right now. Are you saying it's going to grow as long as yours?"

She tilted her head endearingly, eyebrow quirked in a way that made her expression lopsided. It was adorable.

"Most likely, yes."

"And it's..." she paused, pointing toward my rear. "Prehensile?"

I nodded, and could feel my eyes crinkling at the corners. "Those terrible twos will be something."

She looked confused for a second, before a pleasant pink blush rose to her cheeks. "Terrible...Oh! Right, for him! Haha, yes, I imagine..."

She trailed off, still eyeing the waist of my coveralls. I gave a slight cough, and gestured to the bassinet.

"It, uh. Should be done in a few days."

She shook her head, her smile wavering. "It's very kind of you. To go through all the trouble."

"It's nothing. You both need a place to sleep, after all. He'll be more comfortable if he can have his own space."

She walked past me, stepping toward the crib, laying a hand on its wooden edge and giving it an experimental push. It rocked steadily, not even creaking as its weight shifted back and forth.

I found myself missing her face as her position placed her back to me, although that view was also quite nice.

My gaze focused on her round rear. *Hmm.* Very nice.

"You've been awfully considerate, considering you don't even want us here."

That snapped me out of my dirty thoughts.

"I didn't say–"

"I know that sleeping with me is the last thing you want."

Wait, what? What had given her *that* idea?

I shook my head, even though she couldn't see me. She was still staring at the crib, back to me as she spoke all of this. "Betsy, that's not—I didn't mean…" I sighed. What *did* I mean, exactly?

She mistook my pause for an admission of guilt. "It was delicious. Dinner. Thank you for making it. For taking care of me. I've never had a caretaker be this nice before without expecting something in exchange, and I kinda… don't know how to handle it."

"What?" My eyes snapped to the back of her head, my mind a mess of confusion. "What do you mean, something in exchange?"

"Like, are you really this nice? Or is this just a different kind of mean? Because if the whole point of me staying here is sleeping with you, if I really need your semen to make this work, then what is the rest of this even for?"

I stared at her, mouth agape. I wasn't trying to be nice *or* mean. I was trying to be decent. I was trying to do the right thing. I took a step toward her, when she spoke again.

"Maybe I should just give up and go home."

"No!"

The volume of my shout was too loud, even to my own ears. Even to Daisy, who mooed in alarm. I sent a silent apology her way as I took three long strides across the barn. I landed on the other side of the crib across from Betsy and slammed my hands down on the top bar. The resulting bang shocked her into meeting my gaze.

I grabbed her wrists, her small, delicate, human wrists, and hoped to whatever god might actually like me that I could manage to say the right thing for once in my pathetic life.

"I do not want you to leave."

The honesty of the admission struck me as I said it. How was it that, in only the span of a few hours, I'd gone from feeling like her presence was a punishment to feeling like my farm would have something missing without her?

"Then why won't you give me what I need?"

I opened my mouth to speak, when a strangled cry sounded from somewhere outside the barn. In a second, I'd placed it.

Apollo.

"That's my cue," Betsy sighed, tugging her hands out of my grasp. "I guess I'll see if I've got anything to spare."

I stood there silently, like an idiot, and watched her leave the barn to return to her child.

CHAPTER 13

BETSY

Dear Petra,

Figured I'd send you a one week check-in. I'm hoping you're doing well. I haven't gotten a letter from you yet, but I am sort of in the middle of nowhere, so I'm sure mail can take a little longer to get here...

Apollo is growing so fast. Unbelievably fast. This demigod thing is no joke. Can you believe he can actually stand now? He's not even crawling, although that might be hard with the way his legs are. Same with walking, although my roommate thinks that he might take his first steps before he's a month old!

I can't help but feel like it would have happened already if ~~I wasn't so useless~~ my milk supply was better. He needs so much, and I feel like I'm just barely keeping up...

But he's standing. When he sleeps, his nose wiggles in the cutest way. Did I tell you Felix made him a crib? My roommate, that is—his name is Felix. Did I already tell you that? He's super handy. And a great cook. And he—

My pen stopped on the page. What on earth was I saying?

Since the night I'd caught Felix talking to the goddess in the barn, he'd kept his distance. Most mornings, by the time I'd wrestled Apollo into a new diaper and fed him what I could and walked out of the bedroom, my roommate was long gone. Off on his tractor, planting corn or spreading manure or painting the barn or who knows what else he did all day.

He usually didn't come back into the house until it was practically dark, and even then, he got right to work making dinner for both of us before heading right back out and working on some other project until I couldn't stay up any longer. I didn't even know if he slept. By the time I got up and around in the mornings, the only hints of him getting any rest were the blanket and pillow flung across the old couch in the living room, and a bowl of some kind of breakfast waiting for me on the table.

While taking care of a baby minotaur was a full-time job, I had a few hours a day while he napped or watched PBS on the ancient television in the corner that I had some peace. And despite the involuntary nature of my living situation, I still appreciated the fact that I was a guest in Felix's house.

So I did what I could to earn my keep.

So I'd taken to tidying up the little farmhouse: washing

dishes, folding Felix's bedding, doing laundry in the big claw-foot bathtub and hanging all three of our clothes to dry on the line in the front yard.

If I ever caught sight of the big minotaur out on the farm, he'd quickly turn tail and walk away to another task, as if he hadn't seen me.

But for those couple of hours before dinnertime, I'd feed Apollo and put him down for a nap and then wait for him. He'd stomp in the back door—fur damp from an outdoor shower—and I'd greet him with a big glass of water and a towel for his still dripping mane. I'd sit with him in the kitchen, chopping veggies or stirring something for him. We'd talk, and he'd tell me about the farm. I'd tell him about my life with Petra. And in those moments when it was just the three of us, chatting and preparing dinner together while Apollo slept in his custom bassinet, it felt almost like a dream.

Like something out of the Brady Bunch. Like a real family, that loved and took care of each other.

But last night, the baby had cried out while we were talking, hungry once again, and I'd watched as the openness in Felix's expression shut down. He turned back to the stovetop, refusing to look at me as I nursed for the few minutes I could. And the easy peace between us was shattered.

The big man finished cooking, dropped a bowl on the table without looking at me, only to take his own and carry it out the door as he headed once more to the barn without a word.

Apollo and I both cried after that, hungry in ways I couldn't fully explain.

It took until long after dark, but he'd eventually cried himself to sleep. I'd sat at the kitchen table, head in my hands, and must have drifted off—because the next thing I'd known, Felix's giant, warm hand was on my back, and he was gently nudging me awake.

"You need your rest too, mama. You should get to bed."

The words had been murmured, low and sweet. The kindest thing he'd said to me all week. And I couldn't bear it.

"It doesn't matter. The time between feedings is getting shorter and shorter, and I'm not keeping up. He's hungry, Felix. My baby is hungry."

The room had been so dark, the sun having long since set and the only source of light the soft glow of the moon and stars through the window above the sink. His broad face and heavy brow obscured by shadow as he stared at me, the only indication being the slight glint of the reflected moonlight on his deep, glassy eyes.

"You are doing everything you can."

"It's not enough."

"That's not true. You're a good mom, Betsy. Few parents give as much of themselves for their children."

My eyes had slowly adjusted, and I'd seen the sincerity in his expression. But I couldn't help but think that with his help, I could do more.

"Why did you lie to the goddess, Felix?"

His shoulders had tensed, his hand had frozen on my back, the slow circles he'd been rubbing stopping short at my words. I'd been angry, and was out of reasons not to confront him.

"It isn't fair to you, Betsy. You don't deserve—"

"Deserve what? To suffer? To watch my child starve?"

"To be separated from your friends and family and society, only to be forced to have sex with a monster."

I'd tried to catch his gaze when he'd said that, ready to argue, ready to fight for my baby—but he'd turned back to the door. As he'd left, I'd heard his words, but been too exhausted to follow him out to the barn.

"Nothing good can come of it, Betsy. I only destroy everyone I touch."

That had been the only reason I'd gotten from him before I had turned in for the night.

Apollo cried out, and I scribbled a quick, unsatisfactory ending to my letter to Petra before sealing the envelope and slipping it into my pocket. Then I changed and fed my baby.

I knew he was still hungry, but I gave him a pacifier and gathered him up in my arms. I figured I could take him for a walk down the driveway to the mailbox after my own breakfast. The exercise would be good for us both.

A little fresh air.

"Morning," a rich voice lowed from the kitchen when I stepped out of the bedroom. It was a little more gravelly than it had been last night, and my stomach fluttered a bit at Felix's morning timbre.

He was here. Making breakfast. For once, he hadn't run off to the barn at the break of dawn.

My heart pounded against my ribcage as I froze at the threshold, startled by the change in routine. Despite my frustration with his distance, I'd gotten used to having the day to myself in the farmhouse. Eating the cold oatmeal Felix had left for me on the table, then settling Apollo on his blanket in the living room while I set about washing dishes and listening to the drone of Sesame Street playing in the background.

Felix's back was to me as he worked at the counter, the smell of coffee wafting in the air and making my mouth water. I missed caffeine.

"Morning." I returned his greeting, taking in the muscles of his broad, bare back tensing and shifting as he flipped something in the pan on the stove. "You're, um. You're changing up the routine today."

And not just because he was late getting out and about. He wasn't wearing overalls today.

He wasn't wearing *anything,* I realized, as my gaze traveled down his spine to the thick fur that coated his hindquarters and down his muscular calves before his legs tapered into stiff ankles and dark, sturdy hooves. All the while, his tail swayed to and fro.

His *prehensile* tail.

He used it to grab the salt shaker off the counter and sprinkled some into the pan.

Quickly, I darted my eyes away, where they landed on the couch in the living room. The large quilt he used each night was folded over the back, and my chest squeezed. When I turned back to the kitchen, I was surprised to see he'd also turned around, and I had a full-frontal view of my naked roommate.

Now, I'd learned quite a bit about minotaur anatomy during my week at the farmhouse. Because their lower halves were covered in thick fur, and their upper halves seemed to be covered in a fine layer of peach fuzz-like hair, they ran a lot warmer than humans did. I'd learned this the hard way, when Apollo had wriggled his way out of his shirt and pants on the first sunny day I'd taken him outside on a walk around the farm. Felix had laughed at me, himself shirtless, as I struggled to contain the little guy as he'd kicked and pushed at me with all his might when I attempted to tug his clothes back on. It was then he'd informed me that, until he'd been banished to Minnesota, he'd never once needed to wear clothing to keep warm, even in the relatively mild winters in the Mediterranean where he was from.

However, I'd yet to see Felix out of overalls. But apparently it was supposed to be warm today, because my minotaur roommate had made the executive decision to go about his farmer's duties *au naturale.*

Instinctively, my eyes zeroed in below Felix's waist. Then, I corrected, pupils flying to the ceiling as heat rose to my face, only for my curiosity to take over once more and focus right back. But each time, I couldn't quite process what I was seeing.

Because, I actually… wasn't. Seeing his dick, that is. Instead, there was just a furry… sack just kinda between his legs. Almost like a dog.

Oh. *Oh.* Right. Because his lower half was *literally* that of a bull.

My face, if possible, got even hotter as I shook my head and distracted myself by adjusting my hold on Apollo. Of course, I'd seen a minotaur dick before. A tiny one, every time I changed my son's diaper. But I hadn't realized that that furry little dick sleeve that I had to wipe and powder was so similar to what a fully-grown minotaur male would have going on under the hood.

Well, not *completely* similar. There was one… *big* difference.

Felix's tufted tail swished from side to side, peeking out from behind his wide body as I took him in. That was another thing I'd discovered: tails were a lot more useful than I'd given them credit for. Watching Felix dart around the kitchen, stirring something on the stove with his tail coiled around a wooden spoon while he reached in the cupboard for a bowl or a spice jar was impressive to say the least.

In Apollo's case, however, it was mostly annoying. I'd started cutting holes for it in his dwindling supply of diapers. I wondered how long it would take for my son's tail to grow as long and useful as Felix's. The rest of him was certainly growing at an alarming speed, despite his less-than-ideal feeding schedule. He was already human toddler-sized, and I'd switched from holding him in front of me in both arms to a side carry a few days ago. Even now, his little hooves swung on either side of me as I stood with him in the kitchen, one arm under his diapered butt while another steadied his shoulder against mine.

"Supposed to be a hot one today," Felix said, turning back to the stove and transferring something from the pan to a plate. "I went ahead and let the furnace go out. We'll probably only need it at night for the next few weeks as the days get longer. Will that be alright with you?"

I stopped ogling his hypnotic tail and nodded. "Oh! Um, yeah, that'll be fine. If I get chilly, I can just wear a sweater or something."

"I finished planting the fields yesterday. So I have a bit of a lighter schedule now, and was thinking of plotting out the vegetable garden for the summer." Before I could respond, he handed me a plate with two giant, round pancakes on it. I grabbed it, blinking, and he pointed to the refrigerator with his spatula before turning back to the stovetop. "Eat. There's fresh butter and milk in the fridge, and honey in the cabinet there if you like them on the sweeter side."

My stomach growled as I reached for the plate, eyes as round as the steaming flapjacks. This was a lot to take in. Felix, up and cooking in the kitchen when I woke up instead of already out in the field.

It was a pretty big change from the usual cold bowl of scrambled eggs or oatmeal that awaited me most mornings.

They smelled *divine*.

I put the plate on the table, where I noticed a new, third chair had appeared since yesterday.

But not just any chair. A high chair. The perfect size for Apollo. Complete with a lifting and locking table to keep him safely in place as we ate.

I raised an eyebrow, but didn't say anything. Felix didn't seem the type to take compliments well, as he mostly deflected all of my thanks for his work on the crib before. Instead, I simply lowered my baby into the chair, secured him in, and went to the fridge.

The milk was already in a vintage glass pitcher, so I grabbed it along with the butter, which was stored in an honest-to-gods butter bell. I couldn't help but smile at all the old-fashioned table settings.

This place really did seem to exist in a different time.

Even the honey was stored in a porcelain crock in the shape of an old round beehive, with a small lid with a notch where a wooden honey dipper poked through.

I didn't know anything about living on a *farm*. I was a city kid, through and through. Raised in the system, with public school and government cheese and microwaved popcorn as a treat. But here, there was no microwave. No frozen meals. No takeout.

For the past week, I'd been relying on Felix to cook for me. Sure, I might have tidied up a bit, washed some sheets and a few pairs of overalls, but all things considered? I'd barely lifted a finger since moving here.

And today, he was planning out a vegetable garden, where he likely grew the food I'd been eating this whole time.

This was not an easy life. Felix was a true homesteader. And I was only just now piecing all of that together.

We were in the middle of nowhere. There were no grocery stores out here. And even if there were, it's not like Felix could just hop in the car and swing by the Super One and grab a dozen eggs.

He was a *minotaur*.

Which meant this milk came from the cow in the barn. As did the butter. The honey was likely from a beehive he kept somewhere, and the eggs were probably from actual chickens.

Maybe I'd misjudged Felix. Maybe his long days working

the fields weren't because he was ignoring me. Maybe living on a farm was actually just that much work.

"I only destroy everyone I touch."

His words from last night echoed in my head. How could he say that, when he'd built a crib and a high chair for my baby? When he'd been providing for me since we'd arrived? When he cooked for me, grew all of our food, and he let me sleep in his bed?

By the time I returned to the table, two glasses, a fork, and a cloth napkin had mysteriously appeared. I shot a glance back to my massive, furry roommate once more, shaking my head at his endless generosity.

"Would you like some milk?" I asked, pouring myself a tall glass.

I couldn't remember the last time I'd had pancakes for breakfast. Since our emancipation, Petra and I had lived off mostly hot dogs and cereal and whatever else we could get cheap from the convenience store. If it was a special occasion, maybe we'd have a taco night or make hotdish. But neither of us were particularly good cooks, as none of our foster parents had ever taught us.

"Yes, please."

I set the second full glass at the setting across from mine, then sat down to dig in. As I spread the thick, yellow butter and drizzled honey onto my plate, it finally sunk in just how screwed I really was if this was my life now.

It's not like Felix would just wait on me hand and foot forever. Eventually, I'd need to learn how to contribute to this kind of homesteader lifestyle. I'd have to learn how to cook more than frozen pizza or cereal. I'd need to *farm.*

Humbled, I took my fork and wedged out a sticky, buttery, double-stacked slice from the stack, and shoveled it into my mouth.

And I just about orgasmed on the spot.

"Oh my godzh," I groaned around the mouthful, the rich sweet-and-savory softness melting like pillows on my tongue. "Theezh are *amazhing*."

Had I *ever* eaten something this delicious?

I followed the heavenly bite with a swig of cold milk, which was hands-down the best I'd ever tasted. It was rich and creamy, and *sweet*—closer to a vanilla milkshake than any milk I'd ever had before.

How was it even possible for milk to taste this good? If this is the farming life, then sign me up. I'd learn how to milk a cow and egg a chicken if it meant I could have breakfast like this every morning!

"Fucking a," I cursed, licking a smear of cream from my upper lip as I set down my glass, "Are you a *chef* or something?"

CHAPTER 14

FELIX

Betsy didn't wait for a response before indulging in another giant bite from her stack of pancakes. Warmth exploded in my chest as I watched. Before I even knew what was happening, my cheeks puffed in a proud smile as her eyes lit up with every bite.

Since that night in the barn, when she'd almost pulled my cock out of my overalls and ended up in tears, I'd done everything I could to avoid another situation like that. It was clear from her crying that she was not pleased by her sudden change in circumstances. And who could blame her? She was quite literally dumped onto my doorstep with nary a concern for her own needs or desires. She may have had sex with Zeus, but that did not indicate her consent to bedding just any member of the minor pantheon. Especially when she was being coerced to in order to keep her calf alive.

She was under so much pressure as a new mother. It wasn't fair for her to consent to something only to provide for the needs of others. I couldn't accept that. *Wouldn't* accept it.

So I decided to give her space. I could provide for her as

best I could, while giving her as much freedom from my presence as possible. If seeing me made her feel guilty for not following the whim of the gods, then I'd make sure she didn't have to see me if she didn't want to.

And yet, she always seemed to be in the kitchen when I came in from the barn. She'd insisted on helping me with dinner, despite the fact that she was not at all skilled in food preparation. She looked at a chef's knife as if it might grow a mind of its own and stab her.

Even in spite of that, she tried. She made conversation. She'd done laundry—something I was immensely grateful for. Despite her circumstances, she *tried* so hard. And her resilience and kindness surprised me.

Perhaps what was even more of a surprise, though, was my own reaction to her presence. I'd known she was beautiful; I'd been attracted to her since I first saw her step onto my property. But cooking for her, talking with her, being in her presence…

It *did* something to me. Caused a twisting in my gut, a pull in my very core, that became harder and harder to ignore the longer she lived here.

I glanced over at little Apollo, sitting patiently (for once) in the high chair I'd built for him. It was another late-night project I'd embarked on after seeing how often Betsy would glance into the open door of the bedroom over the course of dinner each night. She didn't like for him to be out of her sight, and it wasn't right for her to have to hold him whenever they weren't in the bedroom.

It took a little longer than I'd hoped, as I'd needed to cut, shape, and sand the pieces much more intentionally than I'd needed to when I repurposed the manger for his crib, but I was pleased with how the end product had turned out. I couldn't resist being here to witness her reaction to it once I'd placed it in the kitchen.

And when I saw how delighted she'd been when she noticed it standing beside the table, I couldn't deny how proud—how *happy*—it made me.

That feeling only grew as I observed her eating my pancakes.

Despite the fact that I'd been feeding her since she arrived (after all, I was already cooking for myself, so why not include her?), I'd yet to even consider the kinds of foods she liked or disliked. I never asked her what she wanted for breakfast or dinner, I simply made enough of whatever I was having for two.

But watching the way she devoured her breakfast, I realized what a terrible mistake that was.

I needed to figure out every single one of Betsy's favorite foods. All of them. And feed them to her every day for the rest of my life.

"Are there any more?" She asked around a still-full mouth of food, and a strange tug in my stomach made me stutter.

"Y-yes," I muttered, pointing to the plate of extras on the counter.

"Hell yeah!" She leapt from her seat, bounding over to collect another three pancakes and slather them in butter and honey. She also poured herself another glass of milk, and the sight of the near-empty pitcher instantly dimmed my mood.

Right. For a moment, I'd forgotten.

The real reason she was here.

I took a bite of my own breakfast, not nearly as ravenous as Betsy appeared to be. That made sense though, seeing as she had two bodies to feed. Once we were done, and I'd gathered our dishes and put them in the sink, I snatched up my pile of garden plans and carried them over to the table.

Betsy was already preparing to get Apollo out of his chair, and I put a hand on her arm. "Wait."

She looked up at me, her hazel eyes curious and guarded. The jovial woman she'd been while eating pancakes was gone —or at least, was hidden behind the role of responsible mother she had donned to wear for the rest of the day.

Who had she been before Apollo had come into her life, I wondered? Who was the Betsy that Zeus had met and courted, before abandoning her?

"Uhhh, Felix?" She glanced down at my arm and back up at my face, tilting her head. "What's up?"

"Stay a moment. I'm planning the garden, which you should have a say in."

"Me?" Her nose scrunched with tiny wrinkles as she furrowed her brow. I had the sudden desire to trace the troughs with my thumb. To hold her head and press my lips to her forehead.

I coughed. *What was wrong with me?*

"Yes. It's what we'll be eating off of for the next year, after all. I've got the standard vegetables that are good for cellaring and canning, of course, but we have plenty of room." I shrugged in my chair, tapping a pen against the paper plots of the fields to hide my nerves. *Here goes.* "What do you like to eat?"

It was the most words I'd managed to string together in one breath since she'd arrived. But I couldn't bear the thought of her leaving the kitchen just yet.

Her hand dropped from the high chair, and then she pulled out her own seat and lowered herself back to the table. I spread out my plans, gesturing to the lines and squares that represented the corresponding rows of soil in the back field. Her eyes widened as she studied the papers, glancing every so often to the kitchen window as if to imagine it.

"I've uh... I've never gardened before. Not that I won't

help—I will, I can, I just… I'm sure whatever you choose will be fine. You seem to be really good at all of this."

She waved her hands as she spoke, encompassing the whole of the farmhouse and the acres of land with her small, soft fingers. A pink blush rose from her neck to her cheeks, and I marveled at how I could have ever thought of this woman as a nuisance.

"It is not difficult. Would you," I swallowed, realizing the step I was about to take. "Would you like to learn?"

The second I saw her eyes widen, my mouth went arid. I grabbed my glass of milk, upending it in one ambitious gulp, obscuring her face with the glass as she pondered her answer.

You idiot. The last thing she wants is to spend more time with you. So you offer her a gardening apprentice program? Taking away the only iota of freedom she has away from you so she can toil in the fields every–

"I'd love to!"

CHAPTER 15

BETSY

The second he offered it, I knew I had to pounce on the opportunity to learn from Felix.

Not only would this make me less worthless around the farm—something I was only getting more and more nervous about the longer I lived here—it also gave me an opportunity to spend more time with him. Get to know him.

What made Felix tick?

I wanted so badly to understand him better. He was so different from every man I'd ever met. Since the age of fifteen, I'd never lived with a man this long without him making a move on me. I didn't know what to make of it. Whereas most guys I'd known only had one thing on their mind, Felix seemed to think about everything, all the time. My needs, Apollo's, the chickens' and cow's, his crops and his tractor… he took care of everyone and everything around him, and never asked for anything in return.

I was used to earning my keep wherever I lived, but with Felix…

I wanted to.

I wanted to learn more about the farm. I wanted to help in the kitchen, the garden. But I also wanted…

My eyes drifted down to the table again, imagining his furry lower half below it. I was so intrigued by him. And while *he'd* made it clear that he didn't want a repeat of that night in the barn, I'd often wondered what it would have been like if he hadn't stopped me.

I'd never *yearned* for someone like this before. Was it the post-partum hormones? Or was it something more?

"G-great!" He stuttered, the mahogany fuzz of his face tinting a delightful burgundy. *Gods*, those dimples. His smile was infectious.

I'll admit it: when I first arrived on the farm, I'd been a bit intimidated by the sheer size of Felix. Close to seven feet tall when you included the horns, and broader than even my not-so-dainty body, it had taken a moment for me to feel comfortable around him.

But the longer I lived with my grumpy, burly roommate and my minotaur son, the cuter I found the features that made them so distinctly…*monstrous*. The pale ivory horns that poked from their hairline, parting the tufts of their shaggy hair. Their wide, huffing snout that wrinkled whenever they laughed. The wide, earnest eyes that were so deep brown they were almost black.

Looking at him next to Apollo, I could almost imagine that the two minotaurs were related. That maybe, if my life had been different, if Petra and I had been adopted by a kind, country family out in the sticks of southern Minnesota and I'd stumbled upon this hottie behind the bleachers of the county fair, instead of running into Zeus on my mad escape to Lollapalooza at my first taste of freedom…

Behind the bleachers of the county fair??

Alright, Betsy. That's enough daydreaming.

With a cough, I came back to the present, only just realizing that Felix was excitedly pointing to the diagrams in front of him and explaining things I should absolutely be listening to.

"—reserved for potatoes and carrots, simply because we'll need the extra root vegetables in order to get us through the winter. They cellar well, and if you like pickles, my lacto-pickled carrots are one of my favorite treats on long, humid summer nights." He lifted his eyes from the pages spread between us, shrugging at me with a sheepish smile. Without realizing it, I'd somehow scooted closer to him while he was talking, and those big, soulful eyes contained so many more shades of amber and earth than I'd previously thought. "Do you?"

I started, blinking myself out of the spell he'd cast on me. "Do I what?"

"Like pickles?"

I grinned. "Oh, Felix. I have a feeling this is going to be a fun project."

* * *

TURNS OUT, "FUN" may have been a bit generous of an adjective to describe the arduous task of plowing, fertilizing, planting, and sustaining a two-acre garden. While planning out the various plots of vegetables had been exciting, staking those plots took hours.

After we'd sketched out a basic map of the various crops we planned to grow for ourselves, Felix had rolled up the schematics and risen from the table, telling me to gather up Apollo while he collected the tools we needed. By the time I'd given my baby a frustratingly short feeding, changed his diaper, put on his little socks and shoes and dressed him for the outdoors, the farmer was ready for us—out standing in his field with his furry ass hanging in the breeze.

He held up his staking tools: a quiver of thin wooden dowels and two square, 1"x1" sticks connected by a 6-foot piece of twine. He explained how the two of us would use it, leapfrogging each other down the side of the field and marking each stretch of string with one of the dowels, to measure out even rows as we worked.

Fortunately, Apollo had a grand time as we set to it: plopping himself down into the freshly-turned earth of the garden and digging his stubby little fingers into the ground. Within minutes, his tiny pants and t-shirt were covered in dirt, his shoes and socks ripped off and splayed about him in a semicircle, his face blotchy and mottled with the rich, dark soil. I sighed, worrying about the lack of sunscreen for his sensitive baby skin, but Felix had waved away my concern with a snort.

"His skin is tougher than you think. Trust me. If anything, the time outside will be good for him. He'll be walking soon, and being out in the elements will prime his hooves for country life."

"You talk like he's meant to be a farmer!"

"Well, many minotaurs and cryptids take well to it." The big minotaur blinked at me after measuring out six feet between two rows. "That's what most of the immortals that have been banished from Olympus do."

"There are *more* of you?"

He winced, shoulders rising in a way that made me think he was preparing to backpedal. "Not many. But… let's just say, Apollo isn't the first demigod to be born with a tail."

I considered this, waiting until Felix had stuck another dowel at his feet before I carried my stick past him to mark off another row. "So… does that mean you're also a demigod?"

"Not quite," he grunted. "I'm what happens when the gods curse your mother to fall in love with a magic bull."

"Oh! *Oh.*" I couldn't decide how I felt about the image that popped into my head. It rung a bell, vaguely, from the myths I remember learning back in school. But I'd never been a particularly good student. Something about the Minotaur of ancient Greece and a princess and a… labyrinth? "How'd you end up in Minnesota?"

He paused for a moment, studying me with squinted eyes, and I couldn't tell if he was trying to figure me out or if the sun was in his face.

He started walking out the string before he responded. "It's my punishment."

"Punishment? For what?"

Another long pause. When he finally answered, his jaw was clenched. "I wronged Hephaestus, the blacksmith god."

"Ah. Bummer." I didn't ask for more clarification. We continued marking out rows in silence for a few seconds. "I don't know, though. Minnesota isn't so bad."

"*That's* your takeaway? You're not going to ask me more about what I did to deserve it?"

"It seems like you don't want to talk about it," I answered honestly. "So I figured I'd change the subject."

I'd learned quickly that asking too many questions usually gets you kicked out of a home faster than just shutting up and putting your head down. Was I curious about Felix's origins? Absolutely. Especially since a strange goddess kept appearing and trying to convince him to sleep with me.

But I'd been given free room and board by the gods, and too many questions would get annoying. I wasn't about to piss off the hands that fed me. Not on purpose, at least.

I glanced back toward the house, keeping an eye on Apollo. He was content as could be, sucking away on his pacifier while he made little mountains of the rich soil around him.

"I don't know, though," I added quietly, taking in the peaceful surroundings. "For a punishment, this isn't so bad."

"This is my purgatory. My true punishment was served after I 'died' over a millennia ago at the hands of that human hero."

"Back in the day? *Millennia ago?*" I gaped at him. "Wait, what do you mean, *died?*"

Literally every word he just said sunk in a second after I processed the last. It was a slow unraveling of meaning while Felix continued pacing out rows and dragging me along on the string behind him.

Forget not asking personal questions. He'd just confessed to being a zombie!

"Wait a minute," I sputtered out before he had a chance to reply. *Human hero...* "Are you telling me you're *the* Minotaur from Greek mythology?"

He straightened, staring down at me before reaching into his quiver for a dowel.

"You had sex with The Actual Zeus, and you're surprised about the fact that I—your minotaur roommate—is the one from legend?"

I paused for a moment as that sunk in. Eventually, Felix tugged my feet back into walking along the field's edge, and I took the dowel from his outstretched arm.

"I just... you were *killed*. By Hercules? Achilles?"

"Theseus," he grumbled. "Yeah. I was in Tarturus for a while, in the pool with Tantalus. Then I pushed boulders with Sisyphus. But my time with Prometheus was the worst. Getting my liver pecked out by hawks."

A pang struck my chest at the thought of Felix, serving out hellish sentence after sentence. "That's *awful!*"

"Yeah, it's not my favorite era."

"But what did you do to deserve it? It couldn't have been that bad."

He was bent over the stake as I said it, and at those words, he froze. For a moment, I wondered if he'd hurt himself, but just as I was about to offer him a hand, he shook his head.

"I... I don't want to talk about it."

He straightened and tugged the string again, and I walked it to the next row. I desperately wanted more details, but that for sure sounded like one of those too-personal-to-ask-about situations.

But my mind was reeling. How is he still here, on earth, if he's technically dead? Also, has he died multiple times, if he wasn't sent to Tartarus when Theseus killed him? Who sent him back to earth, and why?

We staked out a few more rows in silence. All the while, I snuck quick glances at Apollo (still playing) while I chewed my lip, trying to come up with something safe to talk about.

"But... you eventually became a farmer? Like the rest of the minotaurs?"

Thankfully, he jumped on the subject change. "Yep. The gods realized that us immortals were better utilized toiling on Earth with the mortals than filling up the centuries withstanding endless torment. Plus, Hades started to lose interest in coming up with more and more punishments for me. With billions of humans taking up the underworld, he's got more than enough to keep himself busy."

"You make yourself sound more like a tool than a person."

He huffed. "Aren't I?"

I stopped. He tugged on the string again, but this time, I didn't move. Instead, I just stared at him, hands on my hips, as a scowl took over my face.

"No, Felix. You aren't a *tool*. You're a human be—well, a minotaur... man. You're your own minotaur man, and you deserve better! You've done your time. You shouldn't have to live out all of eternity being a pawn for the gods!" I threw my hands up, frustrated that he apparently thought so little of himself.

Felix? *My* Felix? The one who farmed this entire giant property by himself and did carpentry in his spare time? The one who made the best pancakes I'd ever tasted?!

He huffed again, and it was quickly becoming my least favorite sound he made. "We're all pawns of the gods."

"*I'm* not!"

He met my eyes then, and the pain and pity swirling in his expression was enough to make my chest hurt. Then he glanced over my shoulder at Apollo, before looking back to me.

"You especially are, Betsy. You, me, Apollo—we're all just here at the whims of Zeus and all his cronies. You wouldn't be here if you weren't."

CHAPTER 16

FELIX

Dozens of emotions flashed across Betsy's face in the second following my outburst, before she tucked them away under the surface. She didn't reply immediately, instead, she snatched the stake on her end of the measuring string and marched the five paces out to mark the next row. When I handed her a dowel from my quiver, she swiped it from my fingers angrily, shoved it into the loose, dark ground, then glared at me to mark the next one.

I sighed.

"Betsy, I'm sorry. I didn't mean to offend you."

"Who said you offended me?"

She crossed her arms, the stake flung out behind her elbow like a weapon.

"All I meant was, the gods do not concern themselves with our desires or feelings. But they will use us to their ends however they see fit."

"How, exactly, are they using me, Felix?"

I sighed once again. The mid-morning sun suddenly felt too hot on my face, the dirt too dry beneath my hooves. What I had hoped would be a peaceful collaboration between the two of us had turned into an argument around my least favorite topic.

I'd been a pawn for the gods since the day I was born. I was used to their despicable treatment. Tartarus or Earth made no difference to me; every world ruled by their mock justice was a type of hell I simply had to endure.

That was the thing about being immortal. There was no escape from the drudgery of life.

The closest I ever came was when I worked the land. There was something comforting in the cycle of the seasons, the pattern of life and death amongst the plants. That was one invention of the gods I quite enjoyed, truthfully, made all the sweeter by the reminder of Demeter's own torment as the summer turned to fall and turned to winter, when her daughter Persophone returned to Hades.

It wasn't only mortals and lesser deities that suffered under the rule of the Three. Even goddesses of the major pantheon had to deal with the consequences of the brothers' rash decisions.

I snorted.

"You were once a pawn of Zeus's, when he filled you with his seed. Now you are a pawn of Hera's, as am I—here to grow and nourish the Brothers' spawn while he is most vulnerable."

"The Brothers?"

I measured out another row. "Zeus, Hades, Poseidon. The Three. The Kings of the Worlds."

"Zeus didn't make me his *pawn*. I *chose* to have sex with him."

She plucked a dowel from my quiver as I gaped at her. Not necessarily because she elected to have sex with the king of the gods, but that she thought it was, in fact, *her* choice. Like he didn't use his powers and wiles to coerce her. "*You* chose it?"

"Yeah, I did. And you know what? It was pretty great. He's a good lover." I snorted again, and she stuck her tongue out at me. "Whatever! He is! Not that you'd know anything about that."

"Excuse me?"

We stood facing each other in a stalemate, as I refused to move another inch until she explained herself.

Betsy covered her mouth with her hands, eyes wide. "Nothing. Forget I said anything."

"Do you doubt my virility, human?"

I crossed my arms and watched the color bloom to her cheeks as her eyes darted below my waist, before flashing back up at me.

"No! No. That's not what I meant. I mean, not that I've like, thought about you… you know what? Nevermind."

We stared off for a moment, before I shook my head. "You are clearly gods-touched, Betsy."

"What's *that* supposed to mean?"

I shoved my stake into the ground, placing my hands on my hips. How frustrating. This was the last conversation on earth I wanted to have, yet here we were.

"None of us *choose* our fates. You have been influenced by the gods. Do not believe for a second that you chose Zeus—*he* chose *you*, and has the power to work his influence to obtain anything he desires. He's been doing it for thousands of years. Anytime any of us think we are immune to the gods' power, we're fooling ourselves. We end up making decisions that don't make sense, taking unnecessary risks, getting–"

Getting our loved ones in trouble. Losing everything we hold dear.

"Getting what? Knocked up?"

She was glaring at me now. I took in all five-odd feet of her, from her dark brown locks plaited into frizzy, pigtail-braids down to the tips of her dirty sneakers. Her hands propped on her round hips, cocked at a defiant angle. The anger and frustration etched into the lines of her tired face.

Damn. I'd offended her.

I brushed my shaggy mane from my forehead, snorting a bit to clear the field dust from my nostrils.

"That isn't what I was implying."

"Oh really?" She squinted at me, shifting her stance to her other hip as she crossed her arms across her full bosom. "Go ahead, hit me with it. I've heard it all before. Just another annoying kid, some useless victim of the system. Shipped from home to home, leeching government resources only to become some kind of welfare queen. Same old story, right? Single mom, shacking up with an irresponsible man and landing herself in a pit of trouble all because she couldn't bootstrap hard enough. Despite the fact that I've been working since I was sixteen!"

"I didn't mean—"

"I know what it means to be *used*, Felix." She cut me off, and I shrank from the bitterness of her words. Instantly, I felt about two inches tall.

She'd mentioned her sister, Petra, who was not a true sister by blood. But other than that, I'd learned very little of her childhood. This must have been why. She'd suffered. And she hadn't wanted me to pity her for it.

Her voice dropped lower, and her hands lowered to her sides. She clenched her fists. "I know how it feels *not* to have a choice. But it wasn't the gods that put me in that position— it was regular old humans. Men, mostly. The gods have actually been pretty great so far. I liked being with Zeus. Hera saved my life. And sure, it's hard taking care of Apollo, but in the end? I chose to keep him. Because I don't want him to have to go through what I did."

"Betsy…"

There were tears in her eyes now, and it pained my heart

to see it. I wanted to reach out, to hold her, but she shrugged away from me when I stepped forward. My breath grew shorter as I watched, dumbfounded, while she steamrolled on.

"And sure, I get why someone might think that's irresponsible. After all, I'm not exactly the best mother, am I?" She sniffed, tears now streaming down her face. "From foster care to food stamps to being foisted off on you to take care of me and Apollo, because we're just that helpless!"

She snatched her stake back up off the ground, marched to the next point along the field, and jabbed it into the ground. Then she shoved her hand out in front of her, fingers wiggling expectantly.

"Well?"

I just stood there, unsure what to say. Ashamed that I'd offended her when that was the opposite of my intention. Devastated that I'd reminded her of something so terrible. I didn't mean to *blame* her for her situation. Far from it. If anything, I'd been trying to absolve her of responsibility.

Responsibility that she seemed intent on taking up, regardless.

"Gimme the damn dowel, Felix!"

When I didn't react immediately, she stomped toward me, loose dirt kicking up at every step. She reached up to my shoulder, her arm stretching straight up while she balanced on tiptoes, only to yank me down so she could reach into the quiver at my back.

The movement brought her close, closer than she'd ever been to me before. My snout buried into the sun-warmed crown of her head, and I inhaled the sweet scent of her hair on accident as she drew me into her.

Gods, that scent. Sunshine and baby powder and honey.

Delectable.

She secured a dowel and went to pull away, but I wrapped

my arm around her back. She'd tied her everpresent flannel overshirt about her soft waist, and my thick fingers bunched in the pleats of the fabric. Her breath hitched, and it awoke something inside me, something that had long been dormant.

Damn this woman. How dare she have such spirit, such *determination*, to fight so hard to rise above her fate? How dare she make me question everything I thought I knew about the gods? How dare she struggle so much, harbor so much pain, and refuse to let me comfort her?

How dare her body feel so soft and welcoming, and fit so perfectly inside my arms. How dare she be so lovely, so fiery, so—so…

She jerked her head back to face me, and seeing her face this close only intensified the feelings I couldn't put into words. I pulled her closer, surrounding her with my arms, burying my face into her hair.

"You are *not* helpless. You are not a bad mother. You fight harder than anyone I've ever known."

She tensed, not a single hair on her head moving as I spoke. But when I breathed the last word, she lifted her arms and sank into my embrace.

My other arm slid to her hip, relishing in the give of her thighs. I hoisted her body against mine, and she wrapped her legs about my waist. A low rumble built in my chest, and her grip tightened. My heart raced, and my lungs strained for breath. Her scent surrounded me.

Sunshine, baby powder, and honey…

I pulled away enough to meet her eyes. She held my gaze, cheeks burning a fiery pink beneath her long, dark lashes as we stared at one another. The sun shone brighter, warming my shoulders and back. The air grew warmer, too—in fact, my whole body grew hot under her focus.

Her hazel eyes sparkled, and it sent shockwaves down my spine. My whole body tingled under her scrutiny.

"Zeus is a damned fool," I muttered, every muscle in my body clenched tight for fear of letting my feelings loose. "They all are."

"What?"

Her plush, pink lips parted around the word, and my breath froze.

This was dangerous. It was stupid.

And it was playing right into the gods' meddling hands.

My body screamed in silent rebellion as I loosened my grip on Betsy and lowered her back to the ground. She swayed a moment on unsteady legs, so I kept a light grip on her elbow as both of us adjusted to the influx of space between our bodies.

Too much space, my instincts grumbled. But I held firm to my resolve.

"I do not think those things about you. Any of them."

She blinked. Shook her head. And blinked again. "What?"

The gods had done something to this woman. They must have. Her lips were unnaturally pouty, her eyes too round and innocent to be fully-grown human. Hera must have done more than simply heal her from her traumatic labor. I wouldn't be surprised if Aphrodite herself had intervened to craft the most enticing woman on the planet to deliver to my doorstep.

This was never a problem when I was first exiled here to live out the rest of my eternal existence alone, to toil the fields in perpetuity. Was it a little boring? Sure.

But boring, I could bear. Boring did not set my blood racing in angry torrents through my veins. Boring didn't disrupt my routine, infiltrate my home, and drive me to distraction.

Boring didn't rip my heart from my chest and stomp it into the ground.

Why had she suffered so much? She'd done nothing to deserve it. Any of it. I, at least, had been punished for my own wrongdoing. But Betsy?

The entire world had taken advantage of her. I refused to do the same.

I couldn't erase her pain, but I could give her that, at least.

It took the utmost of my strength to tear myself from the woman in my grasp. I looked down at the stake still pinned into the ground at my feet, unearthing it and pacing to the next row. We were almost to the end of the field, where we would circle back in the other direction. Then it would be time to draw the rows with the wheel plow.

I pulled two dowels from my quiver, handing one to her. She took it silently, brow furrowed as she chewed on her plush, perfect lip.

We finished staking off the rows in silence, and when we reached the far edge of the field, I took a breath.

"Betsy–"

"Felix, I–"

We both stopped abruptly, before smiling shyly at each other for a moment. Then I waved for her to go first.

She demurred a moment, staring at a pebble she was toeing into the ground. "Look, whether the gods forced me here or not, I just want to say that…"

She trailed off, her eyes growing wide as dinner plates as her focus shifted toward the house.

"Apollo!"

CHAPTER 17

BETSY

$\mathcal{I}$ ran to my crying baby, who'd stumbled after rising onto his shaky legs in an attempt to find me. I wasn't sure how good his—or any infant demigod's—vision was at only eight days old, but there was no way he could see me when I was all the way at the end of the field. Every thought in my head vanished as I raced to comfort him.

Of course, he'd fallen—unable to find his footing in the loose dirt beneath his tiny hooves. His cries grew louder as I jogged as fast as I could, until I was close enough to see the shiny tears streaming down his chubby face.

"Oh, honey, I'm here, I'm here!" I kneeled next to him, gathering his filthy body into my arms and nuzzling kisses into his shaggy tuft of hair. "Let's get you cleaned up and fed, huh?"

He seemed more than eager for feeding. Even as I held him, he squirmed to stand back onto his feet, pawing at my shirt. I looked down at my cheap digital watch. Just over an hour had passed since Felix and I started staking out the garden, and Apollo was already clamoring for a second breakfast.

My boobs didn't even feel heavy yet.

"Alright, buddy, I gotcha." I looked back over my shoulder at Felix, who was still standing at the other end of the field. I couldn't make out his expression, but his horns were tilted as he stared in our direction. A warm tingle from our earlier interaction zinged down my spine.

I wish I knew what was going on in his head.

"I'm gonna go take care of him," I called out.

He nodded.

Half an hour later, a freshly-washed Apollo was suckling greedily at my aching nipples, struggling to get the final drops I had to offer. I was standing at the foot of the bed, with my baby leaning against me as his hooves dented the quilted comforter. When the pressure of his gumming brought tears to my eyes, I yanked him off one boob and switched to the other.

It was hardly better. I was out of milk. I hadn't even recovered from his post-breakfast feeding, and despite the ever-present tenderness of my breasts nowadays, it was clear that I just couldn't keep up with his growing demand.

"Dammit," I muttered as he hollowed his cheeks in an effort to suck out every last drop.

It was then I heard a soft knock on the bedroom door. I hastily covered myself with my flannel overshirt, draping it over Apollo's head.

"Come in."

"Betsy, I—"

I'm not sure what Felix had been expecting to find, but the second his eyes darted down to my loosely covered chest, his face tinted a fiery red. His words stopped abruptly, and for a moment, the two of us just stared at each other until he cleared his throat.

"The rows are all staked out."

"Great."

"I should probably–"

"Ah!" I winced as a lancing pain shot through my nipple. Instinctually, I pulled Apollo away, glaring at the little man with anger I knew he didn't deserve. "Fu–*ugh*, buddy, you can't bite me like that! The tap's dry, okay?"

He pouted at me with his big, confused eyes for a second, and then—

"WAHHHHHHH!!!!"

His wails pierced the still air of the bedroom, and I scrambled for his pacifier. Gently, I set him down on his rump while I searched the room for it. Out of the corner of my eye, I was barely aware of Felix approaching the bed to steady the baby while I shuffled through the makeshift changing table I'd made of the dresser.

"I'm sorry I interrupted–"

"It isn't your fault," I replied over the din. "He's either crying or feeding eighty percent of the time anyway." *Where was that fucking pacifier?* "If I could only find his–aha!"

It had been hiding behind the tub of baby wipes, which was close to empty at this point. Barely a week since we'd moved here, and I was dangerously close to being out of baby supplies. How long until I ran out of diapers? Two days? Three?

I scurried back to the bed and wedged it into Apollo's mouth. His eyes widened in surprise for a moment as he adjusted, then suckled for a few seconds, before he spit it out and started crying even more loudly.

And that was the final straw.

I sank to the floor, face buried in my hands as I joined him with a wail of my own. What else could I do? Even if he *would* drink formula, we were miles away from the nearest convenience or big-box store. I was almost out of supplies, patience, and absolutely out of milk.

I'm not sure how long I sat there sobbing—seconds?

Minutes?—when a warm, solid presence shifted beside me. I peeked through my fingers to see Felix sitting awkwardly on my right, baby Apollo on his furry lap while he held the rubber pacifer against his mouth. The baby squirmed, but eventually settled, eyes fluttering closed as my roommate held him firmly and patted his back with his giant hand.

"I don't know what to do, Felix," I said at last, when Apollo seemed to finally drift off in the minotaur's strong hold. "At this point, he might starve."

"Do you have a bottle? It's almost time to milk Betsy, I can–"

"He won't drink cow's milk. Or formula. I tried everything at the apartment back in the city."

He frowned at me, his eyes pained. "We'll figure something out."

"We?" I stared at him. His gaze was locked on the sleeping baby, who he'd shifted into a more traditional hold, rocking him against his chest. He looked so small in Felix's massive arms, his torso so much broader than mine. My chest tightened as I took in the two of them together, and I wondered not for the first time just what I'd gotten myself into.

"Yes, we. I'm not going to let you suffer anymore, Betsy."

My heart skipped in anticipation. "What are you saying?"

He sighed, rising to his feet and carrying Apollo over to the bassinet. He laid him down and tucked him in, then turned around, bracing his hands against the wooden rail before answering. "You need my seed. Fine. It's gross, but maybe we can sneak it into your food somehow. I'm a decent enough cook, I'm sure I can… disguise the taste. Make it more palatable."

I snorted. "What, you want to jerk off into some pancake batter?"

He shrugged. "It's better than the alternative."

Better than the alternative.

"Wow." I raised my eyebrows, shaking my head in disbe-lief. "You will literally do *anything* to avoid having sex with me, huh?"

"That's not–"

"Why?" I interrupted, flabbergasted. "Are you not into chubby girls?"

"What?" His nostrils flared, and he shook his head so hard his ears flapped. "No! Betsy, my attraction to you is *not* the issue. I'm worried about you!"

"Me?" I gaped at him. "I'm the one who *needs* it, Felix."

Was *this* the reason he'd been avoiding me all this time? He'd been worried that I didn't find him attractive?

He swiped a hand over his face, his gaze dark. "That's just the thing. You *need* it. The last thing I want to do is force you." He lifted his eyes to mine, and they shined with sympa-thy. "Especially after what you just told me? Betsy, I've wanted you since the moment I saw you. That's never been a problem. What *is,* is the fact that you're being forced into yet another impossible situation. What kind of man would I be if I took advantage of you like that?"

My heart stopped.

That was what had been holding him back?

I stared at him, really looked, taking him in from the tip of his horns to the bottom of his hooves. This minotaur was kinder and more considerate of me than any *man* had ever been.

And for some reason, that realization made me so horny for him I could barely see straight.

I wanted Felix. I'd known that for certain since the moment I'd dropped to my knees in the barn. But he'd held back. And when I'd thought it was because he wasn't attracted to me, or resented me, I understood.

But now that I knew he felt the same way I did?

What am I waiting for?

He must have taken my silent waffling for agreement, because he pushed himself away from the crib and started walking to the kitchen.

"I'll look in the refrigerator. There's bound to be something I can bake–"

"Stop, Felix."

He froze at the edge of the bed, turning to face me. I crawled toward him.

"I don't need you to bake me anything. No–scratch that. I don't *want* you to."

His eyes widened as I sat back on my heels, right in front of him. He swallowed, and I watched as the lump bobbed in his throat.

"Y–you don't?"

"No." I put my hand on his thigh, and a thrill shot through me as the loose sack of skin between his legs grew taut. "I want to taste you raw."

CHAPTER 18

FELIX

I want to taste you raw.

Betsy was kneeling at my feet. Her hand was on my thigh. And she'd just told me in no uncertain terms, that she wanted me.

My throat grew dry as I took in the sight of her in my bedroom, alone—a scene I'd purposefully tried to avoid since she'd first set foot inside my house.

I'd only come in here to check on her after everything that had happened in the field. I wanted to make sure she was okay. To help her.

Not…

I want to taste you.

Her words were like a pulse in my brain. Throbbing through my veins, sending a hungry ache below my waist.

The room was dim; the only light source was that shining in from the half-open door to the kitchen and the slight gap in the bedroom curtains. Besides the now-sleeping Apollo, it was just her and me, the two of us wedged between the bed and the crib, caged in by the door and the dresser.

Her flannel was loose about her shoulders, the cleft of

space between her breasts exposed, the sides of the shirt draping suggestively over her nipples. I couldn't see them, but the slight curves of each tit, nestled beneath the fabric, was enough to make my lower stomach ache with need.

"What–what do you mean?" My voice hitched as she rose up on her knees, placing her head dangerously close to my waist. Her breasts swayed with every movement. I had to bend my neck to look down at her: those green-flecked eyes twinkling in the slim ray of light breaking through the curtains.

She couldn't have meant it.

Could she?

She inched closer. "You know what I mean, Felix. I want you.."

I couldn't speak. I couldn't move. I could only look from one beautiful feature to the next: her strong brows, her sparkling eyes, her plush lips, searching for any hint of insincerity.

I did not want to be like the gods. I didn't want to take advantage of her.

So why can't I look away?

Her eyes peeked up through her long, dark eyelashes, and she took a deep breath. Her chest expanded with it, opening the gap between the sides of her shirt even more.

Oh, *gods*, I could see her areolas. They peeked out more with every nudge of her knees, pressed closer as she reached her hands forward. The gap between those tantalizing mounds collapsed into a singular line as she pushed her arms out and placed her palms upon me, landing on the sensitive spot where the fur of my thighs transitioned to the finer hair about my waist.

The sensation I'd been fighting since she'd called to me, the one that burned hot licks of fire through my core, flared with a vengeance as her delicate fingers traced the lines of muscles at my hips. *Fuck fuck fuck...*

When she leaned in and the peaks of her nipples brushed against my thighs, when her shirt opened completely and bared her entire torso, there was nothing I could think of to halt my body's reaction. Nothing I could do but blush profusely as the flared head of my rising erection poked through its prepuce.

The room was deadly silent as the shiny, red flesh hardened between us, and Betsy's eyes widened until I could see the whites completely circling the dappled green centers.

"Holy moly, Felix," she muttered, and fuck me if the puff of air exiting her lips didn't almost make me come on the spot.

I gripped the top bar of the crib with my tail to keep my balance. Every muscle in my body seized as I fought for control. "Please look away," I hissed, hearing how strained my breathing sounded. "I swear to you, I will not force myself on you. I'm not about to take advantage–"

"Take advantage?" Her lashes fluttered as she smirked at me. 'Felix, I'm the one doing the taking here."

I wheezed. "Huh?"

The sight of my cock bouncing mere centimeters from her plush lips was doing something to my brain. I couldn't parse the meaning of her words. I just knew that I needed to leave the bedroom right now, before things got out of hand. Before I ended up making a decision I couldn't take back. My tail coiled tighter.

I hadn't exposed myself to a woman in millennia, and for good reason. Acting upon my desires only led to ruin, and I would not expose Betsy to such consequences.

I prepared to leave, but then something happened that derailed me from my track of good intentions. In fact, it so thoroughly and abruptly severed my line of thought, that my entire body shuddered in reaction.

She wrapped her hand around my cock.

A noise that I could only describe as a wretched moo tore itself from my throat, as my mind went blank.

Thousands of years.

That's how long it'd been since I'd felt a hand on my cock.

No one, not even I, had touched it since Celedonia.

And even she had not had fingers as soft and tantalizing as Betsy's.

"If you're going to give me your seed anyway, I'd rather drink it straight from the tap."

I couldn't speak. The sensation was too great, too all-consuming, too altogether glorious that my brain had flipped off. I was reminded of my time in Hades with Tantalus, thirsty for water I could not drink, hungry for fruit I could not reach, only now…

Now it was like every forbidden, hungry thought I'd ever had about my roommate had been amplified to a hundred. And I was being forced to watch, helpless, as the impending train crash of our destinies edged me closer and closer to oblivion.

She leaned forward, squishing those perfect breasts into my fur, mouth opening wider and wider to accommodate the wide flare of my cockhead, as she inched closer. And then, when her lips were a hair's breadth away from making contact, as I held my breath and stared longingly down at her beautiful face, she paused and met my gaze.

And she hesitated.

"Um… if that's okay with you."

The nervousness in her expression had my lungs in a chokehold. Silence stretched uncomfortably long as the two of us teetered on the point of no return.

Did I want what Betsy was offering? Unequivocally. I

would have been an idiot not to. She was a perfect specimen of humanity, an individual as beautiful as she was selfless, whose strength of will around her heartbreaking circumstances left me speechless.

But it was those very circumstances that made me pause.

Was it okay to want this?

With her at the pinnacle of desperation?

Forced into my proximity by the gods?

Despite my circumstances, despite my rage, despite my preference for solitude… I only wanted what any creature on this earth desired.

To *be* desired.

She said she wanted me. Wanted to *taste* me. Could I believe her?

Would she have ever chosen me of her own volition, had her hand not been pushed into submission by forces greater than herself? Me, the most wretched of creatures?

"Do you truly want me, Betsy?"

"*Gods,* Felix. More than anything." Warmth filled me, only for my body temperature to ratchet up to a thousand and her next words. "Please let me drink you up."

My whole body shuddered. I don't know what I did to deserve such a taste of heaven in my perpetual purgatory, but I wouldn't question it.

I closed my eyes, letting her words sink in, and in every fiber of being I knew: I could not say no to her any longer.

I nodded.

CHAPTER 19

Never in a million years would I have thought a single nod could send a shiver through my spine.

But Felix was not a normal man. And the fact that a simple bob of his head was granting his consent for me to stick this—quite frankly, *incredible*—cock into my mouth?

I was drenched from the very thought.

My jeans were a swamp of desire as I knelt in front of the giant minotaur, thighs clenched as a surplus of want pulsed in my panties. If my past hadn't already ruined me for human lovers, seeing Felix panting at my touch would have been the final nail in the coffin. He was so undeniably hot, with his rippling muscles and perfect physique. Even the thick hair covering his legs turned me on, especially when I could tangle my fingers in his thick coat and bury myself in the scent of him: warm and earthy and something else… something I couldn't place, that just made me want to get more of him.

One hand gripped the fur at his hip while the other

stroked up and down his long cock, until I felt that it was fully erect between us.

And my gods. What a cock.

I didn't want to keep comparing him to Zeus, and gods knew Felix would hate it if he knew the thoughts whirling through my brain as I took him in, but I couldn't help it. It was the only reference I had that held a candle to him. Because every other man I'd slept with before—Zeus included—was *nothing* compared to Felix. In every way: from the strength of his character, to the size of his package.

I mean, I guess it made sense, considering he was half-bull and all. But I hadn't been expecting his shape to be so different. As he hardened, the smooth, red shaft poked free of the hairy sleeve between his legs, and the more I stroked him the longer and thicker it became. Seven inches, eight, nine… while the length was beyond impressive, it was nothing compared to its girth—especially at its flared tip.

It took a few moments of stroking for me to even know how to approach it. I could feel the heat radiating from his body as I'd stared up at him from beneath my lashes and waited for his consent to take him in my mouth.

When he finally dipped his chin, I unlocked my gaze from his deep, dark eyes and took in the meal before me.

And then I opened my mouth as wide as it could go.

I pumped up and down with my hand, the rumbling of his chest encouraging me as I bent my elbow to make sure to get his entire length. Then I tipped his shaft to my lips and touched the ridge running along its underside to my tongue.

His musky flavor exploded on my tastebuds as another low moan crooned from his lips. My mouth watered, and it was as if my body had been waiting for him. I couldn't slow down. I opened wider to force the circumference of his head past my lips as I stroked down with my fist, my fingertips coming together as they slid back to the base. Something primal awoke in me when the taut, smooth skin of his head hit the back of my throat, and suddenly I was groaning. Humming. My eyes fluttered closed as I slurped around the width of him, rubbing up and down all the while.

"Hades' gate," a low, husky growl sounded above me as a huge hand fell upon my shoulder. Felix bent at the waist, his torso hovering over me and casting me into shadow as I pumped him eagerly. "Betsy—ah! Ah, gods, slower please, it feels too–"

I raised my head, releasing him from my lips with a wet *pop.* A tortured *moo* broke through his chest as his eyes glazed, his fingers tightening around my deltoid.

Drool leaked at the corners of my mouth, and I found myself feeling as dazed and lightheaded as he looked. Why did he ask me to stop? When all I wanted was to…

I squeezed my fingers up the length of him once more, gathering the slick of my spit at his head and using it to glide the way back down. His breath hitched, and I felt the pressure of calloused fingers below my chin as he tilted my face up to look at him.

"Betsy, your mouth is…" His deep, cavernous eyes darted down to my lips, and I licked them self-consciously. The black of his pupils spread outward, until I could no longer tell where his gaze was focused. *"Tantalyzing."*

"Do you want me to stop?" *Please gods, no.*

His heavy breathing flared his nostrils, making the ring in his septum rock with each exhale. "No."

"Thank the gods." I descended on him once again.

"Ah, ah–!" he howled, his voice catching when I swirled my tongue around the full circumference of the flared head, stopping at the bottom to lick into the fold of skin that encircled him. It wasn't quite a full foreskin, as it never completely covered his head, but it did push and pull with my hand as I stroked him, and it eased the glide up and down.

But not enough. I reared back once more, using his hand on my shoulder for leverage, and spat some of my excess saliva into my palm, before wrapping my grip around him once more. My hand, slickened, swept up his cock from base to tip, and I followed with my lips as deep as I could take him on the way down.

I felt him buckle forward as he hit the back of my throat again, and I gagged a little around him. A shiver rocketed up his spine that I could feel shaking his hand, and it made me proud to know that I was making him feel good. I knew how badly he'd been trying to stay away from me, how much he'd wanted to avoid hurting me.

But I just couldn't wait any longer.

And while in the back of my head, my physical need for Felix's cum kept me motivated to stroke him to completion as quickly as possible, there was a deeper, more secret voice that urged me to keep him on the edge for as long as I could. I wanted to enjoy this. Enjoy *him.*

I loved the feel of his cock in my mouth, its weight on my tongue, the smooth glide of my palm against his foreskin. I loved how I could feel his muscles jump beneath the fur in my grip, loved the heat of his harried breaths rushing over my neck and shoulders as he steadied himself above me, straining with pleasure from every pump and suck.

And yes, I wanted his cum. I needed it.

But I also didn't want this moment of closeness to end.

Could it be both? Was it okay to want *and* need somebody the way I did Felix?

I could smell his intoxicating musk with every ragged inhale through my nose. I tasted it with every lick, and each time I felt myself get a little bit wetter from the scent. He was just so *good.*

If I forgot about the circumstances that brought me here, if I forgot about the goddess and Zeus and even Apollo for just a moment, I could imagine that Felix and I met completely serendipitously. That this sexy monster of mine had seen me from across the field and known instantly that I was the woman for him, his own sexy little human cow he could take for himself and keep in his barn, and the two of us could live and date and fuck for happily ever after.

It was a delicious little daydream. And I let myself believe it, for as long as it took to coax the sweet release building in his core from his balls.

When his breathing hitched again, and another moo started to build in his chest, I released the hand that had been holding onto his fur and reached between his legs. His balls hung there, low and heavy, and I gently curled my fingers around them to test their weight. His lowing climbed in pitch, turning into a moan as his hips bucked forward, sending his flared head past the back of my tongue and all the way down until it blocked my airway completely.

"Ungh!" I swallowed around him, eyes watering as I fought to breathe through my nose and suck every last ounce of pleasure out of him.

He roared, and I felt the heavy sack in my hand retreat up into his body as his balls squeezed. That was the only warning I got before a torrent of cum streamed into my throat, so deep I couldn't even taste it, aside from his musky scent filling my nose as his hips bucked into my face. I pumped my hand around his shaft furiously up and down the remaining inches, feeling the pulse of his glans as his release traveled up his length before erupting from his tip and down my throat.

I continued to swallow, again and again, feeling the way the inside of my throat squeezed around him and made him shudder. Everytime I thought he was done, another jet would pulse into me, until I felt full of it. Eventually, the firehose slowed to a trickle, and then finally his body slumped over mine.

I gasped around him, pulling back and taking in huge gulps of air as I released him from my mouth. My hand, though, still encircled him, gripping lightly around his base. I moved the other one back to his thigh.

Once free, he dropped to a knee, taking my hand with him as he reached around my back and under my shoulder to pull me into him, rearranging us until he leaned his back against the crib and cradled my side into his chest, my butt seated firmly on his lap and my legs thrown out perpendicular to his.

I felt a soft tickling up and down my arm, and in my periphery, saw the tufted end of his tail stroking me gently. Affectionately.

He slid my hand off of his softening penis, and I gathered the last few drips of cum from his tip as he did. Then I lifted my fingers to my mouth and greedily sucked each and every drop.

At last, I tasted it. Rich and salty and…something else. Something a little sweet, almost, like…

Oh my gods.

I couldn't help but laugh as I pulled my fingers from my mouth.

Felix tilted his head toward me, eyebrows lifting in concern. "What? What's wrong?"

"Milk," I chuckled, wiping the drool from my face. "Your cum tastes like milk."

CHAPTER 20

FELIX

I could feel the heat rise to my cheeks as the sweet, succulent Betsy lapped up my release on her fingers like honey. It was so incredibly lewd, such a lurid picture that left me as speechless as the act we'd just committed.

My gods. This human woman had just made me come.

Of all the tortures I'd endured at the hands of the Olympians, this was by far the sweetest.

"You're… quiet," Betsy murmured at last, looking up at me in the dim light through those long, dark eyelashes of hers. "Was it… okay?"

"Okay?" I snorted. "Gods, Betsy. It was earth-shattering."

The blush that crept up her round face in response was almost enough to quicken me to erection again. She was just so *cute.* I squeezed her more tightly in my arms, letting them sink into her ample waist and boost her bosoms higher on my forearm.

The weight of them was exceptional. I still struggled not to stare at them, a nagging voice in my head informing me that, now that she'd ingested some of my seed, they'd perhaps swell even *larger* with milk for Apollo.

Apollo!

I jerked forward, clutching her to my chest as I bucked my head around to check in on the babe, who—miraculously —was still slumbering in his blanket swaddle. I let out a breath as Betsy stabilized herself with a hand on my shoulder.

"He's sleeping?"

"Yes," I exhaled, my heartbeat returning to normal. "I'd, uh… in my moment of vulnerability, I'd forgotten–"

"It's okay, big guy. My horny goggles were on, too, I get it." She patted my pec, then tilted her head. "How old is he, comparably, to a human right now? He won't remember this, will he?"

"Oh, no," I asserted. With far too much confidence. "I hardly remember anything prior to my own young adulthood."

But I'd been alive for many, many years. And my childhood had been something of a blur, until I'd been relocated to the labyrinth.

I barely remembered my mother.

Had she made the same sacrifices that Betsy made for Apollo? Had she, too, been ostracized from her family, exiled from society? Or was her fate even worse?

I felt a yearning in my heart, so deep as to be almost imperceptible, for a mother I'd long forgotten. I wondered if the gods also planned to pluck Apollo from his mother, to condemn him to a fate like mine.

No. I wouldn't let them.

I tilted my head, feeling Betsy's soft brown hair scrunch beneath my cheek. A few flyaways fluttered and tickled my snout, as I closed my eyes, breathing in her scent.

With her this close, I could feel the initial tensing, and

then slow relaxing of her muscles as she sank into my embrace. We stayed like that for minutes, maybe hours, the silence as natural and lovely as the wee hours in the barn before sunrise. Before long, her breathing steadied, until a soft snore alerted me to the fact that she'd actually fallen asleep in my arms.

How had I let her burrow her way into my heart? How was it that two weeks ago I was content to serve out my exile in peace, and now the very thought of being without these two felt like it was ripping me apart?

Oh, Felix. What are you going to do?

* * *

"Aн! A ha! Ha ha, ha ha ha!!"

The manic laughter shocked me out of the deepest sleep I'd had in centuries. I toppled from the living room couch, almost gouging the rough pine floor with my horn as I scraped my head against the boards.

In the early afternoon, far later than I cared to admit after she'd dozed off on my lap, I'd tucked Betsy into my bed for a well-deserved nap. Once I'd left her and Apollo to themselves and closed the door behind me, I'd had a mind to go back and plow the garden. But I'd thought I could get away with a short catnap on the couch before returning to the endless farm chores that awaited me.

So much for that.

"What is it? What's wrong?"

Scrambling out of the blanket, I galloped into the bedroom, to find Betsy gazing at the sheets in disbelief. A quick glance out the bedroom curtains was enough to inform me I'd overslept, revealing a vibrant sunset casting an orange glow over the fields.

And over Betsy, who was laughing with tears in her eyes.

"Leaking, Felix. I'm leaking!"

Right on cue, a weak cry sounded from the crib, which only grew in volume the longer Apollo waited for his mother to respond. Betsy sprung from the mattress, grinning from ear to ear as she bent over the top bar of the bassinet and reached forward to retrieve her baby.

I didn't want to be rude. So I averted my gaze to the young minotaur as he reached up greedily. And then, I didn't have anywhere to look at all.

Because he immediately squashed his mother's breast between his two tiny hands and crashed himself right onto her nipple.

I didn't know where to look. While I couldn't deny that ogling Betsy's exposed body wasn't quite as taboo as it had been before our adventures earlier today, this turn of events brought me crashing back to reality. *This* was the reason she'd brought me to ecstasy: to feed her child.

It was a means to an end, nothing more.

But did I really believe that? When I'd seen for myself the heat in her eyes when she'd stared at me with my cock in her mouth? When she'd fallen asleep in my arms afterwards? When I could feel my heartstrings tug longingly at the sight of her nursing her child before me?

The line between what was attraction and what was merely necessary for survival blurred beyond recognition, and it made it difficult to know for sure.

I could no longer deny it: I wanted this woman. But did she actually desire me? Or was her body's reaction to me just an effect of my minotaur nature? Of my *essence*?

"I'll leave you to it," I murmured awkwardly, turning back to head for the door.

"Felix, wait."

I froze with my hand wrapped around the doorknob,

daring to glimpse back over my shoulder. And that was when I let myself truly *see* her.

Backlit by the window, strands of gleaming, brown hair glinted around her in a copper halo. Her green eyes sparkled with tears as she knelt on the floor, lightly cupping a hand over Apollo's back as he stood on his little legs before her. His tiny tail flicked back and forth happily as he drank.

Her shirt hung open, framing her naked chest and stomach, her strong, thick thighs parted to allow him to stand between them. She was a vision, nurturing while undoubtedly sexy, and I thanked the gods that her lower half was still clothed.

My control was already hanging by a thread.

She met my gaze. "Thank you. You have no idea how much this means to me."

My throat was thick with guilt and longing. *She* was thanking me? For what? Allowing her to whisk me off to realms of pleasure that I assumed impossible?

I shook my head. "Betsy, I do not deserve your thanks."

"As if!" She snorted, pointing at her chest. "Be serious right now. This right here? This would not be possible without you. I know you didn't ask for this. Gods know I never thought I'd be begging a full-grown minotaur to let me suck his cock for bull-baby batter, but..."

She trailed off, and my breath stopped. The very air between us seemed to freeze in anticipation of her next words.

"I promise I won't ask for anything else from you. As long as I can feed my baby, and we can co-exist peacefully like this, I'm happy. Ecstatic. I'll help more with the house and the garden and even the farm, too—you don't have to make accommodations for me or anything. I don't want you to change your whole life for me."

I stood there, with my hand on the doorknob, completely at a loss for words.

She… didn't want anything to change?

How could she say that, when *everything* had changed?

"I don't understand," I admitted. "My life will never be the same, Betsy. You and Apollo have already upended everything I've ever known. How can you say that you don't expect me to accommodate you, when you're living in my home? Sleeping in my bed?"

My priorities had reordered themselves the second they'd been dropped off at my driveway. My day revolved around making her breakfast and supping with her at night. I didn't want to imagine my home without her in it. Even now, the sight of her in my bedroom was comforting to me. Knowing that she was here, was happy, was safe—that mattered more to me than the farm itself ever had.

The second she'd wrapped those perfect lips around me, my life had changed forever. That wasn't something she could just… take back.

Her forehead scrunched, and concern flashed in her expression. She glanced toward the rumpled bedspread, then at Apollo, then back to me. Her eyes sparked, lips setting in a determined line.

"I'll earn my keep. I will."

"Betsy, that's not—"

"Whatever you want. Whenever you want. Just promise to keep coming inside me, Felix, and my body is yours for the taking."

Felix gaped at me. Which really wasn't surprising, considering what I'd just said.

It sounded pathetic. Desperate. A grown woman, literally bartering with an ancient, mythical monster to trade sexual favors for room and board. But holy shit—it had *worked*.

Swallowing his semen had made my minotaur milk come in.

And he was right. He'd given up everything for me: his home, his bed, his way of life. He'd spent at least two all-nighters making a crib and a high chair, had taught me how to breastfeed my own child, had fed me every morning and night since I'd arrived.

And what had I given him in return?

A blowjob? A few batches of laundry and dishes?

It wasn't nearly enough. And sure, I might be able to help out with farm chores here and there or teach myself to cook, but even that would probably grate on his patience for as long as it took for me to learn how to do it all.

I couldn't let this fall apart. I wouldn't let myself be a burden on him, not when he'd given me so much. As a kid,

I'd been basically helpless: completely dependent on my foster families for all my basic needs. But I was *better* than that now.

I could earn my keep, dammit. I wasn't about to be a drain on anybody: not the gods, not the system, and especially not Felix.

Because I *liked* him. A lot. I was stupidly attracted to him, and the physical chemistry between us only burned hotter now that we'd broken the tension. And he wasn't *just* sexy— he was a good person. Generous, caring, considerate... he took care of us, providing for me and Apollo without a word of complaint.

Or at least, no complaints to *me*, directly. To the goddess who'd brought me here? That was another matter entirely. And knowing how much he'd resisted us being here in the first place made his sacrifice all the more impressive.

Felix was the last person I wanted to see me as a burden. Because once that happened, this arrangement would fall apart. And I needed him.

I wanted him.

It was scary how much I was beginning to care for the big guy, especially considering my history with Olympians and relationships.

And sure, he seemed to like me alright for now. But I didn't know whether that was in spite of the gods or because of them. It was clear he didn't like being put in this situation with me and my biological imperative for minotaur semen. He viewed it as more fuckery from the gods, and I think that was part of why he'd fought so hard against it.

But once he'd given in, and I'd seen how much he'd liked it? How much *I'd* liked it...?

I couldn't fuck this up. I couldn't lose him. My skills in the bedroom had been good enough to keep Zeus entertained for half a year. Certainly, I could keep Felix happy at least until Apollo was weaned, right?

He deserved to be happy. And his post-orgasm haze was the happiest I'd seen him since I'd arrived here.

"You—you're offering me sex in exchange for…" He seemed to find his voice for a moment before losing it again mid-thought.

"For everything. You're generosity, your kindness. You've been feeding me, helping me with Apollo, letting me stay here. Not to mention making it possible for me to nurse my son." I gestured to the baby between us, who had just about drained my left breast dry. I was still a bit shell-shocked at that: I'd managed to keep feeding for ten minutes without running dry. And it was all because of Felix. "It's only fair that you get something in return. I'm not expecting you to take care of us for nothing."

His expression stayed blank. "That's what you think this is? A *transaction?*"

A lump formed in my throat.

Is that what I thought?

No, a small voice in my head whispered, practically begging. *That's not what you want it to be.*

But I swallowed it down. Sure. I'd always wanted life to be more than that. I'd wanted a family who would love me just for being me. I'd wanted to fall in love, to find someone who could be a true partner to me: someone whose goals aligned with mine, to take on the world together.

But the only person who'd ever been that for me was Petra, and she'd been taken from me. I'd fallen in love with the literal King of Gods, and even *he* wasn't better than any other guy using me for a good time. No family had ever kept me, no boyfriend had ever stayed.

I couldn't afford to take anything for granted.

At this point in my life, after I'd tried and failed time and time again to look at life in any other way, was it really worth it to keep the hope alive? That relationships could be anything more than transactional? That I could be accepted and cared for without having to give something up in return?

I adjusted Apollo in my lap, turning him on his hooves and directing him to my other boob. He switched eagerly, his eyelids drooping sleepily as he truly filled his belly for the first time since he'd been born.

Maybe it *was* possible, but I'd been looking at it the wrong way. Maybe *I* had never experienced that kind of love. But what about my son? Somehow, I loved him more than I'd loved anyone in the world, and he hadn't done anything other than just be born. Providing for him filled me with joy and pride, enough that it was worth every hardship.

No one had ever loved me the way I loved Apollo.

And I doubted anyone ever would.

I shrugged, pushing down the hurt.

Felix's big, beefy knuckles paled as he squeezed the doorknob, considering. A muscle in his jaw twitched, and I worried for a second that I'd read him entirely wrong. I couldn't read his expression: at one moment he looked angry, the next, sad.

After what seemed like an eternity, he sat down next to me on the bed, his legs brushing against my shoulder as I kneeled on the floor. I tilted my head at him, and he threaded his fingers into my hair at the nape of my neck.

"No, Betsy," he murmured, holding my gaze. "I won't agree to that."

CHAPTER 22

FELIX

Every bone in my body threatened to snap when Betsy had made her ridiculous proposition. Using her body as payment? For me…doing what, exactly? Enjoying her? Making sure she and her son didn't starve?

No. That wasn't who I was. That wasn't how I worked. Every *deal* I'd ever made was something that had been forced upon me by the Fates. I'd never gone along with this because I'd gotten the impression that Betsy would be *earning her keep*. The idea that she somehow owed me anything was preposterous.

I don't want you to change your whole life for me.

But I already had. Gladly.

But that was the rub, wasn't it? No matter how much I started to care for Betsy and Apollo, no matter how beautiful the future I'd let myself imagine for us… it couldn't last. However long this arrangement continued, however many weeks or months she and Apollo needed was fine with me. But after that, once he was weaned and she no longer needed me…

Working this land for the gods was my permanent

punishment for killing Hephaestus's daughter, but Betsy had done nothing to deserve exile like I had. Nor had Apollo. I knew not what the gods had in store for them, but I couldn't abide if they were damned to the same fate as me.

The two of them deserved better than to be cast outside of society for the rest of their lives. Seeing Betsy and her son so happy, so young, with a world of possibilities in front of them, had put my selfishness into perspective. Her body might have betrayed her, the world might have too, but she was bright and strong and resourceful. She was determined and fierce. Hera had saved her for a reason, I was sure of it.

I didn't know Hera's plan. For now, Betsy and Apollo needed me in order to survive. But once the babe weaned, I doubted the queen of the gods intended for them merely to become *farmers*.

My chest tightened. Ah yes, the gods and their *plans*. They planned for Betsy and I to have sex. Had they planned for me to get my heart broken, once again, and remind me just how despicable and unlovable I truly am?

Perhaps Tartarus was too good for a monster like me. No, *this* was my Hades, my eternal damnation, and I'd be loathed to forget that.

I let my hand cup the back of Betsy's neck, reveling in the feel of her soft hair, her warm skin. I took in the tiny minotaur suckling at her breast. What was *his* fate? Was he doomed to live at the whim of the gods his entire immortal existence, just like me?

No. *No.* Not like me. I wouldn't allow it.

It wasn't his fault he was born a monster. Nor was it Betsy's. I might be damned, but neither of them would suffer my fate.

"You won't?" Betsy's nervous tone broke through my depression, and I met her questioning eyes. "Does that mean you're not… you won't…"

Fuck. I'd made her upset.

My fingers squeezed. "No! Betsy, I want more with you. More than anything, I–"

My throat catched, the words getting stuck as I realized I *did* want more. I wanted her, I wanted them. I wanted to explore Betsy's incredible body and show her her inherent worth. I wanted to prove to her that she had nothing to prove to me.

"I want this to continue. I want *you,* and yes—I will give you my seed. But there is only one thing I want in return."

She tilted her head and adjusted her legs. Glancing down briefly to check on her son, she settled into the new position, leaning more heavily against my hand. "Anything, Felix. Just say the word."

I took a deep breath, letting the heat of her closeness, the scent of her, fill me with strength.

"It pains me to know how much you've suffered in the past. But I cannot imagine your future is anything but bright. You are strong, and beautiful, and when I see you with your son... you are going to be a magnificent mother, Betsy. You already are." Her eyes shone, and my gaze bounced between the hazel orbs. My throat tightened. "That's why, when Apollo is weaned, and you no longer need me... you both must leave."

Her face pinched together, and I could tell she was about to argue with me. I shifted my grip, cradling her jaw and sealing her lips with my thumb. "Please, listen to me. You will be able to have a better life if you don't get attached to this place. The more Apollo knows about me and my life here, the worse it will be for him. I'm not about to let another minotaur be raised in exile. If he grows up around me, in this place, if he thinks that this is all there is..."

Understanding dawned in her features, before they settled in her lips in a hard line. In less than a second, I watched any affection she might have had for me disappear, shutting down and locking away with a terse nod as she agreed to my terms. When she spoke, it wasn't to argue or question. If anything, her voice rang of the kind of resignation that only came from accepting one's circumstances as irrefutable.

"Right. You're not here to play stepfather."

Her words shocked my spine like lightning. I pulled back, eyes widening. "What?"

The leap she'd made was so far from my intentions that I scrambled to find the source of her misunderstanding. *Stepfather?*

The idea was so foreign, so *impossible,* I'd never have even considered it. But that she'd said it aloud, a vision of Betsy and Apollo and I living here on the farm like a loving, human family blossomed in my head like a rose: beautiful and alluring. Is that what I'd been doing this past week? Playing house? Building baby furniture, providing for a beautiful woman and her child, planning out the garden with them in mind...

My chest ached. What if that were every day? Waking up next to Betsy, making her and Apollo breakfast, coming in from a long day on the fields to a kiss on the cheek and an evening at the kitchen table, the three of us together...

But that kind of future wasn't possible. The gods would never allow it.

After what I'd done? After the life I'd ruined?

Never in a million years would the Fates let me have a family.

My snout curved down into a grimace. "The very idea is laughable."

"Laughable." She stared, eyes unfocused, at the crib.

Apollo's head fell back lazily from her breast, a bead of milk still clinging to its tip, and she patted his back absentmincedly. His eyelids fluttered and he swayed on his tired legs, little hooves stumbling as he let out a wet, bubbly burp.

The sound made her smile, and my chest clenched as I watched her lift the little boy by the armpits and kiss him between his tiny horn nubs.

"That was a tasty dinner, wasn't it, big guy? You look about ready for a nap, again, huh?"

She wrapped him up in a cradling hug, and he didn't even squirm. Just leaned heavily against her as she held him to her chest and rose from her kneeling position on the floor.

"Oh shi–"

I was there in an instant, catching her as her knees buckled. She and Apollo toppled forward, pressing into my chest as she lost her balance, and I wrapped my arm about her lower back, supporting her. I shifted them in my hold, moving one hand to the curve of her hip to steady her.

"Pins and needles," she grunted, face twisted in a grimace as she rocked gingerly from foot to foot. I held her firm. "My legs must have fallen asleep from kneeling for so long–"

"It's okay, I've got you."

I leaned forward, lowering her to a sitting position on the bed and taking Apollo. He was already conked out, falling fast into a deep, restorative slumber that only a full stomach could bring about.

Carefully, I lowered him into his crib, tucking his blankets around him. His cheeks were so chubby and round, his mouth open in the perfect little pout below his tiny snout. Dark eyelashes brushed along the soft, pink skin as his eyes winked closed and his breathing evened.

I gave the cradle a few rocks until I was certain he was asleep, then turned to check on his mother.

She sat, slowly rolling her ankles and chewing her lip. I almost sat down beside her, but then she tilted her head at me, and I realized what a stupid idea that was.

You're not here to play stepfather.

"I should probably make us something to eat, too," I murmured, breaking the silence. "Why don't you wash up? I'll have it ready in a bit."

"You don't want any help?"

The idea of spending another second in her presence right now, with all of the conflicting feelings warring in my head, was suffocating.

"No, no. You rest."

I turned away from her, my own legs shaky as I walked toward the kitchen. I heard her breathe in, as if she were about to say something else, but I shut the door behind me before she could.

I sagged against the wooden door, hanging my head in my hands.

This is how it had to be. If she and Apollo were to have a chance at happiness, then I couldn't let myself get attached. Couldn't let *them* get attached.

I never could have guessed just how hard that would prove to be.

CHAPTER 23

BETSY

I fell back onto the bed, exhausted despite the nap I'd gotten earlier.

Why was it that everything between me and Felix felt about a million times more complicated now?

Nothing was different. We were in exactly the same boat we'd been in since the very beginning. If anything, we'd finally clarified our expectations of each other.

So why did it feel like my stomach had been replaced with a ball of lead?

I'd known this was temporary. That Felix would eventually get tired of me. After all, I wouldn't need to breastfeed Apollo forever. Felix had told me that demigods grew up way faster than humans. He'd probably be eating solid food by the end of the month.

And then everything would go back to normal. I guess.

What's normal *for a minotaur, though?* I chewed on my lip some more as I thought that over. Though I'd seen her and Felix talking once or twice, I hadn't gotten a visit myself from the goddess since her automaton driver buddy had dropped me off here. So I had no idea what instructions the gods might impart when it came time for me to go back to Minneapolis.

Including what to do with Apollo.

"When Apollo is weaned, and you no longer need me... you both must leave."

Which was fair, I guess. But what place did my minotaur baby have in the world of humans?

What place did *I* have?

And why did giving up the potential of something more serious with Felix make me feel so... heartbroken?

I groaned quietly, reflecting back on how far the two of us had come. When I'd first arrived, I thought he'd wanted nothing to do with me. But then he'd cared for me, for Apollo. He's made us feel at home. He'd made me feel *wanted*.

And then I'd tasted that big ol' cock of his, and I wanted *more*, dammit. I knew he did, too.

The unwelcome reminder that there was a biological clock ticking down our time together made me desperate to make the time we had together count. He'd done more for me than just about anyone I'd ever been dumped on, and I wanted him to know how much I appreciated it. Appreciated *him*.

I wonder what kinds of things Felix was into in the bedroom. He was a farmer. Part bull. Did he have a milkmaid kink? Or was he more of a French maid kind of guy?

Costumes were in short supply this far out in the middle of nowhere, but I could probably braid myself some pigtails. Pick some wildflowers to put in my hair...

Working in an adult toy store for as long as I had, I knew about all sorts of weird kinks and sexual fantasies. Zeus and I had explored a ton of them during our relationship. I'd liked some more than others, but overall the experience had been freeing. For once, I wasn't just selling the equipment, I was testing it out. And it was *fun.*

We'd tried roleplay, bondage, tantric massage, pain play, and just about every kind of penetration you can do with two people. Apparently, I'd been the first partner he'd had who'd ever agreed to try pegging with him, which we'd done a *lot.*

He was also into bestiality, which was no surprise. I hadn't really been on board with that, ironically enough, although we'd done some fishy foreplay in a lake that I'd rather enjoyed. I'd drawn the line when he'd wanted to try fucking me as a horse, though. Especially when, at the time, my belly was large enough that I'd needed to be more careful during sex. The further along I got, the harder it was to try new kinks—especially the freaky ones.

He left me soon after that.

I hadn't had much time to process our break-up. I'd kinda been six months pregnant at the time, and the holy hormones racing through my system made it hard to parse out how I'd actually felt about it all.

Maybe years from now, I'd look back on the past year and think that he *was* just using me after all, like Felix had said. Maybe my willingness to dive headfirst into kink with him had actually been some misguided plea for attention. Maybe I'd known the whole time that he'd leave the second I said no.

But weirdly, I didn't regret it. And maybe that was naive of me, but I'd had fun with Zeus while it had lasted. And it'd given me Apollo.

There was one thing I did regret: not asking him more about his family. Now that I've heard more about Felix's past and his relationship with the gods, I was so much more curious about the dynamics between them all.

What was Olympus like? Did the gods get along with each other? What happened to all the other minor gods and goddesses and immortals that we never hear about anymore? Felix said there were other minotaurs out there beside him and Apollo, but *where?*

I wished I could talk to Petra about this. Not the kink stuff, necessarily—she was a little too straight-laced to be interested in all of that. But we'd always helped each other through first dates and break-ups, and she was the closest thing I'd ever had to a sister. I longed for a pizza night where we could stay up and vent to each other about men and how inscrutable they were. She might have been just as much in the dark about all of this as I was, but at least she would be able to put a positive spin on the whole thing.

Oh, right! My letter!

It felt like days had passed instead of mere hours since I'd written that thing.

I got up and hopped into the bathroom, shrugging out of my shirt and jeans so I could give myself a sponge bath. I smelled like sweat, sour milk, and a little bit like the bedsheets that had dried out in the sun after I'd washed them a few days prior. Regardless, I needed a fresh shirt.

After I'd washed up, I attempted to put on a bra, but it felt tight and restrictive against my sore nipples. My boobs muffined over the tops of the cups, and after a quick glance in the mirror confirmed just how ridiculous I looked, I reached behind and undid the four rows of clasps.

My chest sighed with relief.

"Well, shit," I muttered, looking at the fabric cage in my hands. "I guess that's one downside to my supply increasing."

I dug through my open suitcase on the bathroom floor, but the few tank tops I'd brought with me were all dirty. And the idea of wearing one of my flannels buttoned up over my naked chest was enough to make me flinch. I didn't need my nipples chafing against the shirt pocket seams.

I pulled on fresh underwear and some exercise shorts, then put my hands on my hips. Well, fuck. What was I supposed to put on for my walk out to the mailbox?

I scanned the room, taking in the white-washed walls and the small, checkered hexagonal tile floor, the enameled claw-foot tub and the big, farmhouse sink before my eyes landed on the bathroom door. The hook mounted to the middle of it.

And the large, silky, minotaur-sized bathrobe hanging from it.

Hadn't he said, over a week ago, that I could borrow his robe if I needed it?

I gave my boob a tentative squeeze, and hissed.

Ufda. Yeah. I'm sure I'd get used to my new boobs eventually, but right now? I couldn't bring myself to shove them into a tight, dirty tanktop.

I plucked the achingly soft bathrobe off its hook, gaping a little at how smooth the fabric was. Was this something Felix had gotten from the gods? I didn't know what silk felt like, but this was the kind of fabric I'd imagined whenever someone had mentioned it. Thin and light, it slid like water up my arms as I draped it over my shoulders.

I shivered. *Fuck.* I could get used to this.

He *had* mentioned I could wear it...

So I will, I decided, tying the fabric belt around my waist and tucking the cinched section under my heavy breasts. The quick adjustment raised the hem off the floor just enough so that the fabric hung down to my ankles, which was good enough for me.

Another quick cinch, and I was confident it would stay in place as I walked Petra's letter to the mailbox. I slipped the letter into one of the big pockets, left the bathroom, and with one last look at my sleeping baby in his crib, opened the bedroom door.

"It's almost ready," Felix called out immediately, not even turning to look as I stepped into the kitchen.

"Okay. I'm just going to step out for a quick walk."

"A wa–?"

His question died on his lips as he turned around and saw me standing there in his bathrobe.

The spatula he'd been holding clattered into the pan.

I gestured to the garment. "Is this okay?"

His deep, brown eyes darkened until they were almost black. A pink tongue darted out from under his wide snout as his gaze swept down my body from head to toe, lingering on the cross-section of fabric that billowed a little above the tie. His tail twitched.

I saw his Adam's apple bob as he swallowed.

"Y-yes. It's perfec–fine. Perfectly fine." He coughed, picking up the spatula, and his eyes darted back and forth between me and the pan. "Don't stray too far."

"Yep!" I chirped, scurrying across the tile floor and slipping into my sneakers at the back door. Then I got out of there as fast as I could.

I gasped in a gulp of fresh, evening air as I shut the door behind me. I'd barely been able to breathe in there under the weight of his stare.

The energy emanating from him in that kitchen as he saw me in his bathrobe was pure, unadulterated lust.

Now that I'd seen him with his cock in my mouth, I knew without a doubt what he looked like when he was aroused, and *that* was one pent-up minotaur.

And that was just from seeing me in his bathrobe? I could only imagine the look on his face if he knew the types of outfits I'd sold at the sex shop…!

I booked it down the driveway, boobs aching with every bounce on the way to the mailbox. But this time, it wasn't just the aftereffects of Apollo's feeding that was making my nipples swell.

It was the thought of pleasuring my minotaur after dinner.

CHAPTER 24

FELIX

She was wearing my robe.

My robe was draped over every curve of her body. That luscious, perfect body. The one that Betsy had agreed to let me use any way I wanted.

It was all I could think about as the two of us picked at our roasted squash and wild rice pilaf, with a side of sauteed soybeans in cheese sauce. I'd made us something hearty, serving her an extra helping to keep up with the increased demands on her body. The little noises of satisfaction she made when she first tasted it was a bonus, and I beamed with pride as she dug in.

But pride wasn't the only emotion rising within me.

Were her breasts...bigger?

My cock was already painfully hard under the table, and that was with me *avoiding* staring at the way the silk fabric of my robe puckered above her waist. She'd tucked the excess length of fabric under her chest, and the weight of them secured the fabric as easily as the belt. The thought of how delicious those weights would feel pressed against my own chest instead—or even better, with my cock sandwiched between them…

My bowl clattered to the table. I couldn't eat another bite. I was full. Had been for minutes.

Betsy glanced at the empty bowl in front of me, then up to my face. "Done with dinner?"

"Yes. You?"

She nodded, pushing her own bowl and the one spoon she'd managed to find in a cabinet somewhere into the center of the table. She used it for every meal, as I didn't have any other silverware that was appropriately sized for a human. Cutlery was one of the few things missing from this house when I'd been stationed here, decades ago.

In my mind, it would always be Betsy's spoon. Even after she eventually moved on.

"It was delicious. Thank you."

"You're welcome."

I could feel my pulse thundering in my temples. We sat there across from each other at either end of the kitchen table, staring unblinking into each other's eyes, for a full six seconds. I know it was that long, because the only sound was the ticking of the analogue clock that hung above the kitchen sink.

Tick. Tick. Tick. Tick. Tick. Tick.

"Apollo's probably gonna be asleep for another hour yet," she said, reaching out her slender fingers and tapping them lightly against the smooth wood. "I'm sure he'll keep me up half the night, but for now, he seems to be content. What do you propose we do?"

"Usually, I work in the barn at night…" My voice cracked, fading away into nothing as her fingers danced between us. *Gods,* I couldn't move. I was transfixed. The easy, friendly rapport we'd maintained impeccably over the last few days had completely evaporated now that she'd sucked my cock, and suddenly I couldn't think of anything else.

I had held it together admirably as I'd prepared dinner earlier, promising myself that no matter how effortlessly sexy she was, I wouldn't act untoward. I'd respect her boundaries. Unless she initiated, I wasn't going to pursue anything more sexual with her. *She* called the shots.

I reminded myself of that. I couldn't take this woman for granted. In fact, the less I indulged myself, the easier it would be when she left.

I'd keep my dignity, and she hers. No one would get invested, only to have the rug pulled out from under them.

It was better that way.

She smiled at me, her eyes twinkling. *Gods, she was beautiful.* "Do you want to go to the barn, then?"

I coughed.

"Yes." I rose from my seat, and she followed suit, grabbing up the bowls and her spoon and carrying them to the sink.

"Alright. See you soon, then," she said, turning on the faucet and letting the water run hot.

"Good night."

It's better this way, it's better this way... I repeated the mantra to myself all the way to the barn, where I gathered up a bale of hay and a few scoops of grain to fill Daisy's trough for the evening. She mooed at me in greeting, and I filled her water and brushed her down before getting everything ready for her evening milking.

The rhythm of the routine lulled me back into a more peaceful state of mind. *This is more like it,* I thought to myself as I carried the milk can over to cold storage for processing into cheese later in the week. *Daisy and the chickens: they're the only women I need. I see to their needs, and they provide me food. Anything else just complicates—*

The can clattered from my grasp, spilling milk all across

the rough pine boards of the barn floor. In the back of my mind, I heard Daisy lo in alarm at the crash, but I was too shell-shocked to do a godsdamn thing about it.

Because standing in front of me, buck-naked save for her sneakers, was Betsy.

"As far as fantasies go, this one's a little outside my comfort zone." She stepped closer, the rubber soles of her shoes making a light *slap, slap, slap* sound across the wet floor between us as her hips swayed far too appetizingly. "But hey, no use crying over *spilled milk*, right?"

"What are you doing?" I practically wheezed, my throat tightening with every step. Her breasts were most definitely larger than they'd been this morning, and they swayed to and fro in opposition to her hips, accentuating her already generous curves. My mouth went dry.

"You said you wanted to be in the barn tonight. Well, here I am. Ready for whatever fantasy you desire."

I shook my head, eyes still locked onto her perfect body. "Betsy, I…"

"Tell me, Felix. What about being in a barn does it for you? Do you want to be my big, strong farmer and I'll be your curvy German milkmaid? Or is it more primal than that? Do you want to just fling open those big, double doors and take me out in the open, under the stars?" She looked over my shoulder, staring pointedly at Daisy munching away in her stall. "Or do you like when *she* watches?"

She winked at me.

And I finally found my voice.

"Betsy, stop! This is all a big misunderstanding!" Somehow, I managed to tear my eyes away from her and grab a towel from the workbench. I knelt down, sopping up the mess I'd made all over the barn floor, doing my best to avoid brushing up against the shapely, naked legs that did their best to distract me from my task. "I came in here to finish up the evening chores. I had to milk Daisy, and get all of the chickens back into the coop for the night…"

Those fingers, the same ones that had wrapped themselves around my cock earlier, scratched lightly across my shoulders.

"Felix."

I froze, screwing my eyes closed and refusing to look her. The view from this angle would be torture. I wouldn't be able to hold back.

I felt her skin press into mine as she crouched down beside me, her scent invading my senses like the first day of spring. I trembled.

"Why are you doing this?" I croaked. "I know you said you'd—but I didn't—you don't have to throw yourself at me, Betsy! Trust me, I know how appealing you are. I know how good your body feels. That's all the stimulation I need, okay? You don't need to act out some fantasy on my account."

I risked opening my eyes so I could show her I meant what I said. Just being in her proximity eating *dinner* was next to unbearable for me. But seeing her like this, out here, offering herself up like some kind of Saturnalia offering…

She tilted her head at me, chewing that damn lip again, and it made me wonder if anyone had ever given her lips the loving, gentle treatment they deserved.

"If that's what you want…" she began, seeming to consider her words. Then she stood, and I had to scoot back and crane my neck to avoid sticking my face directly between her legs. She crossed her arms, and finally I felt like I could look her in the eyes without her plump, pink nipples staring back at me.

She cocked her head. "But you know, it's okay if you *do* have them. Fantasies, I mean."

"Look, I don't know what Zeus made you do to please him when–"

"Zeus didn't *make* me do anything." She stepped forward again, dropping her arms and crouching down until she was level with my gaze. I gulped. Her green eyes were fiery as she poked a finger into my chest. "Now listen close, Felix, because I'm not going to say it again. I like kinky sex. I like acting out fantasies. And I like *you*. And right now, I'm telling you that I want to help you fulfill whatever sexy desires you want for as long as I'm living under your roof.

"You might want to see this as some kind of divine punishment from the gods, and I understand that you didn't ask for me and Apollo to come here, okay? I get it. But however this arrangement came to be, it's clear that we're attracted to each other.

"I'm gonna get your semen inside me one way or another. And you can either *choose* to make the most of it, or you can *choose* to mope around the barn like some kind of shaken up coke bottle ready to pop until the next time my boobs dry up.

"So here's what I'm going to do. I'm *choosing* to get up," I followed her movements as she straightened her legs and turned around, waving her perfect, round ass in my face with her hands on her hips. She surveyed the barn for a moment, then walked over to one of the empty stalls, where a few loops of rope hung from a saddle hook. "I'm *choosing* to take this rope and tie it around…" she studied the open frame ceiling with the rope in her hands, before pointing to one of the central supports. "*This* beam. This one looks pretty strong, yeah?"

I stood, shaking my head as I approached her. "Betsy, what are you–"

"Oh yeah," she said, after she tossed one of the loops up and over the beam, making the soft parts of her body jiggle with the movement. A strangled noise came out of my throat. "This oughta hold."

"Hold *what*?"

"My wrists up." She took a length of the dangling rope and twisted it into a perfect taut-line hitch, before grabbing the other end and securing it back to the saddle hook, adjusting it until the loop hung about six feet off the ground. Then she returned to the loop, slipped her hands inside, and tugged them down, cinching the rope tight about her wrists. "This way, when I *choose* to stick my ass out like this," she leaned her hips back, spreading her large, cream-colored cheeks wide as she sunk her weight into the stretch, letting the rope at her wrists support the pose, "I don't have to worry about my balance while I bounce on your cock."

I couldn't breathe.

"That is, of course, if *you* choose to serve me up my nightly dose of minotaur cum from behind."

And with that, she whipped her dark hair over her shoulder, sending it cascading over her back as she stared me dead in the eyes.

My cock was flying at full mast, hard and straight and practically shaking in anticipation. I'd been hard since she'd first waggled that delicious ass in my face. Hell, since she'd surprised me by showing up in the barn in nothing but her sneakers while I went about my evening chores.

My heart was pounding harder than it had in centuries, and my brain was trying to twist itself into denying this fantasy she was offering up.

But in the end, any brain I had left ended up tied into a knot that rivaled the one securing her wrists to the support beam.

It had been millennia since I'd fucked a woman. And it appeared that many, *many* innovations had been made in the field since I'd been active. My last partner was the daughter of the god of engineering himself, but even she hadn't been nearly so inventive or imaginative as this heavenly siren before me.

How long could I continue to resist her call?

And more importantly, *why* did I feel like I had to?

She was right. At this point, it wasn't the gods who were punishing me. I was punishing myself. Doing the gods' work *for* them.

And I'd be damned if I was going to make their job easier for one second longer.

"So what's it gonna be, Felix? Are you going to choose to live out your exile in misery? Or are you going to fuck me like the virile bull you are?"

CHAPTER 25

BETSY

I'll admit it. I might have pushed it a little far with that last line. Waggling my ass like a matador with a red cape had been more than enough to catch my minotaur's attention.

And when I finally saw the last thread of his reserve snap, I relished the charge.

The rough-hewn boards of the barn floor shook with every stomp as he eliminated the distance between us, grabbing my hips without mercy and lining up my dripping entrance with the flared head of his hard, pulsing cock.

I *really* wanted him inside me. I was putting on a show for him, yes, but I'd be lying if I said I wasn't doing it for me, too. I'd seen the kind of man Felix was under the stoic, monstrous exterior, and I believed that he was the most caring and selfless male I'd ever met.

And he was hung like a bull.

He deserved to enjoy a little wild and crazy sex. He deserved to break his dry spell with a woman who would rock his fucking world, and if I couldn't be that for him, then what the fuck was I good for?

I couldn't cook. I couldn't farm. I could barely pay rent on time for my shared apartment with Petra.

But I was *good* at this, dammit. I was good at taking cock. I was good at fulfilling fantasies.

And I was good for Felix. Even if I was getting the better end of our little deal.

"Is this how you want me to give you my seed, Betsy?" He growled, and I could feel the rumble of his chest everywhere our body made contact. "Fucked from behind in a barn like an animal?"

That's it. There's the beast I knew was in there.

"Yes! I don't want you to hold back. I want you to fill me up with your giant bull cock and then pump me full of your cum!"

His grip tightened on the swells of my hips, neatly trimmed claws digging into my flesh hard enough to leave bruises. I felt myself lift from the ground, my toes barely scraping the floor as he raised me into the air with his brute strength and settled me against his lap.

I couldn't move. The rope at my wrists didn't offer nearly enough leverage to pull myself off of him and ride his cock like I'd promised. I'd miscalculated. He was taller than I'd realized, significantly so, and I'd forgotten that when I'd set myself up in this position.

So when the flared head of his tip notched itself between my cheeks, and he pulled me down on top of him in one, fast yank, there was no resistance keeping him from burying his entire length all the way into my pussy.

I gasped, the force of his cock knocking the very air from my lungs. Oh, *gods* he was big, and he was *thick*. His head, in particular, dragged along the inner walls of my pussy, spreading me to my absolute limit as the rest of him slid home. Thank the gods I'd been wet for him since dinner, because I needed every drop of arousal to ease the way for his giant cock. He filled me, tip to hilt, and I squeezed down, shuddering around him.

It was like nothing I'd ever felt before.

And it was *amazing.*

"Yes, yes!" I shouted, tears stinging my eyes as I pulled helplessly at my ties, wiggling for more. "Give it to me, Felix!"

"*Fuck,* Betsy," he grunted, the puff of air sending strands of my hair flying as he buried his snout into my neck. "It's no wonder you caught the eye of the gods. You are magnificent. You feel so good."

"How good?" I panted, baiting him to move me again. I wanted to be impaled by this cock again and again until we both fell apart. Thank Hera she'd repaired my pussy with her magic after having Apollo, because I don't think even postpartum would have been enough to keep me from this dick. My thighs were slick with arousal seeping from the place our bodies met, preparing me for the load my body knew it needed.

Call it hormones, call it the will of the gods. But I needed Felix like I needed air. And I wanted to hear how badly he needed it, too.

"How good is my pussy, Felix?"

His breathing was heavy and labored as he answered, "it's incredible."

"Then fuck me like it. *Show* me how incredible it is!"

He let out a growling sound that was something between a moo and a yawp, before pulling his hips back and thrusting into me once again.

I keened as I felt that fucking flare spread me open from the inside out, massaging my inner walls with every stroke.

At the apex of his thrust, his head dragged against a magical spot deep within me, and a tugging sensation flared in my belly. He pulled out and pushed in once more, hitting it again, and a familiar pressure began to build.

Oh fuck, oh fuck. He was homing in on my g-spot like a missile. And my orgasm was approaching like a freight train. I couldn't hold back.

"Fuck Felix, it's so good! Do it, fill me up with your seed!"

"No!"

And before I could even blink, he pulled his cock out of me with an audible *pop!* I shuddered as my pussy fluttered uncontrollably, squeezing around nothing, the emptiness unbearable after how full I'd been less than a second ago. Just like that, my body swung forward, and my sneakered feet caught the ground as he disappeared behind me.

"What are you–"

But as quickly as he'd left, he reappeared, a three-legged stool in his hands. He planted it about four feet in front of me, then stepped over it, bending at the waist to grab my legs.

"Felix!"

I wriggled in his grasp, but once again he used leverage to his advantage. He plopped his ass on the stool and took me with him, pulling me forward until my thighs were open and perched on his shoulders and my body was suspended between the rope around my wrists and his strong, calloused hands clutching my ass cheeks.

I stared in disbelief down the length of my torso, right into his big, dark eyes—the pupils of which were blown wide with lust.

A huge grin spread across his lips, and his snout crinkled with mischief. I felt my eyebrows rise as he stuck out that long, pink tongue of his, and licked a slow path up my slit, keeping eye contact the whole time.

When the tip of his tongue reached my clit and he flicked

across it, my hips jerked. His grip on my ass tightened, and he licked again, lighter this time.

"Ah!" I gasped, core pulsing as a different kind of pleasure built, focused and tight and hot beneath his tongue. "Felix!"

"You're forgetting something, Betsy," he growled, pushing out the words between laps.

"What?" The word came out as barely more than a puff of air. He'd turned my brain upside-down when he'd reoriented me, and I hadn't gotten the chance to adjust before he'd buried his face between my legs.

"This isn't for me."

"It's all for you!" I screamed. "I want to make you come and fill me up with your—"

"No!"

My heart sank as he lowered my ass to his chest and narrowed his eyes on mine. My chest heaved as I caught my breath, and I wondered for a moment if I'd done something wrong. Was this too much? Had I offended him somehow?

Was it the German milkmaid thing?

"I'm sorry, Felix, I didn't mean–"

His eyebrows sank deeper into a scowl, and his grip on me tightened. "*Do not* apologize."

My mouth snapped shut, and I searched his eyes to figure out why he'd pulled out of me. Was he hurt? Had he gone soft? Had he come already, and I'd missed it somehow?

'Why did you stop?"

In response, he curled his massive arms around my thighs and spread me even wider. My breath hitched as he tilted his head down, stuck out his long, pointed tongue, and licked a slow, meandering path all the way from my ass, through my folds, and finishing with a lingering flick to my clit.

I moaned.

"Let me make one thing clear, Betsy. This morning, when you sucked my cock? That was the *only* time I will *ever* finish before you. Do you understand? I don't care what you think you need to prove, or whatever you think you might owe me. I'm not coming without you. And from this point forward, you come *first*."

He punctuated this monologue with another lick up my slit.

"That's not—" I panted, as he delved his tongue even *deeper*— "necessary-"

"*Fuck* necessary," he hissed, and it came out so muffled and wet amidst all the other lewd noises he was making down there I almost didn't believe I'd heard him correctly. "You need my essence? You need me to fill you up with my cum? *Fine.* But I *want* yours first. You can't walk into my barn looking this tempting, smelling this good, tasting this sweet, without expecting me to take it from you. Gods be damned. You need my cum to make your milk come in, but I need yours for completely selfish reasons."

My head was spinning. He'd moved his mouth off of my clit, electing to use his fingers while he explained his second condition. My thighs were pinned to his shoulders by his massive arms, and he had one hand spreading my pussy lips wide while he circled at my clit with the other. Every now and then, he'd dip two of those thick fingers inside my channel to collect some of my slick and swirl it around my swollen bud, working me up into such a tizzy, my vision was beginning to blur at the edges.

"*Fantasy*," he growled, and the word rumbled up my spine like an earthquake. "You want to know my fantasy? I want you to soak my face with your juices, Betsy. I want to make you gush and drink you up. Your milk might be for Apollo, but your cream is for me."

His fingers moved faster and faster over my clit, spinning me higher and higher, until the dam finally burst. My legs snapped straight behind him with the force of my release, and my thighs clamped around his snout as I came with a fury.

His ears twitched in delight, tickling the inside of my thighs as I fell apart around him. Somehow, despite the vice grip I had on his face, he still managed to lick his tongue between my lips, lapping up my release as he continued to tease that sensitive spot relentlessly through my orgasm. My wrists yanked at the rope bindings as my whole body bucked. I was completely at his mercy, and he knew it.

He licked and fingered me relentlessly as I continued to scream, wedging my thighs apart and burying his face deeper even as my body tightened like a spring. I was panting for breath, my arms ached, and still he pleasured me.

Never would I have imagined Felix would be this hungry for me once he let his walls down. I'd offered him any fantasy he'd desired, and by the gods he was milking the opportunity. Slurping up every last drop my body had to give, and then some.

But even if I'd known what my minotaur had in store for me, I wouldn't have changed a thing. Not even with my clit screaming from overstimulation, nor my wrists chafing in their binds. I was coming harder than I ever had in my life, and I knew that this orgasm was just the first of many.

Because the look in Felix's eyes was that of a hungry, sex-starved beast. And I was about to be a five-course meal.

CHAPTER 26

FELIX

atching Betsy blink herself back to earth after her orgasms was more satisfying than I could have ever imagined. She tasted like pure honey, and her thick release coating my tongue was enough to make me ready to blow my own.

But not yet. I'd been admiring those perfect, milky breasts of hers since I'd first laid eyes on this woman. And I'd be damned if I came inside her pussy for the first time without being able to fully appreciate them.

Slowly, once I was sure she could handle it, I lowered her feet back to the ground. She stood, supporting her own weight once more, and I chuckled as she stared at me with glazed eyes.

"Are you going to fuck me now?" She teased. Her voice was hoarse from screaming my name, and it was the most beautiful I'd ever heard it sound.

"Not here." I wrapped one arm around her for support while the other reached up and loosened the binds about her wrists. I rubbed the blood back into her hands, looped her arms about my neck, then scooped her into my arms and cradled her to my chest. I carried her like that out of the barn.

"Where are we going?" She asked, shivering in the cool night air. Temperatures dropped quickly when the sun set this time of year. I pulled her closer, letting my body heat surround her. I was far more suited to the Minnesota weather than she was, despite being born in the Mediterranean.

One of the perks of having fur.

"Hay is not nearly as comfortable as modern bedding for what I have in mind," I teased her. "Although I will admit, you may have convinced me that the barn is a more flexible space that I've given it credit for."

She nuzzled into me, and I felt her grin.

I continued to carry her even as we stepped into the house, through the kitchen, and into the bedroom. "We're going to wake Apollo," she whispered.

"And what better place for us to be when he wakes up?" I whispered back. I set her down onto the bed, tugging on the pull cord of the floor lamp in the corner before returning to remove her shoes and socks. She giggled as I struggled with the laces, and I held a finger to my lips in a *shhh*-ing gesture.

When I finally had her feet bare, I slid my hands up her ankles, then calves, all the way to those delicious thighs, tracing the lines of her body with reverence as I settled between her legs.

"You'll need to be quieter this time," I murmured close to her ear. I then traced a line of kisses from the soft skin under her earlobe, down the side of her neck, across her collarbone, before dipping at long last to the wide, mouth-watering curve of her breast. "We're not in the barn anymore."

She gasped, loudly, and I gave her a warning look. She clapped a hand to her mouth, and I felt the buzz of her moan travel down her arm as I gently took the peak of her nipple into my mouth and sucked.

A few drops of her sweet, rich milk gathered on my tongue, and my eyes practically rolled back into my head.

Delicious.

I wanted it. Oh, how I wanted every last drop. But I pulled away, leaving trails of teasing licks up and down the swells of her breasts, alternating from right to left until she practically keened with desire. I didn't drink from her any more—I knew not to indulge in what wasn't mine—but the taste of her still lingered in my olfactory senses.

I let it serve as a reminder of why she was here, and what we were doing this for. After all, this was only temporary. She needed me to provide for Apollo, and the gods had put her here for that purpose.

But I couldn't allow her to think that that meant her pleasure didn't matter to me. I was done letting the gods dictate who served and who received. I'd watched this woman do nothing but sacrifice for her son since the day she'd arrived on my doorstep, and I was tired of it. It was time this human was spoiled. She was more worthy of worship than any Olympian I'd ever met, and by the heavens, I was going to prostrate myself at the altar of her body and prove to her that it was more than just a vessel for the gods.

I flicked her sensitive nipples lightly with my tongue while I cradled her heavy tits on either side, careful to mind how tender they were. She'd swelled visibly in less than a day after swallowing my cum the first time, after all. Her body had adjusted so quickly, it had to be painful.

Guilt gripped me at the thought that *I'd* caused that pain. Her body was changing to accommodate *my* seed, *my* potential offspring, even after it had already changed so much. It wasn't fair. Her body was already perfect. Why did it need to change for me?

I lifted my head a few inches so I could take her all in. Her flushed, rosy skin. Her broad shoulders and hips. The way her body dipped and swelled, welcoming and undulating under my grasp. I traced my fingertips from her shoulder, down her arm, across her elbow to her stomach, marveling in the cartography of her.

I wanted to map every peak and valley. Needed to preserve it for the centuries to come.

"What's wrong?"

My eyes snapped to hers at the whispered question, interrupting my mental snapshot.

"Nothing," I whispered back, before lowering myself to her body once more. "You are perfect."

I nuzzled into her neck, sliding my hands between the mattress and her ribcage, letting my body surround her. Then I lifted her breasts, pushing them in from the sides, gently supporting their new weight as I worshiped her with my tongue and mouth. Over and over, I grazed my snout lightly across her stretchmarked skin, so lightly that goosebumps pebbled in my wake. Air stuttered from her lips, shivers cascading down her spine with every stroke.

A silent symphony of pleasure.

I couldn't say how long I focused there, only that I could have listened to her soft gasps and shuddering breaths for hours if she'd let me. I wanted her to relax fully in my hold—to set down the burden of care she'd shouldered since she'd started growing that little demigod inside of her. Gods, I wanted to take it from her. Carry it for her.

How magnificently would she bloom, without the weight of Olympus pulling her down?

I longed to see it.

Moisture beaded at the peaks of her breasts, indicating that feeding time was fast approaching. Apollo still slept soundly in his crib, but for how much longer?

I wanted so badly for this moment to last forever, to carve out a time in eternity that I could enjoy her body without end.

But my sack hung heavy with seed, and I trembled with the need to release it inside of her. It was now or never.

"Are you ready for me?" I whispered, reaching between her legs to feel her wetness with my fingers. She spread easily for me, even slicker than she'd been when I'd finished fingering her in the barn. Heat flared within me.

She nodded, hand returning to her mouth in anticipation.

I knelt between her legs, centered my achingly hard shaft at her entrance, and thrust inside.

It was all I could do to keep from crying out. Instantly, her heat enveloped me, rocketing up my spine and sending me into a pleasure spiral. I heard her muffled cry through her fingers as she, too, struggled to stay silent. Her channel clamped down on me with a vengeance, especially my cockhead, walls of muscle squeezing me relentlessly as I pushed myself forward, inch by ecstatic inch until I was fully seated inside of her.

Betsy's back bowed off the bed, eyes squinting shut as she muted her pleasure with her hand.

I rocked back into my hips, glorying in the drag of that tight pussy around me as I did so. I could feel that velvet pocket milking me, coaxing my cum. I could barely focus.

Was this Elysium? The holy circle of the afterlife that I'd been denied? My vision was spotty from the current of pleasure rippling through my core. I reared back until only the widest part of my flared head was notched inside of her, took a breath, and then plunged back inside.

Her green eyes spun white as they rolled back into her head, and I reached out to her. Posting myself on elbows, I wove my fingers through her dark, silky hair, pressing my forehead to hers as I struggled to contain myself.

I'd never felt so good as I did in that moment, completely enveloped by her body. It was pure bliss. So perfect, it was unbelievable.

"You okay?" I breathed.

"So okay." Her voice cracked, and my fingers tightened in her locks.

"I'm afraid I'm going to hurt you. It feels too good. I–"

"Don't stop."

Her gaze locked with mine, and the longing I saw there pulled my insides taut. My entire body was a spring about to snap. The beast within me was a hair's breadth from the surface.

It was terrifying.

"Once I start, I'm afraid I won't be able to," I grunted. I had barely moved inside her once, and the pressure of her sweet cunt was already driving me to the brink. I wanted to charge, and I wanted to *buck*. Every instinct inside me roared at me to *move*, to take this woman with reckless abandon.

But my mind screamed back that this was wrong, that it was dangerous. I knew what happened when I succumbed to pleasure without considering the consequences.

What if I hurt her? What if, once I started fucking her in earnest, I couldn't stop? I was so much larger than a human man, surely I'd do damage.

What if this was another punishment from the gods, and my resolve was the only thing keeping me from destroying her?

"Please, don't stop. You've had me on the fucking edge since you carried me in here," she hissed. "Felix, *please*. You're killing me here!"

Terror clutched me. *No, not again!*

A strangled noise pinched out of my throat, my lungs frozen. I couldn't see, couldn't think—

When a small, soft hand cradled my cheek.

Betsy's face came back into focus as she tilted my mouth to hers.

"Please, Felix," she whispered against my lips. "I need you."

And then she kissed me.

Warmth seeped from her lips to mine, spreading with every dart of her tongue and gentle nibble. I felt it thaw the cold fear that had gripped me, sinking into my skin, my bones, my heart.

I need you.

My chest squeezed as she said those three little words, differently than before. This was a pressure like a hug, gentle and grounding, and it combined with the way her body wrapped around me to give me strength. Even though I knew she hadn't meant for her words to sound so serious, the honesty of her plea came through loud and clear.

This woman needed this. Needed me. *Wanted* me. To help bear her burden, to ease her fate. I was the only one who could give her what her body required. And in a moment of pure selfishness, I was grateful for it.

Because if there had been anyone else who could have provided her this gift, I never would have let myself give in. I wouldn't have allowed myself to succumb to her charms, to hold her, to kiss her, to taste her.

I never would have *felt* her.

Gods, the way she gripped me! With her lips locked on mine, her arms encircling my back, and her pussy embracing my cock in its entirety, I was completely surrounded.

I could drown in this woman, I realized. *I want to.*

So I did.

A low rumble shook my chest as I finally allowed myself

to move. My mouth opened wider, tongue darting out to tangle with hers as I reared my hips back and drove forward, filling her from both directions. She moaned into me, and the sound traveled straight to my core.

My cock twitched inside her, and I pistoned my hips again—gaining speed now as the instinctual desire to flood her with my seed overwhelmed every other sense. My vision tinted red, the blush of her cheeks seeming to spread to consume her entire body as the beast inside me took over.

I hammered into her, and her stifled moans pitched higher, more frantic—cutting off with the apex of my thrusts in shorter and shorter intervals.

"Ah!" She gasped, wrenching off my mouth as her body bucked beneath me, her stomach pressing into mine as her hips jerked upwards. "Fuck, Felix!"

All concerns around volume flew out the window as her cries unraveled me completely. The bull was in control now, rutting wildly, as the pleasure inside me wound so tight I thought my soul might explode right along with my cock.

The sounds of her soft, supple flesh smacking against my furry legs grew louder, wetter. My speed increased as her channel grew slicker and slicker, her juices soaking my fur more and more with every thrust.

"I'm coming! Coming! Felix, please, I need–"

"Tell me!" I roared, the swelling at the base of my cock nigh unbearable.

I would give it to her. I would give her *everything.*

"I need you to fill me with your cum!"

Like a dam bursting, my cock erupted inside her. All at once, my balls and my core tightened, sending a torrent of fluid gushing from my cock in such a fury I could *feel* the jet of it pulse through my shaft. Instinctually, I redoubled my grip on Betsy's body beneath me, crushing her hips to mine to force the load inside, as deep as it could go.

I knew what would happen next, but it still caught me by surprise when the bulge of my knot inflated, squeezing the last drops out of the head while simultaneously sealing the opening of her pussy, locking us together so my seed could take hold.

Betsy's entire body twitched, legs straightening behind me as her hips shuddered uncontrollably, the rest of her shaking with the force of her orgasm.

"I can feel it, I can *feel* it," she keened, arms shooting out and grasping my forearms. Her fingers dug into my skin, pulling herself even more tightly against me. "Felix, *Felix*, your cum is filling me up!"

My eyes fluttered closed as her pussy spasmed around me. *Fuck. This is what it feels like to breed a human,* I thought.

It was different. So different.

Betsy's body and mine locked together, the pieces of our puzzle snapping into place as if it were inevitable. There was no buckling, no grinding, no friction whatsoever. It was just *right*.

And the most perfect part of all was the way Betsy's body reacted. A look of absolute euphoria glowed upon her face, chest heaving with exhilaration as her eyes sparkled. She met my gaze, laughter mingling with the sounds of her orgasm as sensation rolled up and down her body.

A grin split my face as I took her in, every inch of her radiant with pleasure.

As the shuddering of her release slowed and we both came back to ourselves, the world around us entered our focus. The soft, rustling sounds of Apollo fussing in his crib let us know that our moment was coming to an end.

For now.

I didn't think about how all of this was temporary—how it *had* to be temporary. For now, Betsy and I needed each other: she needed me to bolster her milk supply, and I needed her for…

Well. Now was not the time to worry about that.

At last, her grip loosened on my arms, and I felt her slump back onto the sheets. A small puddle of her juices had formed underneath us, but she didn't seem to mind. I followed her down, turning us on our sides. We were still locked together with my knot. Betsy's eyebrows raised, and she looked down at the place we were joined as if noticing it for the first time.

"Um, Felix? Are you…stuck?"

"It will go down in a moment. Once your womb has absorbed all of my seed."

Her eyes widened. "Really?"

I nodded. "I assume it's part of the biology around all of this. Your body needs to absorb the minotaur seed to produce for your minotaur calf. So, until it does, my knot seals your entrance to keep it all from leaking out."

"Your knot." She blinked. "You didn't have a knot this morning."

My face heated. "This morning, it wasn't necessary. It doesn't form when I stroke myself, either—I assume it's a response to the amount of fluid and the, uh, the surrounding pressure." I coughed into my hand. "With your mouth, uh. Your body absorbed it more quickly. Since it was deposited in your stomach."

I avoided her curious gaze, my cheeks burning. A devilish grin quirked the corners of her lips. "Wow. Your penis literally can tell the difference between a mouth and a pussy. You Olympians really are mythical, aren't you?"

I laughed uncomfortably. "Blame it on the titans."

She hummed. "So how long does it take this way? To absorb, I mean."

I opened my mouth to answer, but before I could, a yawn took over my reply. It was then that I noticed that the sun had set completely, the only light in the room emanating from the solitary floor lamp. It cast a warm and cozy glow, perfect for snuggling.

I pulled her into me, settling her head into the crook of my shoulder and letting my chin rest on top of her hair. My eyes drifted closed.

"Not long, I'm sure." Another yawn. "Twenty minutes, maybe. Half hour, max."

Lying in my own bed with Betsy in my arms was so comfortable after more than a week of sleeping on the couch. It was catching up to me. I felt myself sink into the soft mattress, taking her with me, and we laid like that for a moment. Long enough that my mind drifted into that halfway place between wakefulness and sleep—the world at once closing in and fading away.

It was in that state of mind that I heard her murmur something. And I couldn't be sure if it was real or a dream.

"Is it bad that…that I wish we could stay like this forever?"

I squeezed her closer, and the soft embrace of her body pulled me fully into sleep.

If I'd learned one thing from living on the farm with Felix, it was that no creature on earth slept more soundly than a minotaur with a full stomach.

Despite the fact that he'd literally been less than ten feet away from us in his crib, Apollo hadn't so much as gurgled the entire time Felix and I had been fucking like animals on his giant bed. I'm pretty sure our lovemaking rivaled the noise of a construction site: all that drilling, slapping, moaning, and roaring had certainly rocked *my* foundation.

We'd put up a good effort at first, what with our whispers and me covering my mouth with my hand. But once he'd thrust his entire length inside me and hit that spot that turned my vision into a kaleidoscope, I knew I wouldn't be able to hold back.

And I didn't. My voice was gonna be hoarse for a week.

And yet, it wasn't until Felix had grown soft inside me and his knot had deflated (his knot. *Knot!* Talk about a kink to explore!) that Apollo finally stirred to life with an ear-splitting cry.

Yep. *That* was my little minotaur.

But just like Apollo had been completely oblivious to the deafening coitus earlier, Felix snored right through the baby's cries. And after how fast he'd faded post-nut, I assumed he was out for the night.

I disentangled myself from his arms, taking just a second to admire how much his stubborn features softened in his sleep, and then rolled off of him to go take care of my son.

My back ached when I sat up. I'd yet to adjust to all the changes in my body that had taken place in less than twenty-four hours. Motherhood alone had taken a toll, but minotaur semen was something else.

Not only were my boobs easily one—if not two—cup sizes bigger after a couple heaping helpings of Felix's milky essence, but my libido had amped up to eleven. I'd never come so hard, so many times, in such quick succession, as I had when Felix's knot had inflated inside of me. The orgasms just kept coming, with every jet of his release that I'd felt drench my insides.

And that wasn't an exaggeration. I'd literally *felt it* when his cum squirted out of his cock. It sprayed my g-spot like a Super Soaker, a concentrated stream that pummeled my Big-O Button over and over as something inside me opened up, sending me into a climax that just kept building until I couldn't take it anymore. Every muscle in my body had tensed and spasmed at once, an all-consuming electrical storm of pleasure, and by the time I came down I felt like I'd just run a marathon.

All I wanted was to curl back up into Felix's arms and conk out.

But, duty called.

"Betsy?" No sooner had I rocked myself off the bed did a large, warm hand reach out and wrap itself around my forearm. "What's wrong?"

"Apollo's crying, ya big lug." My eyeroll was affectionate. "Can't you hear him?"

"Bring him here."

"He's hungry, Felix. And probably needs a diaper change."

The large minotaur wiped sleep from his eyes and tried to hold back a yawn as he wiggled himself up the bed until his back was upright against the headboard. "That's fine. You can nurse him here."

He patted his lap.

"Do you really think it's a good idea for me to sit my naked ass in your lap while I'm feeding my child?" I shook my head, walking over to the crib and reaching in, grabbing said child under his arms and pulling him to me. "Doing it in the room while he's sleeping is one thing, but while I'm nursing is—"

"I'm not going to do anything inappropriate. I just don't want to let go of you yet." He yawned again, giving me a second to cover up the goofy smile that lit up my face with his admission. "Besides, my refractory period is much longer after knotting. Round two will have to wait until morning."

"Round two?" Despite my protestations, I carried Apollo to the bed and arranged the two of us so I was sitting atop Felix's crossed legs with my back against his chest, and the baby balancing with his hooves on the mattress and his butt propped on my knee. "Don't you mean round six? Seven, even?"

"Is that how many times you came?"

He nuzzled his snout into my shoulder, and my stomach fluttered. I gathered up my left boob in my hand and raised my nipple to Apollo's lips. "In the barn, maybe. I lost track of the total."

I felt the man's grin as his cheek pressed into my neck. "Maybe next time I'll make you keep count."

I gasped as he nibbled at my earlobe at the exact moment

Apollo latched on. The warm, wholesome sensation of nursing swirled with the electric tingles from Felix's lips, and the combination was enough to make my head fuzzy.

I sank against the broad, muscular chest behind me. I wrapped an arm around Apollo's back and Felix circled his about my waist, and together, we made quite the happy little family.

No, not a family, I corrected myself.

Unless…

"This is nice," I said. Felix rumbled in agreement, the slightly rough texture of his snout eliciting shivers as he dragged it up and down my skin with every nip. "Maybe… maybe we could do more of this."

He paused, his grip on my ribcage tightening just a hair as he shifted. "What do you mean?"

"I mean," I sighed, leaning my head back so I could look at him and gauge his reaction, "*this.* Just… snuggling."

The details of his expression weren't clear in the shadows of the room, but I could tell his forehead was wrinkling from the way his horns tilted down, catching the ambient moonlight peeking through the window. Funny, I hadn't realized consciously that his horns moved with his face—but in the week we'd spent together, the deeper parts of my brain had picked up on it.

Subconsciously, I knew things about Felix that I couldn't put into words. Like the way I knew how much he liked whatever food we were having for dinner by the way his tail flicked while he was cooking, or I could read how much he was holding back by the muscle definition in his shoulders.

I tried to read him now, but he was so different from anyone I'd ever known. Even though I'd picked up on so many of his little signals, I felt like I never could be sure if I knew what he was thinking.

Silence stretched between us, the only sound in the room

the soft suckle of Apollo nursing. But then I felt Felix's arms relax a little more, and relief flooded me.

When he finally spoke, his voice was small and cautious, more suited to a mouse than a minotaur. But I sensed the kernel of hope in it, and that was enough for me.

"When would we snuggle?"

"Well… at night. After… *activities*, we could both sleep in the bed. Fall asleep like this, together. We could do that every night, if you wanted."

I paused, waiting to see how he took that.

Slowly, he nodded into my shoulder, his kisses resuming with the softest press of his lips. "Every night?"

I shivered as his snout brushed across my skin, nodding. "Mm-hmm. And every morning, we'll wake up together."

The kisses halted. "You won't sleep in anymore?"

"Well, Apollo will be feeding more regularly now. I can nurse him, then get the two of us ready for the day while you take care of morning chores. By the time you come in to make breakfast, I can be ready to help you."

"Hmm." He resumed his slow, nibbling trail. "Every morning?"

"Why not?"

There was another long pause, and I held my breath. There were a million reasons why he wouldn't want to wake up with me every morning, the first of which being that he'd said he didn't want to get attached.

His kisses slowed, and instead he buried his face in my hair. His breathing slowed as he held me and I leaned into him.

"What would it look like?" He murmured, his voice low and—dare I say—*hopeful?* "Our daily routine?"

"We'd have breakfast together. Discuss our plans for the day. I'd help you in the garden, or take care of the house chores while you handle the rest of the barn stuff, like the corn fields and the tractor and all that."

I felt his snout stretch against the crown of my head, and I suspected he was grinning, holding in a chuckle at my over-simplification of "barn stuff."

"Then?"

"Then, we take a break for lunch. And maybe a quickie."

"What's a quickie?"

"That's when I bend over the sink and you fuck me from behind hard and fast, without worrying about any of the other stuff."

He sucked in a breath, and his hold on me tightened again. He lowered his mouth to my ear, and rumbled, "what if I *like* the other stuff? I told you, Betsy, I don't intend to take my pleasure without pleasing you first."

I squirmed. "Felix. It's not like you're going to tie me up and eat me out for an hour every time we have sex."

He tilted his head, as if he hadn't considered that option. "What if, instead, I use my mouth and fingers to make you climax merely *twice* before I mount you?"

Any of the words in that sentence would have been enough to make me shiver, but specifically, my brain zeroed in on *mount.* I pictured myself, prostrated on all fours in the barn, a bit in my mouth and my tits swinging wildly as Felix reared my head back with a leather rein, as he rutted into me from behind.

I opened my mouth to speak, but the words got stuck in my throat. I coughed.

I suppose we could compromise.

"Uh, sure, yeah, that's fine."

He hummed again in approval, once again burying his snout into the crease of my neck and shoulder. I sank into his warm embrace, enjoying the feeling of safety that enveloped me with Felix at my back and Apollo suckling at my front, the fantasy of being mounted like a broodmare playing out in my head, when a voice nudged me from my reverie.

"And after lunch?"

My face heated. "Right! Uh, after lunch and um… and the other stuff, I'll tuck Apollo in for his nap and feed the chickens, while you, uh…"

Truth be told, I'd gotten sufficiently distracted with the other stuff. On top of that, my baby had begun to fuss.

I sat him on my other knee, rubbing his back as a burp worked its way through his system, and the movement inspired Felix to adjust, too. He sat up a little straighter, hoisting me and Apollo further up his lap where, despite his earlier denial, a chub had *definitely* begun to form. It settled right between my buttcheeks as he scooted me closer, not seeming to notice its insistence as he wrapped his arms right back around my waist, propping up my boobs in the process.

Apollo belched, then came right back in for seconds, attaching to my right boob this time. The soft cadence of his suckling lulled us both into a happy, drowsy state as we cuddled.

"How about this?" Felix piped up after a moment or two, as he shifted to a one-handed hold and used the other to scratch lightly up and down my thigh. "I feed the chickens after lunch, while you and Apollo both tuck in for a nap. Then, the two of you enjoy playtime and television until I wrap up chores and come in to fix us dinner. You join me in the kitchen, catch me up on all that Apollo did and learned while I cook. We eat, and you put Apollo down for the night after his evening feeding."

"So, the same as always?" I smirked.

"No, not the same as always. Because what happens after that is very important." He leaned in close, his fingers growing more adventurous. My pulse hammered faster as his nails stroked a trail up my hip, to my elbow, eliciting a march of goosebumps all the way up to my shoulder and back down as he lightly traced the curve of my breast, brushing his calloused fingertips over my tender nipple. I gasped, trying my best to hold Apollo steady as my whole body began to tremble. "After he's all tucked in and cozy, you strip down all the way to your sneakers and wrap yourself up in my robe. And then you come to the barn, where I've gotten everything ready for you."

"W-what will you have ready?"

"It's a secret," he whispered, as his teasing strokes homed in on the ticklish crease of my waist. I bit my lip, holding back a shiver, which only served to tense my muscles and make them more susceptible to his tickling. It was torture. "But let's just say it's one of those fantasies of mine that you seem so intent on making a reality."

Sweet, sweet torture.

His bulge twitched under me, and I was surprised his whole cock didn't poke from its furry pouch and slide right in with how wet I'd gotten from his teasing. My breathing had grown heavy, and I closed my eyes and counted out slow, even inhales and exhales until my pulse slowed back to normal.

His stroking hand returned to its favored path, running up and down my thigh, as the both of us calmed down.

"And then?"

The stroking stopped as he wrapped me back up in his embrace. "By then, it'll be bedtime. And, assuming I didn't ruin everything and scare you away, you let me sleep with you in the bed again."

I snorted. The very idea that Felix might do *anything* to scare me was so laughable, I couldn't help myself.

"And then the next day," I added, "we do it all again."

"Hmm." He squeezed me tightly, breathing in as he pressed a kiss to the crown of my head. "I like the sound of that."

Hope flared in my chest, warm and bright. What if this could work? Me and Felix and Apollo.

Maybe this was the family I'd been craving all along. Maybe all my failed foster parents and relationships had all fallen apart to bring me here, to this man, and this moment. Maybe Felix was wrong, and this *was* the gods' plan for me.

After all, he'd been lost and lonely just like me before the gods had plucked me from the cities and dropped me into his path. He'd been to Tartarus. He'd served his time. Maybe now, all we needed to do was accept that we could be happy.

My stomach twisted with how badly I wished it could be like that. Wished that *I* was like that: the type of girl that a man like Felix would settle down with. The type of girl with a perfect, happy family.

But hey, it couldn't hurt to dream, right?

CHAPTER 28

FELIX

The next week with Betsy was the happiest of my life.

She and I woke up together, just like she'd suggested when she'd spelled out what our future might look like if we abandoned all pretense and simply... *enjoyed* each other.

And gods, how that perspective changed everything. In the morning, when I fixed her breakfast, it was for no other reason other than I wanted to see her face light up as she forked that first bite of pancakes into her mouth. When I went out to the barn to milk Daisy and feed the chickens, it was so I could ensure the two of us had fresh milk and cheese and eggs to nourish our bodies, which in turn would nourish Apollo's. When I came inside for lunch to see Betsy waiting for me, wiggling that perfect ass in the air as if she could seduce me into forgetting my promise to bring her to climax twice before I came inside of her, I fell to my knees and worshipped her sweet cunt and clit until I'd made her cry out with *three* successive orgasms, before I bent her over the sink and sank into her tight, wet heat and spilled myself inside her.

Of course, we'd forget about my knot, so we were always a little late returning to our tasks for the afternoon, but that didn't keep her from greeting me in the kitchen when I came in from the barn each night to make us dinner. She'd kneel on a folded blanket by the kitchen table and nurse Apollo, telling me how they'd spent the afternoon while I prepared us root vegetable hash with baby kale and soft, pressed cheese.

I delighted in the details she shared; motherhood suited her. She was so taken with her child. The love in her eyes as she spoke of every gurgle and giggle, his impressive strength, his first crawl. He was growing quickly now, and Betsy couldn't hide the smile in her voice as she'd "complained" about the need to baby-proof the cabinets now that he was able to move about the ground on his hands and knees. Of course, I'd volunteered to help in any way I could.

After dinner each night, she'd put Apollo to bed, and I went back out to the barn to prepare for our evening activities.

The first few nights, I'd kept it simple. Laying her out on my workbench and worshipping her with my tongue until she soaked the ground beneath. Tying her wrists to the rafters like she'd done our first night together and mounting her from behind. Turning her around, so she could rock freely on my cock while she grabbed my horns for leverage (something I *particularly* enjoyed, although I hadn't yet confessed to her how sensitive they were). There was no shortage of ways to enjoy each other, and we had done well to explore as many as we had the stamina for.

And then, at night, we'd retire together to the bedroom, and she would curl her back into my chest until the two of us drifted off into sleep.

I knew it couldn't last. Eventually, she and Apollo would need to leave this place. I would not allow them to live with me in exile forever; it wasn't fair to them. Apollo deserved a life where he wasn't punished for my crimes. Betsy most of all, deserved a shot at happiness.

And while she made me happier than I'd ever been, I wasn't so naive as to believe the gods would let her stay with me for all of eternity—or at least, for the chunk of eternity that was her human lifespan. It was enough now, in her early days of motherhood, that I could be her companion and lover and give her the care, support, and orgasms that she deserved. Provide insight into her minotaur child's development. She often explored my body with a curious expression, asking clarifying questions about the differences between it and that of a human male's. And despite my early doubts, she truly seemed to find my beastly form attractive—moreso with each passing day.

Her presence provided me endless joy: whether it was her grateful compliments of my cooking, her pride at watching Apollo grow, or the lusty sparkle in her eyes when I'd catch her looking at my rear. Since she'd arrived, the little farmhouse had begun to feel less like a prison and more like a home. It was brighter with her and Apollo's presence; there was something to look forward to each morning when I woke to fix them breakfast, and each evening when I came in from chores.

Now that we'd broken the tension, and I hadn't hurt her, I felt much more comfortable with the physical nature of our arrangement. Betsy was a vivacious, promiscuous beauty, and I was grateful for her sexual appetite. I'd been nervous that my attraction to and hunger for her body might frighten her, the opposite had proven true. The wilder I became in our lovemaking, the more desires we explored, the more she opened herself to me.

There was one fantasy I still hadn't shared with Betsy, however.

We'd explored every inch of one another's bodies in such a short span of time. I was entranced by every part of that woman: her intelligent green eyes, her plushy lips, her broad hips and curvaceous legs, that hungry pussy... but I couldn't deny that there was one part in particular that featured predominately in my hidden desire.

Well, two.

I hadn't been able to get those perfect, milky breasts of hers out of my head since I first saw her attempting to feed Apollo. They'd broken down my resolve, invading my mind and filling my head with all sorts of perverted fantasies I never would have entertained before.

Maybe it was the bull inside of me that made me think of it, but once the image had popped into my head I hadn't been able to shake it. No matter how hard I'd tried.

I wanted her milk.

And by the gods, I'd tasted every other part of her by now, had I not? I'd licked her supple skin, slurped at her juices, nipped a line of kisses from her ankle to her hairline, and I'd savored every drop of her.

But I needed more. I'd resisted squeezing those full teats of hers with all of my willpower whenever the opportunity had arisen. I knew that Apollo needed her precious milk more than I did, but *gods,* the temptation to bury my face in her sweet bosom and drink my fill! I wanted to *drown* in her, lay under her suspended body and let those udders soak me with their spray.

And I'd learned her supply was already exceeding Apollo's needs. Last night, when I'd come inside to cook dinner, I'd opened the refrigerator and seen two glass jars of milk that hadn't been there before. When I'd asked her about it, she'd confessed that she'd needed to express between feedings that day, that she had become uncomfortably full.

I'd almost dropped to my knees to relieve her pain right then and there.

After all, I wanted to. I wouldn't be taking from her son. And the longer we explored our new dynamic, the deeper our relationship grew… the fewer excuses I had not to confess this deepest, most secret desire. She'd said once that she wanted to fulfill my fantasies, had she not? If it provided her relief to empty her breasts, and she had excess supply, then…

The next afternoon, instead of working on the tractor (which had been having issues since Iris's visit), I got to work with my rudimentary carpentry skills. I'd actually improved quite a bit since Betsy and Apollo had arrived, with building his crib and high chair. But the stakes for this particular project felt higher, somehow. This was not something for a babe. This was a piece of specialty furniture for Betsy and me, and it had the potential to make our relationship far more intimate. With this, she would no longer have to self-express her excess milk into jars over the kitchen sink.

From now on, *I* would be the one to milk her.

I began drafting up a bench that I could use for just such a purpose. I was an experienced dairy farmer, after all, so I was familiar with the concept and the physics of the thing. But milking a human woman would be very different from milking a dairy cow, and not just because the former was infinitely more titillating than the latter. A cow had four, skinny legs, and its teats were long and slender. When I milked Daisy, I squatted on a stool at her side and squeezed the spray of milk into a bucket on the ground. It was uncomfortable work for me, but she was comfortable enough. The anatomy of a cow was such that one could access their udders easily enough from the side.

But Betsy was a whole other animal.

When she was down on all fours—a position I'd become

intimately familiar with in the last week—her thighs touched, and the apron of her belly hung over her lap. Her breasts hung too, of course, but her arms caged them in and pressed them together. To further complicate things, she was short enough on her knees and arms that her nipples nearly grazed the ground when her muscles quaked with her release, and that simply wouldn't do.

For this fantasy to be complete, Betsy would be climaxing throughout—and I couldn't trust her arms to hold up her body while she experienced that much pleasure. Just today after lunch, her legs had given out after merely four orgasms.

No, no. Her luscious body would need ample support during this adventure.

I'd been able to complete the initial sketches and locate the raw materials for my design this afternoon, but it would take a few more days before I was ready to unveil the project in its entirety to my roommate. So an hour before it was time for me to go in for dinner, I rigged up a simpler setup for this evening's activities.

I Macgyvered a burlap sack, some hemp rope, and some carabiners I had lying around into a serviceable swing, complete with two stirrups from an old saddle I'd salvaged and hung from the rafters in which I could place her feet, allowing her to rock freely from a single point in the ceiling without having to rub her wrists raw like the night before. The rest of the saddle I saved in reserve for the other project.

The sack and the rope formed a flexible, reinforced swing that could support the bulk of her weight while enabling the freedom of movement I'd require to rut her with abandon. This way, I wouldn't need to rely only on my arm strength to lift and sink her perfect pussy on and off my cock, and I could save my stamina for the things that mattered.

Like keeping count of her orgasms.

I finished rigging up and reinforcing the swing and Betsy appeared in the doorway, wearing nothing but her sneakers and my silk robe like she had every night since our first joining. My heart beat double-time when I saw the fabric draping over her supple skin, the large cut dwarfing her and emphasizing just how dainty she was in comparison.

It made me positively feral for her.

She surveyed the barn as she walked in: taking in the freshly swept floor, the swing hanging from the rafters, and the pile of materials I'd collected that afternoon for the milking bench I was working on. I'd shifted all of my carpentry tools over to one corner of the large space, opposite the row of stables that lined the eastern wall. The longer this building served as our play space, the more pride I took in its cleanliness and organization.

I wanted this to be *our* space, instead of merely mine. Well, mine and Daisy's, I suppose. Even the dairy cow seemed to appreciate the changes to the space, as I'd become even more religious about keeping her corner tidy and well-stocked with fresh hay.

But all thoughts of Daisy left my mind; the swaying of Betsy's hips attracted all of my focus as she approached me.

"I see you've rigged up some new toys for us," she purred. "What delights do you have in store for me tonight?"

She traced a finger down my sternum, eliciting a shiver that traveled all the way to the tip of my tail. "So many. But first," I dropped my hands to her waist, letting them linger for a moment before I untied the belt of her robe, "let me take your coat."

"Oooh, we're hanging up the robe now?" She raised an eyebrow, eyes sparkling. "Fancy!"

"I got tired of picking up the errant pieces of hay that get stuck in the fabric when we toss it on the ground," I admitted. Not all of my tidying and reorganizing had been for aesthetic purposes. There were benefits to a cleaner barn.

She sighed as I slipped the silk from her shoulders, baring her creamy skin and abundant curves in all her glory. "I appreciate it. The only thing I want poking and sticking me in this barn is *you*."

My cock twitched in response to that, and I left her briefly to hang the robe. Gods, this woman made me wild. It was hard to believe that for millennia, I'd been celibate. It had gotten to the point that I hardly even thought about physical pleasure; my cock had been nothing more than a pissing stick for centuries. I'd lost my connection to my sensuality after so many years of punishing myself for it.

All it took was one human—albeit, a delightful and sexy one—to reawaken desire in my loins. It wasn't just lust for sex she'd inspired, either. I had a lust for life itself, now: an excitement for each day and its mundanities that I couldn't remember feeling since my time in Olympus. When was the last time I'd taken so much pride in the state of my barn? Or planned out the garden with the taste of each vegetable and crop in mind?

She hadn't just stoked my desire, she'd reignited all of my senses again. Taste, smell, sight, touch… even the buzzing of the bees through the pea plants and carrying nectar to their hives each afternoon sounded like music to my ears, when I knew the honey they created would sweeten Betsy's breakfast in the morning.

By the time I'd turned around, she'd walked over to the swing hanging in the middle of the barn. She ran her hands over the various knots and fasteners, tugging to check for strength. I wrapped my arms around her from behind, nuzzling my snout in the hollow beneath her ear.

"It'll hold," I assured her. "I tested it myself."

"*You* did?" She stifled a giggle as I pulled her closer, tickling the back of her knee with the brush-like tip of my tail. Her legs buckled, and her soft weight fell into my hold. Her cheeks stretched in a smile against my own. "I wish I'd been a fly on the wall to see *that*. Stoic, serious Felix swinging from the rafters, wind in your hair…"

As if to demonstrate, she reached up with her soft fingers and tussled the tuft between my horns. My grin grew wider.

"What can I say? You bring out the playfulness in me."

"Good."

She spun in my grasp, pressing her front to mine as she rose on tip-toes and pressed a kiss to my lips. I parted eagerly for her, sliding my arms beneath her ass and hoisting her up until our hips bumped against each other. Her mouth broke away on a gasp as my hardening cock brushed the seam of her legs, and she curled them around my waist in response.

I moaned as my length slotted easily into the cleft between her cheeks, the flesh of her thighs tensing across my obliques. I could have taken her right there, just like that—and had, on more than one occasion.

But not tonight. Tonight, I had other plans.

I tugged on her lower lip with my teeth, pulling her back into a kiss as I walked us forward until the swing bumped against us. Carefully, I placed her into the seat, tracing my lips and tongue from her lips to her jaw and down her torso as I checked the tension in the binds. The rope stretched taut as she sank into the swing, creating new creases in her hips and waist as the fastenings held strong.

I let the seat take her weight and my hands slipped from her ass up her thighs, scratching lightly from hip to ankle, before I tore my mouth from her body.

She wiggled her hips and grabbed hold of the ropes at her side, pushing her knees straight and rocking back. Her green eyes sparked with delight.

"Okay, you might need to install one of these just for this," she said, pumping her legs and swinging to and fro like a child on a playground. I stepped back to give her room, smiling at the juxtaposition of her innocent glee and sexy naked body. She laughed. "What? You mean to tell me you never played on the swings at the playground?"

I laughed. "Can't say that I have." She slowed for a moment, the glow of pure joy dimming a bit. I put up my hands. "But don't stop! I could watch you like this all night."

Her smile reignited, and she went back to pumping her legs again. "Push me!"

I shook my head, this night going in a completely different direction than I'd anticipated, but not an unwelcome one. Walking to the back of the swing, I waited for the crest of her backward motion to reach out and tangle my fingers around the knots at her hips. I drew her into me, until the wisps of her dark brown hair tickled my nostrils.

"Hold on tight," I whispered into her ear, then pulled up and back until her legs dangled from the seat at the same height as my shoulders. She squirmed against me, practically shaking as I held her there, the potential energy crackling with tension.

"Let me–"

"Go!" I finished for her, and released my fingers.

She swung toward the ground, squealing in delight as the pendulum dragged her in its arc, her heels swishing inches above the ground as she stretched her legs out straight in front of her, hair flying back from her face. Then she rose once more, bending her knees under her to prepare for the backwards descent.

"I'm flying!" She laughed, before plummeting toward me once again. "More, again!"

How could I resist?

The glowing red of the sunset flaring through the

windows had faded to a dusky purple when at last she slowed, tilting herself forward and tumbling out of the burlap seat. I rushed forward to catch her, but she beat me to it—stumbling upright before any damage could be done. When she righted herself, she hopped around in a circle, face red with adrenaline and cheeks positively chipmunk-like as her toothy smile stretched from ear-to-ear.

She beamed at me, her hair a wild nest about her head, spreading her arms wide and inhaling deep to catch her breath.

"That was amazing!"

Her happiness was infectious. Before I realized I was doing it, I crossed the barn and scooped her into my arms, twirling her in a circle until her feet flung out behind her.

"Felix!"

The squeaky chirp of my name on her lips only made me squeeze her tighter. I pressed a kiss to her hair as I set her back on the wood plank floor, refusing to let her go just yet. She hugged me back, still bouncing on the balls of her feet, as if her body couldn't contain all the emotion inside her.

When we finally parted halfway, hands falling to hips and heads free enough to look at one another, a pink blush still blossomed across her cheekbones. She sighed, her shoulders lifting and dropping in a satisfied shrug.

"Okay. We can have sex now. I just needed that."

"Needed it?" I tilted my head. A kernel of doubt sprouted in my chest. "Am I not seeing to all of your needs, Betsy?"

"What? No!" She shook her head, pulling away to brush her bangs out of her face. "Not at all! I just meant…"

She trailed off, and the hesitation only grew my concern. I glanced around the barn to find a place to sit.

I pressed my hand to the small of her back to guide her to a closed grain storage bin across from the stables. I sat on it, opening my arms so she could sit on my lap.

She obliged, turning sideways and settling her thighs on mine with her feet perched on the lid of the bin, allowing me to snake my arms about her waist and pull her into me.

"Has our new arrangement been stressful for you?"

She chewed her lip for a moment before responding. "No! Not at all. If anything, the last few weeks have been the happiest of my life! Since you gave me your seed," she looked up at me through her lashes, a pleasant blush coloring her cheeks as she alluded to out first time together. "And my milk came in in earnest, it's been way easier on me. This little routine we've established," she gestured to the barn, "it's nice. So nice. Gods, Felix, you make me so happy."

Warmth spread in my chest, and I shifted a little to avoid poking her with the thickness rising in my lap. Despite her reassurance, it was clear that something was still troubling her. I didn't want my lust to interrupt her speaking.

"But there's something wrong?"

She shook her head again. "It's not something anyone can fix, really. It's just… growing up, you know?" Our eyes met, briefly, before she looked away. "I mean, I didn't really get to be a normal kid. Before, whenever I started to feel like I belonged in a foster family, the mom would get pregnant, or a new, cuter kid would come along that was a better fit. I'd get sent back to the group home until another family took me in. But then, when I was sixteen, I got placed with a terrible couple. I don't even know how they got approved. I figured if that was the best the state could find for me, I was better off on my own. So I ran away. Made it work until Petra turned eighteen and we could find a place together.

"For a while, it was fine. But it was a hamster wheel: work, bills, eat, sleep. Day in, day out. Over and over until…" she sighed. "I thought a vacation would be the answer. But it ended up making everything even harder."

This insight into Betsy's childhood was unexpected. I'd

heard her mention her upbringing in passing: references to foster families or "the system," but I knew very little of what a modern human childhood looked like here in America. Despite living on this particular farm since the mid-1950s, I'd been bounced from deserted field to deserted field dozens of times, across country lines and continents, in order to avoid contact with humans entirely. Growing grain for the gods was tedious and lonely work, made lonelier by the fact that I had to hide it from the inhabitants of the land around me.

The plains of the American midwest, particularly the ones that laid fallow after the dustbowl in the 1930s, had been a perfect place to hide in plain sight. Even when an errant car passing along the country road bordering my property saw me riding on my tractor in the field, my large straw hat and wide, wildflower border along my property kept my silhouette innocuous enough as to not flag anyone's suspicion.

I could not imagine living in a city, surrounded by humans and people of all descriptions, and attempting to forge one's own slice of freedom amidst the chaos of all that. Especially when she'd started at such a disadvantage.

But the monotony she spoke of. That, I could relate to.

"I understand what you mean. About the wheel."

She met my gaze again, then continued. "I saved up for months so I could go to Chicago for Lollapalooza. Just for a break, you know? To get away. Do something exciting, for once. And that's where I met Zeus. Talk about exciting!" She laughed, the sound a bit sharper around the edges than it was earlier in the evening. "It felt like a sign. Like the universe was finally giving me proof that I could be something more than just another cog in the machine."

I gave her a squeeze. "You are *so* much more than a cog in the machine, Betsy."

She shrugged. "It doesn't always feel that way. Even now, after all of that, I gave birth to a honest-to-gods *demigod*, and suddenly everything is different, except..."

I waited for her to finish.

"Except the stakes are so much higher." Her body grew slack, and I tilted her into me. She sank gratefully into my hold, tracing lazy circles in the fine fizz that covered my chest. "On the one hand, every day brings about a brand new challenge to contend with, but on the other, I feel like if I take a minute to catch my breath, everything will spin out of control.

"I love Apollo more than I've ever loved anyone. Every moment of the day I think about his wellbeing, his future happiness, his current happiness. He's growing *so* fast. And while I don't regret the decisions that brought me here and brought him into my life, I... well. I worry what will happen when he grows up. When this is all over. And it feels so... *heavy*, sometimes."

"Does the time we spend together... does it also make you feel that way?" I braced myself for her answer. She's upended my monotony. To hear that she didn't feel the same...

"Oh no! No, no, no! It's wonderful. Amazing!" She placed her hand flat on my chest as she said that, piercing me with her sincere, hazel eyes. "It's... it's almost like it's too good to be true. And then I remember that, as wonderful as it is, as wonderful as *you* are, I wouldn't even be here if I didn't need your cum to make me lactate. My body has changed so much in the past year, you know? Sometimes, it doesn't even feel like it's mine anymore."

She sighed.

I thought about that for a moment, unsure how to respond. Somehow, even after all of the orgasms I'd given her, she still felt as though her body were not her own. I wanted to offer words of comfort, but everything I could think to say felt meaningless in the context of what she was speaking to.

I loved her body. I loved her being here. The hamster wheel of our routine the past few days had brought me joy and excitement I hadn't felt in eons.

But telling her that would only prove that her efforts brought *me* happiness. And that was very different from one's actions bringing about happiness for oneself.

"Being on the swing like that," she broke the silence without lifting her head from my chest. "It was just... *fun*. It was just for *me*. And fuck, Felix. I had no idea how much I needed that."

She tilted her head up, and I studied her face. A calm, sleepy satisfaction had come over her as we sat together, the knot of sadness having loosened slightly as she spoke.

I vowed then and there to make the swing—something I'd intended to be a temporary aid to more adventurous, horny adventures—a permanent fixture in the barn.

But not for sex. For *fun*.

For Betsy.

"You can come out here and swing whenever you want. Whenever you need to steal a moment of joy for *you*." I rubbed up and down her arms, leaning my muzzle into the crown of her head and surrounding her as best I could.

Her lashes tickled my skin, and a moment later, a trickle of tears dampened the space between us.

"Oh, Felix." Her legs folded in on themselves, and she burrowed closer to me. "Thank you."

CHAPTER 29

BETSY

*D*espite the fact that Felix had literally installed a sex swing in the barn, the two of us didn't get it on that night. Instead, I embarrassingly cried for like, half an hour on his lap while he cradled me like a baby, rubbing my back and letting me just… let it out.

And here I thought I was done with the waterworks. The past week had been so much easier than the months leading up to it, I hadn't realized just how much had been weighing on me. But a couple of rounds in the swing had made me feel *weightless,* and that put the whole last year of my life into perspective. The pregnancy, Zeus's abandonment, having Apollo, leaving Petra, dealing with the stress of breastfeeding… my life had completely imploded, and I'd been trying to juggle every new ball the gods had tossed to me.

But even the best juggler needs a break once in a while.

When I'd been swinging back and forth in the barn, feeling the wind in my hair and flutters in my stomach, all those feelings bubbled up. And for the first time, I felt safe enough to just… *let go.*

Once my tears had dried up, and my sobs had turned to

hiccups, Felix gathered me up against his chest and carried me to the bedroom. Again. Where I slept like a rock all through the night. At one point, Apollo had started crying, but when I sat up to take care of him, I felt a large, warm hand push me back down into my pillow.

"I'll get this round," Felix muttered, rubbing the sleep from his eyes. "It's almost sunrise anyway. Plus, you have that extra milk in the fridge. I can give him a bottle and change his diaper. You sleep in."

Too tired to argue, I did.

By the time I roused again, the sun was streaming in through the bedroom window, and my minotaurs were nowhere to be found. Surprised, I pulled on Felix's robe and wandered out into the kitchen, where a bowl of oatmeal was waiting for me with a tinier bowl of nuts and the honeypot clustered beside my spoon. While my stomach growled at the sight, I didn't feel right eating before I knew where my son was, so I ignored the thoughtful spread and headed straight out the door to the backyard.

There, in the garden, was Felix: kneeling in the dirt next to a positively filthy Apollo, who was holding a tiny trowel and smacking it against the ground. I watched, open-mouthed, as Felix made eye contact with my son and held up a seed, then dug a tiny well in the dirt with his finger and dropped it in. Then Apollo—my three week-old baby—looked down at the seedwell, up at my roommate, then gave him a big smile before hammering the trowel down on top of the seed.

"Apollo, no!" I shouted, mortified. Here Felix was, trying to teach my son about the miracle of modern agriculture, and Apollo was violently destroying it.

But before I could snatch him away from unleashing more carnage, Felix waved me off. "No, no, it's okay! Good job, Apollo! Cover up the seed so we can water it!"

I froze, watching as my baby's face furrowed in concentration, and his frantic trowel waving became slightly more controlled. He then opened his hand, letting the tool drop, and twisted onto his hands and knees to crawl to the watering can that I just now noticed was sitting to Felix's left.

He nodded when Apollo pawed at the can, then he lifted it over the newly-planted seed and tilted it so a small shower of water spilled onto the loose ground. Apollo clapped in glee, then crawled a foot down the row and plopped on his furry, naked butt to wait for Felix to dig the next hole.

"You're... gardening?" The question sounded dumb to my own ears, and I regretted it the second I said it. *Obviously they're gardening, you idiot.* Hence the seeds and the trowel and the watering can. *They're in the garden, aren't they?*

But Felix took my confusion in stride, handing the trowel back to Apollo and burrowing another seed into the ground before smiling up at me. "After getting him fed, his diaper needed changing, and I didn't want to bother you by digging around for one in the bedroom. I figured some outside time would give him a little grace if he had an accident, and give you a chance to catch up on sleep." His expression turned serious as he looked me up and down. "How are you feeling?"

My chest squeezed at his thoughtfulness. "Good! Good. I uh, I didn't realize how tired I was, I guess. What time is it?"

He glanced up at the sun. It was a beautiful day; the temperature felt like it had climbed into the sixties and there wasn't a cloud in the sky. A bit chilly for me in just a t-shirt and jeans, but neither Apollo nor Felix seemed to be bothered with their fur and fuzz to keep them warm. "Eh, probably ten, ten-thirty? There's breakfast for you on the table. Sorry if it's cold."

I shook my head. "Not at all! I saw it on my way out here. Thank you, by the way."

He smiled again, his dark eyes crinkling at the corners. "Don't mention it." He picked up the watering can, to Apollo's delight. "Go, eat. We'll still be out here when you're done."

Relax, his tone assured me, *I've got this.*

I took a breath, my shoulders falling away from my ears as his words released a knot of tension I hadn't realized had taken root. The worry I'd felt when I'd opened my eyes to an empty bed and crib dissipated.

Somehow, in just over a week, I'd gotten used to the two of them being there when I woke up in the morning. The routine we'd established had weasled its way into my brain, in a way that felt more natural and more like home than anywhere I'd ever lived.

I wrestled with that thought as I left the two of them to their planting, while I went back inside to eat my breakfast.

By the time I'd wrapped up the morning chores and pumped an extra jar of breastmilk into the fridge, my two minotaurs had planted a whole row of cabbage, carrots, and leeks: a type of onion, according to Felix, that I'd never had before, but no doubt would be delicious in whatever way he planned to cook with them. From the window above the sink, I watched as Felix carried Apollo over to the hose and sprayed both of them down, rinsing away the streaks of mud that covered their fur. After their showers, he observed the baby for a moment, then carried him over to the manure field to relieve himself.

I turned away when the larger minotaur *also* started to relieve himself. While I appreciated my roommate taking on some of the potty training responsibilities, I had no desire to watch a grown bull-man demonstrate the finer points of bathroom etiquette to my son.

The sound of the hose turning back on let me know when they'd finished, the old plumbing of the 1920's farmhouse rattling with the rush of well water through the walls. They hosed off, and a minute later I greeted the two of them at the door with fresh towels from the bathroom. Felix grinned at me, the surprised gratitude in his expression making my heartstrings do that tugging thing again that they'd started doing whenever he acted like *I* was the thoughtful one in our relationship.

"Ready for lunch?" He asked as he tossed one towel over his shoulder and placed Apollo into the one I had unfolded in my arms.

"Sure!" I swaddled the little man, rubbing him down vigorously before laying him and the towel out on the kitchen table to get him into a new diaper. He kicked and fought me while Felix patted himself down, apparently enjoying the taste of naked freedom he'd gotten in the field. Eventually, though, I got him sorted, the battle having tired him out enough that when I carried him into the bedroom for his nap, he didn't raise a fuss.

I closed the door behind me as I walked back into the kitchen, before sinking into my usual chair at the table and letting out a breath. Felix was at my side with a glass of water in a second.

"Do you need anything else?"

His tone had taken on a slightly worried note, and when I caught his gaze, the concern etched into the lines of his forehead only emphasized it.

"Felix, I'm fine." I took a sip of water, if only to put him at ease, before straightening in my seat. "Seriously. I know I probably scared you a little last night, and I didn't mean to. Please. I'm okay, really. If anything, I feel better now than I have in weeks."

And I did. A solid cry and a good night's sleep had been just what the doctor ordered. Not only that, but seeing my baby thriving in the care of someone else for a couple hours had lessened the stress I'd placed on myself in thinking that I was being selfish or irresponsible whenever I let him out of my sight. Despite the fact that my brain *knew* he was safe when he was sleeping in his crib, it was hard to turn off the constant baby-dar I had beeping in my head whenever he wasn't in the room with me.

He was *crawling* now. My baby demigod was *mobile*. That alone had made me start seeing everything from the floor to knee height as a potential hazard.

But that was before I saw him with Felix, and I realized that I wasn't the only adult here who cared about Apollo's safety. I could *trust* him. I didn't have to shoulder this burden alone.

For now.

I plastered a reassuring smile on my face, and it seemed to be enough to reassure Felix that I was, in fact, fine. But as I watched his back while he chopped up vegetables and dumped them into a big pot to make soup, I couldn't quite silence the voice of doubt that wanted to creep in the back of my mind.

Because, it wasn't an imaginary voice. It was Felix's.

"You will be able to give him a better life if you don't let him get attached to this place."

And what was I doing, letting myself get used to the idea of Felix helping me care for Apollo, if I wasn't "getting attached"?

Eventually, my baby would be weaned and, biologically-speaking, I wouldn't need Felix anymore. I'd promised him when that happened, I'd take Apollo and raise him far away from here. Far from Felix and the sway that the gods had over his life. It was the one thing he'd made me agree to when we both gave into the pressure of the gods' demands.

Logically, I understood his reasoning. But it didn't make it any easier to accept emotionally.

Who would help me raise Apollo when I left this place? When Felix and his pancakes and the farmhouse and the garden were all just a distant memory? When I was just a single mom again, with a job and bills and a rapidly growing demigod mouth to feed? How would that even work, in the real world? Would Hera and her goddess sidekick whisk me away again to some other farmhouse in the country, where I was all alone? Or would I find some way to disguise my child's horns and tail and hide him in plain sight amongst the mortals of Minneapolis?

I cleared the table of Apollo's towel and diaper bag, while also attempting to clear my head of all the heavy thoughts about the future. Right now, we were safe. We still had time.

Felix and I ate our lunch, and this time I let him tell me about everything he and Apollo accomplished during their morning together. Every twinkle in his eye as he spoke about seeing how quickly the tiny minotaur learned new concepts, the way his gurgles and babbles made him laugh, filled my heart with a bittersweet longing. I loved this. Sitting down with Felix, talking about my son, making plans for his life and the farm together while we celebrated every step forward.

Like a family. A *real* family. One where I belonged.

I finally felt like I had what I'd always wanted. What I'd always dreamed of.

And I knew it couldn't last.

I blinked back tears as I kept that pasted smile on my face, nodding along to the conversation. I buried them deep, along with all my anxiety around our future, until it didn't threaten to overflow.

When we finished our bowls and tidied up the dishes, I put Apollo down for his nap. And then I let Felix take care of me.

Right there on the kitchen table, he emptied my mind of

everything but pleasure. Brought me to the brink again and again, made me shatter into a million pieces before coming apart inside of me with a vigor that shook me to my core.

As his knot inflated and he embraced me from the inside out, it was all too easy to believe that we could stay locked in each other's lives forever. Brought together by the gods, sealed by forces more instinctual and powerful than either one of us could fight.

CHAPTER 30

FELIX

I put my hands on my hips, admiring my handiwork as I took in the bench before me. It had taken just over a week to put the finishing touches on it, but I was proud of the end product. Almost all of my carpentry and engineering knowledge had gone into making this a perfectly functional and comfortable piece of furniture, albeit one that served a very different function from any other chair, bed, or couch one might find on the property.

I climbed atop it, testing it once again to make sure all of the parts were sturdy and worked as intended. Carefully, I leaned my hands onto the raised, padded platform in the middle of the two-tiered bench while I placed my knees onto the lowered platforms on either side. Leather pads, fashioned from a couple of repurposed saddles I'd found in the stables, stretched over the wooden surface, providing comfortable cushioning for my shins down to my ankles, where some old inverted stirrups could be used as safety straps. Once I was balanced on my knees, I leaned forward until my stomach was prone atop the middle raised platform, letting it take the weight of my torso, while I wrapped my hands around a support bar I'd hung from the ceiling a couple feet in front of the bench. Just a simple metal pipe that I'd wrapped with more leather straps for grip and hung from the rafters.

The resulting position was incredibly suggestive. My tail swished across my spread legs and exposed backside, while the majority of my sternum hung suspended between the padded bench and the grab bar.

In other words, I was completely at the mercy of whomever might walk in and seek to take advantage of me. Certainly, if I'd strapped myself down at the ankles, I could have stayed there for hours while someone had their way with me.

At the thought, my cock swelled, poking from its sleeve and dangling between my legs. Though I hadn't designed this bench with traditional male anatomy in mind, I took note of the fact that there was potential for unisex play with this particular device.

Useful to know, but not my intention for tonight.

I let my head hang, horns resting naturally on my upper arms with them stretched before me like this. Comfortable, and yet the freedom of movement the bar allowed gave the user the chance to adjust to a wider or narrower grip and stretch their neck as needed.

I'd often watched Betsy tilt her head from side to side in an attempt to relieve the neck and shoulder tension she never seemed to be free of. It was important to me that she have ample flexibility, even when strapped into a milking bench.

My eyes fell upon the wooden stool and metal bucket I'd placed suggestively on the ground below the bench. Though my chest was suspended about four feet from the ground in this position, Betsy's would hang considerably lower, placing her nipples just inches above the pail's folded lip. The perfect height for me, seated on the bench, to squeeze, massage, and milk her perfect breasts.

My cock hardened further, and I held back a groan. I could not wait to show her my invention.

Provided, of course, that she was as titillated at the prospect of being milked as I was milking her.

Of all the kinky fantasies we'd explored together, this was by far the wildest. But after she'd bared her soul to me the night I'd shown her the swing, I'd thought a lot about what she'd said regarding her body.

"Sometimes I feel like it's not even mine anymore."

And while my heart broke to hear it, I understood. Just as I felt that I couldn't truly enjoy my life for as long as I was serving my punishment from the gods, because my body and mind were a tool for them to exploit. I grew grain for Olympus, corn and barley and wheat to feed their breweries and bakeries. Even as I planted the vegetables and other garden crops that sustained my own modest needs throughout the year, there was always that awareness in my mind. I lived on this farm because the gods had put me here to serve them. And no matter how many delightful distractions Betsy and I engaged in while we lived here, I knew that "here" was still my prison.

It was why I couldn't let her stay forever. The last thing I wanted was for Betsy to feel trapped at someone else's mercy.

The thought that Betsy had been made to feel that way about her own *body*—that perfect vessel of curves and flesh and zest—crushed me. It had only made me more determined to help her seek her pleasure in any way I could. Despite the fact that she needed my seed, as she'd put it, for Apollo's well-being, I felt a responsibility to make the process of delivering it as indulgent as possible for her.

She deserved it.

And though the project of building this bench had, at first, been inspired by *my* sexual desires, I'd begun to think of it as another way to show her the ways in which her body doesn't exist solely to serve her son.

Perhaps this was just me being selfish. I may have been able to empathize with her feeling trapped, but I didn't know what it felt like to be a mother. Her attachment and devotion to Apollo was as natural and pure and wonderful as it was stressful. The love she felt for him was abundantly clear. I knew she didn't view him as a burden.

But I wished she loved and cared for herself as much as she did for those around her.

The truth was, I wanted to worship her in any way I could. Help her see her body the way *I* did.

She was so much more than a vessel for the gods. Betsy's body was a reflection of everything she'd earned and endured, and she deserved to *revel* in the pleasure of it.

Just like she did when she was on the swing. Since that night, she'd come into the barn while Apollo was napping every day to enjoy it. I'd been sure to cover up my project with a tarp whenever I'd seen her approaching from the farmhouse, puttering about with other chores while she took her seat on the burlap swing and pumped her legs back and forth. Seeing the joy on her face, the smoothing of her brow as she closed her eyes and relaxed into the sensation of flight and gravity, warmed my soul in a way I hadn't even realized it could. To see her so happy, so free… it sparked an ember of hope inside me that had long burned out.

And while I wasn't certain that this fantasy of mine would succeed in giving her that same pleasure or relief—after all, submission to sexual pleasure was very different from the more innocent delight of swinging on a swing—there was a part of me that hoped.

I supposed I'd find out tonight.

CHAPTER 31

BETSY

The evening routine in Felix's farmhouse had evolved quite a bit in the almost-month Apollo and I had been there. My little minotaur was now sleeping through the night, which meant he was up and alert a little later into the evening the past few days. After dinner, he and I would play a bit in the living room while Felix did his evening chores. I'd give him his last feeding and change before telling him a bedtime story (we didn't have any books with us, but I'd gotten pretty good at improvising through what I remembered of Grimm's Fairy Tales). And then, I'd tuck him into his crib and do a quick pumping session before heading into the barn for "roommate time" with Felix. Tonight began like any other, except for one tiny exception.

Felix asked at dinner that I not pump before joining him in the barn.

"Really? But, Apollo hasn't been draining me completely at night. I'm worried I might… you know…"

He'd tilted his head at me, a barely-concealed smirk teasing the corner of his lips. "You're usually so tender after pumping. I want the chance to play with you a little more tonight without worrying about hurting your nipples."

I'd blushed at that. Play with me *more?* "Exactly how much *playing* do you think I can take, Felix? And what if I leak?"

He'd raised an eyebrow. "You've spilled plenty of fluids in that barn, Betsy. A little milk isn't going to hurt anything."

I'd been too embarrassed to argue after that.

But when I'd tucked Apollo into bed and the time came to head to the barn, I felt…*full.* I hesitated in the kitchen in Felix's robe, wondering whether I should just do a quick hand expression or two before going out there, when Felix walked in through the door.

"You ready?" he asked, holding a length of fabric in his hand.

"Uh," I hedged, heat already rising to my cheeks. "Well, I'm wondering if I should…"

I trailed off, and his eyes darted to my chest before he gave me a questioning look. I nodded.

He shook his head. "Trust me." He held up the length of fabric, gesturing to my head. "May I?"

"A blindfold?" I blinked. "What kind of plans have you cooked up for tonight, Felix?"

He just wiggled the fabric again, and I tilted my head forward, acquiescing. Despite our many sexual adventures, we hadn't played around much with bondage other than the occasional wrist tie. Zeus was the only partner I'd had that made a habit of restraining me, and while it had been hot, it wasn't exactly my "thing."

In general, I much preferred Felix's more pleasure-driven approach to sex. It shouldn't surprise me, given how observant he was in the day-to-day, but he had proven himself to be an incredibly responsive and considerate lover. I hadn't even realized how many different kinds of gasps, sighs, and noises I made during sex until Felix had started interpreting their meaning. I swear, every response I made to his actions, be it a lick, touch, pinch, or poke, he'd decoded into an entire spectrum of meaning, ranging from lighter to harder to faster to *a little bit to the left!*

He understood my body like no mere mortal or god ever had. I didn't know if it was a minotaur thing or a Felix thing, but whatever it was, it was *absolutely* a thing I could get behind.

So when he tied the fabric around my eyes and the world went dark, I knew I could trust him to lead me across the uneven ground to the barn. If anyone would catch me before I fell on my face, it would be Felix.

When the ground shifted from turned dirt to wooden plank, and the cool air of the spring evening gave way to the warm smell of hay bales and sawdust, the broad, tall minotaur leaned his snout next to my ear. His warm breath tickled the hairs at the base of my neck as he spoke.

"Before I show you my surprise for tonight, I want you to know that it's perfectly okay to tell me you aren't interested."

"Okay…" I shivered at his closeness, and the mystery of his words. "Is it a kink thing?"

He hummed, and I felt him nod. "You mentioned a few weeks ago you'd fulfill my deepest fantasies. Something about a milkmaid…?"

Heat rose to my cheeks at the memory. At the time, I'd been so cock-drunk from the minotaur semen hangover that resulted in sucking him off for the first time, I'd resorted to desperate measures to get him to come inside my pussy. Something about having him in his mouth had made me ache for him to fill my core, and the resulting actions I'd taken to get him there weren't exactly my proudest moments.

Not that I'd admit it.

I covered up my embarrassment with a raised eyebrow

and a cheeky grin. "Oh? Was I closer to the mark than you admitted?"

"Why don't you see for yourself?"

His fingers deftly moved at the back of my head, and the fabric fell from my eyes. As my eyes adjusted to the light, I tried to interpret the arrangement of wood, leather, and metal in front of me.

My first thought was mechanical bull, what with the leather saddle on the raised center bit. But I eliminated that option when I looked more closely, and noticed that the seat of the saddle was oriented the wrong way for that.

Was it some kind of chair? But it didn't have a seat…

"I hate to burst your bubble, here, but I have no idea what I'm looking at." I scrunched my nose in apology, but my roommate didn't seem upset. Instead, he took my hand and walked me closer to the object, placing a hand on one of the leather-wrapped armrest-looking things underneath and to the side of the saddle.

"This is a milking bench."

His face was completely neutral as he said it, as if he was determined to let me react without worrying about hurting his feelings. But I still didn't really understand.

"A milking bench? Like, for you to sit on when you milk a cow?"

Even as I asked it, I knew that couldn't be right. Felix had a wooden stool he sat on when he milked Daisy, and this bench was in a completely different part of the barn than her stable. She was behind us, actually, in the corner closest to the farmhouse, while we were standing more in the open center of the barn floor, closer to the back wall and away from the workbench, stables, and the cement pad where he kept the tractor.

Actually, the little stool was here too, next to a metal bucket. They were on the floor behind the saddle part, underneath a pole that was hanging horizontally from the ceiling.

"No, Betsy. This isn't for cows. It's for humans. Women, primarily, although I'm sure someone could find more creative uses for it if they desired…" He shook his head, his ears flapping a bit as he cleared the thought from his mind. "But the idea is that you could kneel with your legs here," he pointed to the armrests—or, leg rests, I guessed, "while your stomach rested here," he patted the saddle, "and grab hold onto this bar, giving me full access to your…well, your milk."

His ears twitched as he said that, a pink tinge spreading across his mahogany skin as he explained the bench's intent. I followed his description, painting a picture in my head, and could feel a matching blush bloom on my own face in response.

"So, in this fantasy…I'm not the milkmaid?" I kept my tone as even as I could, even as my stomach flipped somersaults.

"No, Betsy. You're the cow."

I would be the cow. I side-eyed Daisy, who was munching away happily on her hay in the stall in the corner. "You're aroused by the idea of milking cows?"

A look of horror spread across his face. "Betsy! No, of course not! I would *never*!"

"Well! I mean, you did say I'd be the *cow*." I shrugged, relief flooding me, even as something else entirely began to burn in my core. "And you *are* half-bull. It's not the wildest conclusion to reach."

He scowled. "I might be half-bull, but I'm *fully* sapient, and I would never fuck a creature who was incapable of consent."

I tilted my head, squinting. "…but you want to?"

"Godsdamnit, Betsy, *no*! I am not sexually attracted to cows. Mine and Daisy's relationship is strictly professional!"

He swiped a hand through his horns, mussing up his hair in the process. A sheepish look crossed his features as he toed the ground with his hoof. "I'm just… aroused by the idea of milking a woman. A *human* woman. You, specifically."

I considered this, as surprised by the concept of milking a human as I was relieved to confirm that Felix wasn't fucking his dairy cow on the side. To be fair, Zeus had exposed me to some bestiality-related kinks in which cows and cattle played a significant role. But I'd put my foot down at fucking him while he took on the form of an animal, and he'd left me not long after that.

Of course, never in a million years would I have thought that life would bring me a minotaur baby, or a sexy minotaur roommate that made me question how blurry the line between animal and man really was. For the first time, I wondered if Zeus had control over which of his sperm had impregnated me, if somehow he'd filled me with god/bull semen specifically to punish me for poo-pooing his cow kink.

Joke's on him, I guess. Felix had made me look at beasts of burden in a whole new way.

"Just to be clear, is it the human part you're attracted to, or the sapient part? Like, would you be aroused by the idea of milking a female minotaur?" He glared at me, and I threw up my hands. "What? It's a fair question."

At least, *I* thought it was fair. The look on Felix's face, though, seemed to say otherwise. He stood there a moment scowling, arms crossed, his dark eyes roving across every swell and crease of my body until I grew hot under his gaze. I tugged the robe closer, and he moved—walking around the bench and eliminating the space between us until he towered over me. Slowly, he placed his hands on mine and opened my grip on the silk lapels. Then he untied the belt and snaked his fingers beneath the fabric. I gasped as the relatively cool pads of his fingertips dragged across my flushed skin, slipping in between the silk and my curves, brushing the sides of my ribs and breasts as he skated them up to my collarbones and gently pushed the fabric down off my shoulders.

"I'm aroused," he said in a low, rumbling voice, letting the robe fall in a puddle at my feet, exposing my naked body completely, "by the idea of *you* leaking all over my face as I massage your swollen udders."

He grabbed a fistful of my tit in his giant hand and squeezed, drawing the focus of the pressure closer and closer to my nipple as he rolled his palm and fingers. I moaned, the sound sneaking up my throat and coming out instinctively. Drops of milk beaded at the peaks of my *udders*, heat pooling low in my stomach at how dirty that word felt in his mouth. He leaned in closer, hot breath ghosting across my skin as he continued to knead my chest.

"I'm aroused at the thought of you letting go of every preconception you have about breastfeeding. About your milk, and who it's for. Picturing you, embracing the inherent sexiness of your body and the many, many pleasures it can offer you when you stop thinking about who it can serve, and start thinking about how good it can feel to just—" he squeezed, and I gasped. A spray of droplets splattered across his stomach. It was like a spark had ignited in my breast, an ache that was at once heavy and electric, something between the telltale fullness before a feeding and the coiled tension of a more sexual touch.

He let go of me, bringing his milky fingers to his lips and licking them clean, one by one.

"That," he finished, eyes boring into mine as he snaked one last trail of his tongue between his middle and forefinger, "is very, *very* arousing to me."

"Oh," I answered lamely, a little dazed from the dizzy tornado of tingles he'd just unleashed in my belly. In my breasts. In between my thighs. A tidal wave of lust was pulsing throughout my whole body the longer I stared into his eyes, so dark they were almost black, and my brain caught up to everything he'd just said.

"So you understand? What I'm asking of you?" He asked.

I nodded. "I–I think so."

"And you're willing to give it a try?"

I nodded again. More than willing.

"Tell me with words."

"Yes, Felix."

"Yes what?" Our connection smoldered, his desire for my complete knowledge and consent holding back the fire of his lust—barely. It was intoxicating, the way he was drinking me in, his jaw tense with nerves and anticipation as he requested my permission to indulge in this fantasy he'd kept hidden from me for this long.

I grinned.

"I'll be your human cow, Felix. And you can be *my* milkmaid."

"Ha!" Mischief sparkled in his gaze as he barked out a laugh. In a flash, his hands were gripping my ass and he was hoisting me in the air. "Be careful what you wish for, little siren."

CHAPTER 32

BETSY

From his arms, he carefully arranged me onto the milking bench, supporting me as I found my footing—or, kneeling, I supposed—with my stomach pressed against the padded support in the middle. My hips reared back, pushing my ass high in the air while my breasts swung down in the negative space in front of my ribcage. I clasped the sides of the bench nervously as Felix strapped my ankles into the leg rests, and my heartbeat pounded as I realized I was at his mercy.

He laid his palm flat on the back of my calf. "Is this still okay?"

I closed my eyes and exhaled a slow breath, dropping my shoulders away from my ears. "Y-yes."

"Betsy." He moved his hand up my leg and over the curve of my hip to the small of my back, and his other hand appeared before my face. He held it out, palm up, gesturing for me to take it.

I did, and he helped me sit up, until I was just resting my butt normally on my heels. He gave me a shy smile, my considerate minotaur roommate rising to the surface in place of the sexy, bullish dominant he'd been a moment ago.

"Anytime you want, you can sit back like this. If it gets to be too much, or too…"

"Weird?" I supplied helpfully.

He nodded, his Adam's apple bobbing as he swallowed. "Or too weird, yes."

I chewed my lip. "But you want this?"

He sighed, taking a seat on the stool under the bench in front of me. For once, his head was now beneath mine, and the change in angle centered me a little. The warm, incandescent lights of the barn reflected off the ivory of his horns as he mussed his hair again.

"I want *you* to enjoy your body. I want to play with you, yes, and gods, Bets, I want to suck milk from your teats more than I've wanted anything in the worlds. Resisting drinking from your bosom is worse than not being able to drink from Tantalus's lake!" He laughed, a dry, sardonic bark that made his nostrils flare. Then he tilted his head back and met my eyes. "But mostly, Betsy, I want *you*. For as long as I have you. For as long as you'll have me."

A bolt of lightning shot down my spine as the meaning of his words sunk in. This was different than when he'd said he wanted me before. Then, it had been a difference between want and need. Between desire and biological imperative.

But now, he wasn't just reiterating that he *wanted* me. He was saying that he wanted *me*. All of me. Not just my body, not just my orgasms, and not just my milk.

He was acknowledging my autonomy. My past. My features and flaws, altogether. He was telling me that he cared for me whether I indulged his fantasies or not. He wasn't giving me a choice between having sex with him or not having him at all.

He was letting me know that he cared. That he wanted

me to be happy. That he wanted me to enjoy my body, not because of what it could do for him or for anyone else, but because it was *mine.*

There was no doubt in my mind that if I said no right here and right now, he'd take it in stride. We'd enjoy each other another way, and fall asleep in each other's arms as always. But this was a vulnerable part of himself that he was sharing with me. He wanted to drink my milk. Not for nourishment—for *pleasure.*

My supply had been doing just fine for weeks. We didn't need to bang like rabbits two, three, even four times a day anymore like we'd gotten in the habit of doing.

The truth was, we'd been fucking so much because we *wanted* to. If this had only been about feeding Apollo, we could have cut back to a quickie in the kitchen every other day. I had more than enough of Felix's seed; my cups runneth over.

But my milk had always been for one purpose, and one purpose only: raising Apollo. It was my responsibility, and the whole reason I was here.

Slowly, I realized what Felix was trying to say. Giving my milk away to someone other than my son was a way of reclaiming my body as my own. Getting carnal pleasure while nursing a sexual partner? Seeing a big, hot male like Felix get hard sucking my nipples?

My breasts were *mine.* My milk? *Mine.* I had the power to share it with whomever I wanted. It was my choice, and mine alone.

Even giving it to Apollo was a choice. Raising him, loving him, caring for him: I'd chosen to do those things. But this…

This was different.

Felix and I were so much more than just roommates-with-benefits; we had been for a while. We gardened together, we cooked together, we shared responsibilities. He spent time with my son; I did his laundry. I cared about him. And he, obviously, cared about me and my son.

Not because he had to. He didn't *have* to do any of this. He didn't have to care about me, he didn't have to be sweet with me.

He chose to.

Just as I did him.

The choice mattered. I'd always known that instinctively of course, but when life feels like one stream of impossible choices after another, you start to lose track of what you actually have control over. Which choices matter, and which ones are just for show—because an A/B decision that leads to C no matter what, isn't really a decision at all is it?

Get a job, or lose your home.

Fuck this minotaur, or lose your baby.

Those weren't choices. Those were ultimatums.

Felix knew that. That's what he'd been trying to tell me all along. That's what Felix's history with the gods had taught him, and that's been the reality of his world for his entire life.

But despite that—or maybe even *in* spite of that—Felix was offering me a *real* decision now.

No consequences, no ultimatums, no conditions. Just a choice. A: try out this kink, and explore a new way to reclaim my body, or B: don't, and still have a great night.

For as long as he had me, for as long as I chose him, he'd respect that choice. He'd respect *me*.

I leaned forward, stretching out my arms to wrap my hands around the bar suspended above Felix's head. I understood now what it was for. My torso stretched across the empty space above him, my chin brushing his horns as I let my breasts dangle right in front of his face.

His eyes widened, darting to my face for confirmation as he licked his lips.

"I want to give you my milk, Felix."

A full-body shudder wracked him from horns to hooves. His cock twitched, the shiny red head peaking from its sleeve as it grew from his arousal. His eyes darkened as he leaned forward, wrapping his big hands around my swinging tits and testing their weight.

Our gazes locked, I nodded, and he began.

CHAPTER 33

FELIX

The first thought to strike my mind as I cupped Betsy's full, swollen breasts was how *heavy* they were. How strong she was, to carry these swinging weights upon her chest each and every day. My appreciation for just how much they'd grown in the short time she'd been here surged, and my determination to help her enjoy her body to the utmost extent grew even stronger. This woman deserved to be worshipped, and she chose *me* to bow at her altar.

I wouldn't squander the opportunity.

My fingers grasped around the circumference of her milky globes, one hand encircling each, and I gently drew my thumb and forefinger together as I rolled my palms inward—a practiced motion I'd done thousands and thousands of times. Though never with a pair of udders as round and full and magnificent as these.

A sharp gasp, then a long and titillating moan tickled the hair at my scalp as Betsy reacted to the first stream of milk that squirted into the pail at my feet. Her flesh jiggled in my hands as a shiver ran down her spine, and I looked up to see her eyes glaze over as relief radiated through her torso. Of course. She was heavy with milk, full to bursting, and the release of it had to feel good.

"Good girl, Betsy," I assured her, and her eyelashes fluttered at the praise. "That feels good, doesn't it?"

"Mmm-hmm," she hummed, a sound which morphed into another moan as I kneaded her again. Her nipples sprayed, milk splashing the sides of the bucket before dripping down and collecting into the rich, white puddle at the bottom. Again, I squeezed, sliding my hands down closer to her areolas, watching the skin flush red as the pressure released in a steady stream from her peaks.

Her moans deepened, my cock thickening as they took on an almost guttural quality. *She's lowing,* I thought to myself, heat spreading through my core. The reality of Betsy being my human cow was even more arousing than the fantasy, her lusty sounds ratcheting my desire tighter and tighter. *Gods, she's beautiful.*

With several ounces gathered in the bucket, the pressure in her chest had likely eased enough that I could focus more intently. I released her left breast, taking her right in both of my hands and bringing the deep pink tip to my mouth.

Her eyes popped open, watching me, as I flicked the elongated, swollen bud of her nipple across my snout. She twitched as its peak caught the flare of it, her breath catching behind her pouted lips, even as her eyes hooded with pleasure.

"May I suckle you, Betsy?" I asked, my breath hot and damp against her. Her arms bracketed her head, and she leaned against one arm, letting her torso sink into the bench beneath her. The effect was intoxicating. Her back bowed down beautifully, her ass and shoulders arcing up in a lewd, full-body grin, and for a moment I felt myself yearn to cross to her other side and plunge myself inside her exposed, and no doubt leaking, pussy. Lazily, she nodded, and all thoughts of filling her were pushed aside as I tilted my head and wrapped my lips around her teat.

I took her deep, flattening my tongue along the underside before curling it against the cylindrical curve of her nipple. Sucking in my cheeks, I drew her tip to the roof of my mouth, letting my lips massage the tender skin of her areola and unleash a warm, delicious stream into my mouth.

My eyes rolled back into my head as the taste of her milk exploded on my tongue. I swallowed her greedily, massaging her breast with my hands as I suckled in steady pulses with my mouth. My lungs cried out before I got my fill, and I released her with a gasp, exhaling and inhaling heavily while I laved and flicked her with my tongue. It was sloppy and undignified, but the desire for her body had detonated in mine, that first gulp of her milk drowning all but my most animalistic instincts.

I needed more of her. More of her milk. More of her sounds, her moans. Her *pleasure.*

Gods, I wanted to *drown* in her.

"Fuck, Felix," she panted above me, twisting the bar in her grip as she wiggled back and forth. "*Fuck,* your tongue!"

"You like this?" I waggled its pointed tip as quickly as I could, back and forth across the engorged bud, squeezing her as I did. Droplets sprayed and flicked across my face, drenching the fine fur along my jaw in her sweet nectar.

She writhed even more, shaking in my grasp. "It feels…"

"*Fuck* me, tell me how it feels, gorgeous," I growled, needing to know. Was it working? Was she enjoying this as much as I was? Could she feel how sexy, how enticing, how wholly *pleasurable* her body could be?

"It feels *amazing!*"

Fuck yes, it did. "Amazing how?" I dove back in for another gulp of her, and she moaned as her current filled my mouth. I swallowed, then resumed my licking teasing. "Describe it to me."

"It feels…*nngh*…tingly…"

"And?" I shifted her heavy mass into one hand, reaching across to flick her other nipple with my thumb.

"Ah! Oh, gods, and—*mmm*—good. Like releasing a pressure valve."

I pinched the nipple that wasn't in my mouth, and she yelped, before sinking back into a moan.

"I need more than that, Bets. I want to know how it feels when you let go. When I do this," I switched my mouth to her other breast and sucked *hard,* and a jet of liquid streamed into my mouth. We both moaned as my cheeks bulged with the volume of it, and my eyes rolled closed as I savored the sweet, creamy taste filling my senses.

I gulped it down, pulling off her nipple with a *pop!* I looked up at her, seeing the same glazed-over expression in her eyes that I could feel taking over mine, as my head grew fuzzy from her heady flavor.

"Who do these breasts belong to, Betsy?" I grabbed hold of them once again, kneading and squeezing for the sheer pleasure of feeling her flesh mold to my fingers, hearing her milk pour out into the pail.

"You," she moaned, sounding more like a moo than an answer.

"No," I corrected. "Try again."

Confusion lit her face, lifting her from the haze of pleasure we'd spun. The wheels turned in her mind, and I could see she struggled to find words.

I let go of her breasts, bending instead to pick up the bucket at my hooves. I lifted it up, until the rim was inches from her lips.

"Taste it, Bets," I whispered. "Taste how delicious you are.

Take pleasure in your own damn body, because every inch of it belongs to *you*."

Her eyes widened as I tilted the bucket, and she opened her lips to take a sip. I watched as the flavor burst upon her tongue, and her lashes fluttered closed.

I pulled it back. "Don't you taste incredible?"

She released one of her hands, grabbed the rim of the bucket, and tugged it from my hands. Leaning back, she upended it, milk cascading down and dripping on either side of her mouth as she guzzled it, throat bobbing until she emptied the entire pail.

She let her arm fall, and the bucket dropped to the ground with a clatter. I gaped at her.

My cock was harder than it had ever been. Her chest heaved, collarbones rising and falling like waves as she wiped the wetness from her chin, meeting my gaze with pure fire in her eyes.

"I'm *delicious*," she said, almost angrily. She looked mad with lust, pupils blown wide and shining as she panted. "Give me more."

I blinked at her, slowly turning the bucket upright and reaching to milk her to fill it again.

"No," she interrupted. "Not like that. I want you to feed it to me. I want to know what we taste like together, Felix. My milk from your lips."

Heat and pressure went supernova in my belly. I thought *I* might explode, and I fisted the base of my cock in an attempt to keep from spilling my own release into the bucket at her request. My little hucow had bite, and she wanted me to know it.

I grinned at her, tugging at her udder and drawing her nipple to my mouth.

"Yes, ma'am."

CHAPTER 34

BETSY

The moan that rumbled through my chest when Felix sucked my milk straight from the tap and brought his full lips to mine, spilling it inside me as he fucked my mouth with his tongue, was downright feral.

My minotaur lover had unleashed something in me—and I wasn't just talking about my milk. My body was on fire. Every inch of me ached with desire: a tense, coiled itch that yearned to be squeezed and stretched and drained and filled all at once. I ground my hips into the bench, seeking some kind—any kind—of friction to relieve the pulsing heat flaring between my thighs. My tits weren't the only part of me that leaked: slippery liquid gushed from my core and dribbled down my thighs, which I longed to rub together.

But the restraints holding my ankles apart kept me from feeding the fire in my bloodstream. My whole being warred with the tension of wanting to stay stretched out at Felix's mercy, and wanting to finger fuck myself until I collapsed into a wet, shaking mess of pleasure.

I breathed heavily through my nose as Felix flooded my mouth again, dribbles of milk escaping through the hungry movement of our lips as we devoured each other. Our tongues tangling, teeth clashing and bumping sloppily as our lips slanted and pushed against each other.

We hadn't kissed like this, ever. This desperate, moaning, bumping grind of mouths was so different from our usual careful lovemaking. Since that first night, when I'd come into this very barn to seduce him, and I'd gotten the teensiest taste of what it felt like when Felix lost control, he'd reined himself in. Oh sure, he knew how to pound a girl. But now I realized he hadn't truly let his lust take over his senses until tonight.

This was the beast inside Felix. This was the animal inside him, the virile bull he'd only hinted at existing in our previous interactions. And it had taken him to unlock the beast inside of me.

I swallowed, sucking his tongue deep into my mouth as my milk filled my belly. Oh, gods, it was good. He'd been right. I had a whole new appreciation for my body after tasting my milk, after feeling how good it could be to let myself go. I was more than a vessel for the gods, I was more than a mom: I was a complete woman. My body contained multitudes, and I could use it however I wanted.

And right now, I wanted to use it to make both of us come.

"Felix," I said, my voice low and thick from all the moaning and drinking. "I think I'm empty now."

He dragged his tongue across my jawline, sucking and licking a path down my neck and collarbones all the way to my breasts, which felt almost light after all our playing.

He gave my nipples a tentative pull. Only a few tiny drops beaded at the tip, not even enough to fall into the pail below.

I released my grip on the bar with one hand, reaching down and threading my fingers through his hair. He nuzzled into me, his snout pressing into my cleavage as I stroked the base of his horns. He moaned.

"Oh Betsy, when you touch me like that…"

"What, your horns?" I pulled my fingers together and squeezed the smooth, hard protrusion.

And I could only describe the answering sound that rumbled from Felix's chest as a *moo.*

"Yes, my horns!" He roared, thrusting his arms up and gripping my shoulders. "I'm about to burst as it is!"

I stifled a giggle and a moan of my own as I slowly released my other hand and sank into his shoulder. "Well maybe now that my breasts are all empty, you can fill me up."

I stretched back, pushing my ass out over my heels as I curled my back like a cat in the sun, that ache in my core still pulsing for release. My clit was screaming for friction, and my pussy had been clenching around nothing ever since the moment Felix first strapped me to the bench.

He straightened, and even though I couldn't see him, my whole body trembled in anticipation as I heard his hooves *clack-clack-clack* around the bench to stand behind me. When I felt the smooth, hot head of his flared cock slide through my slippery folds, I just about came on the spot.

He flicked it against my clit, and my hips bucked.

"Oh yes, you're ready for me, aren't you?" He murmured, one hand gripping my hip as the other aligned his cock with my entrance. I whimpered as the flare notched into my channel, just enough to tease.

"Yes, please."

"Gods, with you spread like this…" Both hands rubbed over my ass cheeks, before this thumbs pulled the flushed outer lips of my pussy apart. I gave a little whine as he notched ever so slightly deeper inside, before he lifted his thumbs and my slit collapsed back around him. "I could spill my seed right now. What if you were covered in it? All your swells and curves, dripping in white, impossible to tell what's your milk and what's mine…"

I pushed back into him, but his hands kept me from sinking myself fully onto his length.

"Felix," I begged, almost crying with need. *"Please."*

"Yes, ma'am."

He thrust inside me, filling me to the brim in one greedy plunge. My head flew back, all the air leaving my lungs in a cry as that first thrust gave way to another and another, my minotaur wasting no time in establishing a punishing rhythm rocking my cunt. I straightened my arms and leaned my hips back, relishing in the strength of his grip as he filled me again and again.

My breasts bounced with the force of it, swinging to and fro as he pounded me from behind. At one point, he growled, grinding himself against my deepest part as he pulled me back against him. He steadied my hips with one hand, reached around to paw at my breast with another, before tilting back and pistoning his hips up at a new angle. I saw stars as his flared head pushed into the forward wall of my channel, rocking into my g-spot and threatening to send another gush of fluid spilling from my body.

His hand squeezed, and I cried out as a flaccid spurt of milk dripped from my nipple. My body squished in his hold, the flesh around my hips bulging between his gripping fingers, the sound of his hard, pulsing cock splitting me apart resounding in wet, echoing smacks throughout the barn. Sweat, milk, and arousal covered our bodies in a slick perfume of sex, and my head spun with it. Pleasure spun higher and higher, a tornado in my gut, as he pounded me closer and closer to the edge.

"Fuck, you're incredible," he grunted, tilting his head down and sucking the skin at the crease of my neck and shoulder.

I cried in agreement, reaching one hand down to rub at my clit. I was so, so slippery down there, my fingers flew across the swollen bud in frantic swipes. More lewd sounds of slick flesh joined the chorus of our union as I touched myself, and Felix's thrusts grew frantic.

"Are you ready for my knot, Betsy?"

"Fuck," I moaned, more ready than I'd ever been for anything in my life.

"With words!"

"Yes, I'm ready for your knot!"

"Here it comes!"

With a roar, he buried himself completely inside me, shoving my pussy wide as he notched his bulging knot inside me. My walls clenched, the burning stretch inciting a reactive recoil of my inner muscles as they pulsed around his girth. His flare formed a seal against my channel as his seed shot inside me, hammering my insides with a heat-seeking missile of cum. The coil of pleasure in my core snapped, exploding as he filled me, and my entire body shattered around him.

Thank the gods he held me up, because my muscles spasmed uncontrollably for minutes, the orgasm refusing to let up. Every time I thought I might be done, the relaxing of my pussy just sank me deeper on his knot, and the cycle of shaking pleasure started all over again.

The last thing I remembered was the strong, warm grip of Felix's arms around me before I blacked out.

* * *

I WOKE up to Apollo's cries in the middle of the night. Clean and dry beneath the covers, with Felix's soft, fuzzy chest rising and falling with his steady breaths at my back, I concluded that he must have cleaned us up and carried us into bed after I'd passed out from orgasming so hard.

I had to hand it to him. I'd been wary of his little hucow fantasy at first, but the deeper we fell into the role of cow and farmer, with him bending me over on that padded bench, massaging my breasts and feeding me my own milk before rutting me from behind... well. I couldn't argue with the results.

That being said, all that screaming and writhing in pleasure took a lot out of me. I was spent. It didn't help that I was getting woken up in the middle of the night, either, especially when I'd just gotten used to Apollo sleeping through til dawn.

I rubbed my eyes and dragged myself out of bed, moving slowly so as not to wake Felix, but I needn't have worried. The big guy was out like a light. I groaned as I straightened my legs and hobbled over to the crib. I didn't know if I was more sore from the wild sex, or from the overall toll being a new mom took on a body. Now that Apollo was crawling, I was doing a lot more running after him, and the constant up and down was exhausting.

To my surprise, Apollo was already standing on his hooves, tiny hands holding onto the bars as he wailed for me.

As luck would have it, the top bar of his crib came right up to my ribcage, making it the perfect height to facilitate his preferred feeding position. I leaned over it, letting my elbows rest on the wide wooden railing as I steadied his shoulders. His grip shifted immediately from the bars to my boob, and he latched on like a pro, smushing my nipple in between his tongue and his snout and suckling.

I sighed with relief. Somehow, my breasts were already full of milk again, and tender with swelling. I'd wondered if maybe I'd be too sore to nurse my baby after Felix milked me on the bench, but I needn't have worried. My body contained multitudes, it seemed, and I'd recovered quickly.

My nipples even seemed to know the difference between my baby minotaur and my big one. With my baby at my breast, I didn't feel a hint of the wild sensations Felix had elicited from me earlier. Instead, my chest filled with the warm glow of maternal pride.

My milk flowed easily as Apollo fed. That happy, comfortable feeling I always got when the two of us found a good rhythm settled deep in my bones, and even some of my tiredness seeped away.

Me and my baby. Making it work like mothers and sons had done for all of time.

It was hard to believe that barely a month ago, I'd been terrified we'd never be able to have this. And I supposed, if it wasn't for Felix, we wouldn't have.

I stroked my baby's head, appreciating the softness of his fine, dark hair. He'd been born with a full tuft of it between his tiny horns—barely more than nubbins that poked from either side at the top of his hairline. It had already started growing thicker, a fine peach fuzz-like fur filling in around the longer, darker hair that covered his scalp, similar to the fuzz that covered Felix's human-like half. Pretty soon I'd have to give Apollo his first haircut.

I closed my eyes and imagined it: him sitting in his highchair at the kitchen table. He'd be impatient, swinging his legs and barely sitting still, so I'd give him a handful of Cheerios to keep him occupied while I wet a comb and trimmed his bangs with a pair of shears. Felix probably didn't own a pair of regular scissors, after all, so we'd have to make do with whatever he had lying around in the farm. When I was done, I'd carry Apollo with me out to the barn to return the shears, and Felix would give us a big grin when he saw our little guy's fresh new 'do, plucking him from my arms and swirling him around before setting him down on his hooves so he could run around and chase the chickens. Then he'd turn to me, pull me into his arms, and kiss me long and hard and deep, and we'd...

I let the fantasy play out like a film in my head as I played with Apollo's hair, who suckled for a few more minutes before burping and switching to the other breast. We were pros at this by now. I wiped the spittle off his snout with one of the burpcloths tucked around the railing as he dove in for the second course.

The pressure in my boobs evened, and the influx of oxytocin and adrenaline that always flooded my system when I nursed eliminated most of my drowsiness. Apollo started squirming, his hands pushing into my chest to let me know he was done.

I let go of him, wiped him down with the burpcloth, then grabbed Felix's robe from the bathroom door and the backpack I'd brought with me when I first arrived here, which held all the pacifiers and baby toys. I scooped up Apollo and carried him out of the bedroom, closing the door behind me so Felix could catch up on his own rest.

He hadn't started crying again, but I knew he'd be ready to go any minute now. Potty time had become something of a standoff between me and the little guy. Not soon after Felix had started helping out with the little guy, we'd run out of diapers. So the two of us had developed a system for getting Apollo on board the proper minotaur pooping technique train.

During the day, I'd watch for his tell-tale poop signals and carry him outside to do his business, celebrating with praise and smiles whenever he relieved himself in the field that Felix used. It wasn't unlike potty training a dog, to be honest.

But it wasn't ideal. I'd only been Apollo's mother for a

month, after all, and I'd never owned a dog of my own. So I missed his poop signals a lot. Which, in turn, meant a lot of impromptu loads of laundry and cleaning up accidents.

I wasn't keen on the idea of washing out his crib again, so I elected to just wait him out this time until he was ready to go outside.

I set him in his highchair, handed him a toy from the backpack, then tied my robe tight around my waist.

So absorbed was I in keeping an eye out for the poop face, that I didn't even notice that there was someone *else* sitting at the table. That was, until I looked up to check the time.

"Oh my gods!" I leapt about a foot into the air, and immediately regretted it as gravity yanked me back down to earth tits first. My nipples scraped against the edge of the table, and I winced. *Ow.* One hand shot to my racing heart while the other banded across my chest as I caught my breath. "Where did you come from?"

A tall, white goddess with strawberry-blonde hair, crystal blue eyes and sharp features was leaning casually against the back of Felix's minotaur-sized dining chair. Her chin rested on her knuckles, elbow propped up by the relatively tall armrest, and the shimmery, white fabric of her toga-like dress draped elegantly over her legs, which were crossed at the knee. Her lips curved into a knowing smirk as she waited for my pulse to settle.

"Isn't it just like a man to sleep in while the mom takes care of everything."

I frowned at her. Pretty judgy for someone who'd literally *forced* a single mother onto an unsuspecting bachelor mere weeks beforehand. What's worse, her insult wasn't even true. Felix had only picked up more of the slack in recent weeks. I'd begun to see him as a partner when it came to Apollo, actually, despite his early resistance to filling any kind of fatherly role.

Turned out, when he wasn't spending all of his time railing against the gods for saddling him with Zeus's unwanted offspring, he actually seemed to enjoy the hallmarks of fatherhood.

What's more, he was good at it. And I looked forward to seeing how his and Apollo's relationship would grow over the years.

"Iris." That was her name, right? "Long time, no see."

That wasn't entirely accurate. I'd actually seen her twice since the day she'd rescued me from the hospital. But both times, I'd been eavesdropping on a private conversation between her and Felix, and with everything that had happened in the last month, it felt like years had passed since the goddess and I had spoken.

Truth be told, I'd assumed that my dealings with the gods were over now that Apollo was breastfeeding regularly and Felix and I had established a good rapport. Iris seemed, to me, like something of an Olympian social worker. Showed up when there was a gods-related emergency, extricated the problem, and then fucked off somewhere until there was another fire that needed putting out.

And since the gods' little matchmaking scheme between Felix and me had gone well, I'd assumed there was nothing more she needed to do here.

The last time she'd visited me, I'd been delirious with pain and on the verge of death as a pair of demigod horns threatened to tear my vagina apart. And even though I knew that's what had happened, the memory itself was foggy. She and Hera had done something to me, Petra, and the hospital staff when they'd taken over the delivery. Messed with our memories somehow so none of the nurses or doctors would come away from the experience with wild stories about the Queen of the gods stealing a newborn monster and its mother from the nursery.

Trying to remember details from that day was like trying to hold water in my hands—they slipped through my fingers before I could grab hold.

All I knew for sure was that they'd saved Apollo's life and mine that day. And again when they'd delivered me here, to Felix. Then, she'd told Felix he needed to fuck me so my boobs would work, and skated off on her rainbow back to Olympus.

And, sure, the first few days had been rough. But we'd worked it out. And now I couldn't imagine my life with Apollo going any other way.

So why, then, was Iris here?

Her eyes roamed about the kitchen, lingering for a second on the toy that was slowly becoming engulfed in drool in Apollo's mouth. Then she turned to me.

"It's nice to see the two of you adjusting to life on the farm."

Awkward silence stretched between us as I scrambled for something to say in reply. But I hardly knew this goddess. Don't get me wrong: I was grateful to her—as grateful as one could be to someone who'd erased most of their memories of the very thing they did to deserve gratitude.

But her comment about Felix still grated at me. I wasn't sure what the protocol was in this situation. How was I supposed to treat the goddess who'd plopped me onto a farm in the middle of nowhere for the sole purpose of fucking its only inhabitant?

And now that I'd done that, what else did she expect of me?

Luckily for me, Apollo had no such qualms. While I froze, debating about whether or not to make small talk, he stared directly into the goddesses eyes and screwed up his face in a look of immense concentration. His snout wrinkled, he let out a little grunt, and then…

"Godsdammit!"

A *profound* stench propelled me from my chair. Iris's appearance had completely distracted me from watching for his poo signals, and I'd totally boofed it. I waved a hand over my nose as I approached him, lifting him out of the mess in his highchair and trying not to breathe in.

Ufda. I ran over to the sink, plopped him down in the empty basin where he'd be having a bath, ASAP, before grabbing a rag and some white vinegar to clean up the mess.

Iris paled, her nose wrinkling. "That reminds me."

She snapped her fingers, and three packages of diapers, two tubs of wipes, baby powder and diaper cream appeared next to my backpack. I almost wept at the sight. All animosity I felt towards the goddess was forgotten as I took in the pile of baby supplies.

"Oh my gods, *thank you.* How did you know?"

This was like, half a paycheck's worth of diapers and wipes. I wanted to throw my arms around her in gratitude, but the mess in the high chair was more urgent. I wiped down the seat and the wooden legs three times over, running back and forth between it and the faucet to rinse out the rag between cleanings. Once I'd sufficiently eliminated the odor of baby poop and replaced it with the tang of vinegar, I finally addressed the baby in the sink.

The goddess spoke. "A little birdie told me you were running low. It also wanted me to deliver this."

I turned on the faucet and let it run, rinsing my hands real quick and patting them dry while the water warmed for Apollo's bath. Once dry, I allowed myself to take the purple envelope that Iris offered me.

Petra.

My stomach dropped. The sight of her name and return address in her loopy handwriting was enough to bring tears to my eyes. I'd wondered if she'd been getting my letters.

Homesickness walloped my chest like a mallet as I scanned the envelope for a post-date. It had been sent two weeks ago. Why had it taken so long to arrive?

I tore open the envelope and started reading.

Dear Betsy,

Shut up. Who would have thought that you'd wind up on an honest-to-gods farm like something out of Little House on the Prairie! How big is it? What kinds of crops does your roommate grow? Are there animals?? Oh my goodness, if you tell me that you've seen an actual cow in real life (you know, a full one—like with udders and stuff, not a half-cow/half-person that's only got two legs like Apollo), I will positively FLIP OUT. If having Zeus's baby means that you get your own bedroom in a cute little antique farmhouse and out of the projects, then maybe I should try picking up a god next year at Lollapalooza. Do you have any tips? Because let me tell you girl, I could use a break from city life.

Not that you need to worry about me. I'm doing alright. But I miss you like crazy. I decided to try to find a subletter. It's been a nightmare. I'm glad your roommate seems nice. I'd take quiet and polite over the weirdos who've been answering my classified ad any day. Part of me hopes you'll come home before I actually have to fill your room, but I can only swing the rent for another month without someone to split the cost. Any chance your boobs will be fixed by then?

Haha, just kidding! I'll be fine. The most important thing is that you're safe and sound, and I'm happy to hear that Apollo's settling in. You're right: we're tough cookies, and that includes Apollo now, too. He's probably got tougher skin than you and me —literally!

Miss you so so so so SOOOOOO much. Can't wait to hear all about your life on the FARM!! (oh my goodness I will NEVER get used to that! Can you see the stars at night? Can you see the Northern Lights??) If you have a CVS out there and can get film developed, take a picture of the night sky and send it to me so I can tape it to my ceiling in the middle of all my glow-in-the-dark stars and pretend I'm there with you. And while you're at it, take pictures of your roommate, too! I wanna know what he looks like.

I'll send you a picture of whatever roommate I find, too. So you can know exactly who I'm judging for not being nearly as wonderful a roomie as you.
BFFs forever,
Petra

I wiped my eyes, sniffling, as I stuffed the letter and the envelope into the pocket of Felix's robe. She must have sent this after getting my first letter, and because I now lived out in the middle of bumfuck nowhere, it had taken forever for it to arrive. True, I'd stopped checking the mailbox as religiously as I did when I first arrived, once Felix and I had started to hit it off. But it hadn't been more than a few days since I'd gone out there, hadn't it?

Guilt knotted in my stomach as I tried to remember how long ago I'd written. I'd started a letter telling her about Felix's and my first time, but I'd gotten distracted when Apollo started crying halfway through and had forgotten to finish it. Then one thing had led to another, and…

Oh, gods.

I was a terrible friend. A horrible, *terrible* friend.

Had I truly forgotten about Petra once Felix and I started banging?

Steam rose from the running faucet, and Apollo was babbling and banging on the porcelain sink walls without a care in the world, distracting me once again from my letters with Petra. I leaned my hands against the edge of the counter for a moment, attempting to compose myself, before adjusting the temperature back down to less than scalding and plugging up the drain of the basin so I could get on with his bath.

"She misses you."

"No shit, Sherlock," I muttered, before freezing in panic. Unsure of protocol or not, I was pretty sure getting snippy with a goddess was a good way to get cursed. My eyes bulged, and I whipped my head around to apologize. "Oh gods, I'm sorry. I didn't mean—that wasn't-"

"It's okay, Betsy," the goddess soothed. She patted my elbow as I wiped my eyes again, which only got more water on my face as my hands were wet from the sink. "I know you miss her, too."

"I do." Apollo tilted his head at me, patting at my chest with his fingers spread wide as I gathered myself. "It sucks that me being here is causing her so much trouble."

"That's your takeaway?" Iris's brow furrowed, and she snapped her fingers again. The letter appeared in her hand, and I panicked, patting down my pockets which, surely enough, were empty. Her eyes scanned the letter, eyebrows furrowing. "I'm pretty sure she expressed being happy for you. Where was... ah! Here we go. 'If having Zeus's baby means–'" she read aloud, and I lunged at her.

"Give that back! Don't you know it's illegal to read someone else's mail?"

I reached to snatch it out of her hands, but she was quicker. She raised an eyebrow. "Illegal? For whom? I'm the goddess of messages."

"Then you should *know–*" grab, miss. "That it's *rude–*" swipe, miss. "To spy on a private conversation!"

I finally cornered her against the counter and was able to pluck it from her slender little fingers. I stuffed it back into my pocket with a *hmph,* furious at myself for getting it wrinkled and probably smudged. Even moreso, because I knew that the goddess had most likely *let* me take it back. I stormed back to the sink, turned off the water, and squirted out a dollop of baby wash onto another used burpcloth.

I needed to do laundry again. I needed to respond to Petra. I needed to figure out a way to get back to the city so I could help her with rent...

Wait. What was I thinking? Go back to the city?

Where would that leave me and Felix?

"Funny, how much value you place on privacy when it's someone eavesdropping on *your* conversation," she observed. Heat rushed to my cheeks. *So she had noticed.* "I'll remember that next time I spot you peeking your nose through the curtain to spy on me with a certain minotaur."

"That's different," I defended. "First of all, that was weeks ago. And might I remind you, you dropped me here without any word whatsoever about what I needed to do to take care of Apollo. How else was I supposed to learn how to fix what was wrong with me? If I hadn't listened in on your conversations, I never would have found out that I needed to swallow a bunch of minotaur... *essence* for my milk to come in."

"Swallow?" Iris blinked. "Who said anything about swallowing it?"

My face grew, impossibly, hotter.

Great, Bets. You're really nailing this talking-to-a-goddess thing.

She crossed her arms, lips curling into a smirk. "My, oh my, Betsy, you really are quite the little treat, aren't you? I'd heard you and Felix were getting a little…*creative* with the prompt, but I didn't realize you'd kicked it off with such a bang. No wonder Zeus stuck around for as long as he did."

I ignored the barb, carefully avoiding getting suds in Apollo's eyes as I washed his hair.

What was it about Hera and her tribe that made them so judgey about any kind of intercourse that wasn't explicitly sanctioned for serving some purpose other than pleasure? *No wonder Zeus stuck around,* indeed. Was this the kind of attitude that fucked Felix up so much about enjoying sex? Why it had been so hard to get him to fuck me in the first place?

Sex was fun, dammit!

Especially when you trusted someone enough to really let go. To indulge in new pleasures, or refuse without fear of retaliation. I hadn't even realized how many messed-up ideas I'd had about pleasure and sex and my own body until Felix opened my perspective. How many relationships had I been in where I used sex as a tool to keep someone happy? Or really, used my body to make everyone around me happy, instead of worrying about whether or not *I* was happy?

Maybe Iris should take a look at herself and her own attitudes around sex. Maybe then she wouldn't be throwing all this judginess around!

I took a breath, gathering myself before I said something I'd regret. I was still upset about Petra's letter. If I started lecturing Iris about free love and feminism now, I'd likely go overboard and earn myself a one-way ticket to Hades.

"I assume that you showed up here to talk about something other than blowjobs," I finally said, moving on to scrub the lower half of my little man. "Or were you just stopping by to read me my mail?"

Why lecture, when I could just continue to make passive-aggressive comments?

"I also got you diapers," she said pointedly, raising an eyebrow.

I sighed, contrite. "Right. You did. Thanks again."

"You're welcome. But you are correct, this little visit is more than a mail-call. The real reason I came was to check on Apollo's welfare. And yours. A little birdie told me that… Well, I won't get into the details. I just wanted to make sure you two were alright. He hasn't hurt you, has he?"

"Hurt me?" I shot her a look as I rung out the burpcloth before switching into rinsing mode. Apollo splashed his hands. "What makes you say that?"

She waved nonchalantly, but I noticed that even as she did so, she seemed to scan my face and neck. Her eyes darted down to the bruise on the crease of my neck and shoulder, where Felix had left a hickey and a bite mark earlier that night.

I adjusted my robe, pulling it up and closing it tighter around my shoulders.

She shrugged. "No reason. Hera fortified your body when she healed you, after all. If anyone's equipped to withstand a romp with a minotaur like Felix, it's you!"

She said that with the chipper energy of a camp counselor sending me off on a nature hike. I turned off the water and gathered a dishtowel.

But before I patted Apollo dry, I paused.

"What do you mean, a minotaur *like Felix?*"

Something was off in this conversation, and it wasn't just me. Iris claimed that she was here to check on Apollo's welfare, but the entire time we'd been talking, she hardly looked at the demigod since he'd shit in his highchair.

No. Instead, she'd been focusing on me and my sex life. Picking on me for Felix's and my adventures, while checking me over for bruises.

Because she was worried that I'd get hurt… by *Felix*?

The same Felix who'd had so much self-control, I'd had to literally wave my naked ass in his face before he'd fuck me the first time?

The minotaur who'd stepped up to the plate to help me raise Apollo. Who built him a *crib*. Who cooked me breakfast every morning, and dinner every night.

She couldn't possibly be concerned about the Felix who insisted I come a minimum of two times before he'd even let me touch his penis whenever we had sex. The one who never once stopped focusing on my pleasure. Who helped me take the reins of my own pleasure, even, and reinterpret the way I looked at my body and what it was capable of.

That Felix?

Yes, he was giant. And half-bull. And to some people, sure, I guess that might have been intimidating. There was no doubt in my mind that, if he wanted to, he could toss me around like a bale of hay. Gods knew he'd lifted me and carried me and swung me onto the bed or fucked me up against the wall enough times to prove it. He was a strong guy. And sure, I guess that also meant that he was capable of hurting me if he wanted to.

But that was the thing—I couldn't imagine anyone wanting to hurt me *less* than my minotaur roommate.

He was the sweetest, most attentive man I'd ever been with: the truest example of a *gentleman* I'd ever met. Monster or no.

So why was Iris implying that having sex with him put me in danger?

The goddess shifted a bit before answering, her expression guarded. "Let's just say, there's a reason he's been exiled for three thousand years. He doesn't have the best track record when it comes to physical relationships. But I'm happy to hear he's improved!" She clapped her hands, pasting that toothpaste ad-smile back onto her face. "Especially since Hera's hoping to expand this little minotaur daycare."

"Hold on," I interrupted, still stuck on the first thing she'd said. "What do you mean, track record? It's not like he's hurt someone before, has he?"

Not *my* Felix? He might look vicious, but he wouldn't hurt a fly.

The smile fell off her face so fast, I'm surprised it didn't make a crashing sound.

"It's really nothing to worry about, okay? The important thing is, you're fine. As we knew you would be. Now why don't you towel off your little demigod and write back to Petra, hmm? Tell her what you all have planted in the garden. I noticed the peas are coming in! I'm sure she'll love to hear all about that. I'll see if we can get you that disposable camera, too. Although, we might need to establish some rules regarding that."

She made like she was heading for the door.

"Now wait just a minute!" I said, reaching up my hands in the universal sign for stop. "You can't just come in here and tell me Felix 'doesn't have the best track record with physical relationships,' when you literally put me here to have sex with him!"

"I *literally* came here to check on you! And clearly, you're fine, so what's the problem?"

She crossed her arms and tapped her foot. I spluttered at her, too dumbfounded to speak. *Is this the kind of treatment Felix is used to?*

Her forced smile twitched.

"You *are* fine, right?"

Her gaze became more assessing, and I found my voice in a heartbeat.

"Of course! Felix has treated me like a princess since I got here! He's kind and generous, and loving, and…" I trailed off, emotion clogging my throat as I realized just how much I'd come to care for the big guy.

The letter from Petra weighed heavy in my pocket as I fought to figure out what I was trying to say.

"Well that's great!" Iris chirped. "I'll let Hera know. She's found a few other women *in a family way* that have been abandoned by their god lovers, and they're in need of a kind, generous minotaur to help them out with that. I'm glad to hear that Felix will be up to the task!"

My insides turned to lead.

"What? What do you mean 'other women'?" I gripped the edge of the sink as the meaning of her words filtered through. "Iris, you don't mean that you want Felix to…"

"Enjoy the diapers!"

And before I could get another word in edge-wise, she poofed out of existence in a cloud of rainbow glitter.

I fumed as sparkly bits of plastic dust rained over the kitchen, covering the counters, floors, me, and my freshly-washed baby in a psychedelic film of trash.

"Aw, *come on!*"

CHAPTER 35

FELIX

$\mathcal{I}$ woke to an empty bed.

At first, I almost believed that all of the events of the past month had been some sort of elaborate dream. It was easy enough to do, when the pale, springtime sun was peeking through the curtains like it always did this time of year, and the crisp sheets and heavy quilt tangled in my massive limbs. Hooves were not designed for bedding, and I'd quickly untucked the bottom edge of the covers within a few minutes of crawling under them.

And yet, the physical proof of Betsy's presence lingered. Her scent was everywhere—strawberries and cream and sunshine—surrounding me and my senses as I clung to the vestiges of sleep. The sheets beneath the small of my back were still damp from the marathon of orgasms I'd coaxed from her, and the smell of sex lingered in the air. The spirit of her was heady and palpable throughout the room; the imprint she'd left on my heart was as undeniable as the one she'd left in the sheets.

There was a chill in the air, reminding me I hadn't stoked the woodstove before bed. Spring was fickle in Minnesota:

some nights pleasantly cool, others cold enough to threaten a lethal frost, even as late as June. I'd found in the last few weeks, I'd worried less and less about the fireplace at night, as the bed was far warmer when Betsy and I snuggled beneath the covers. Which begged the question: where had she gone?

Just as I was sifting through what of the previous night had been real and what had been imagination, the sight of Apollo's empty crib against the wall brought my brain to rights.

Betsy and Apollo were up already, and the house was cold. I needed to quit dawdling. Make breakfast. Maybe I'd take Apollo out to the field with me again today, show him how to do some repairs on the tractor. Maybe Betsy would even come out there with us, and we could spend the morning together on the farm as a family.

A family.

No. It was dangerous to think that way. As much as I might want it, I knew that this paradise of ours wouldn't last forever. I could still care for them, of course. Help Betsy with little Apollo, prepare him for the world. But in the end, I was destined to toil the fields alone and miserable in perpetuity.

But I hadn't had a check-up from Iris in weeks.

What if the gods had decided once and for all to leave me alone and let me serve out the rest of my sentence in peace now that I'd helped save Zeus's son? Perhaps this favor had been repentance: a life saved, to replace the one I'd taken.

Or maybe after all these centuries, their feelings toward me had simply faded from hatred and disdain to mere apathy. Maybe they didn't care if I decided to live out the rest of my days as a partner to Betsy and a parent to her demigod son.

A parent.

The closest thing I'd had to parents had been the gods

themselves, who'd plucked me from my mother as soon as I was weaned and dropped me into an elaborate maze to play villain to their human heroes. Hermes had kept me company at first, with his various instructions from the Three in charge, but eventually even his visits dwindled. The yearly interactions I had with humans left such a terrible impression, I was still a vegetarian to this day.

When Hera appeared before me, asking me to let the next human set to be delivered to my doorstep best me in battle in exchange for immortality and a better life, I didn't so much as blink. *Freedom,* I'd thought at the time. *She's offering me freedom.*

But my brief second life in Olympus was one of loneliness. No gods wanted to fraternize with an abomination like me. As a bastard of a gods-made beast and a human, I didn't belong in a paradise with deities. I ended up working in the Hades-hot coal forges for Hephaestus, another Olympian outcast, and the blacksmith God.

Only Celedonia, the most beautiful of Hephaestus's daughters, took pity on me. She and I grew closer over time. She kept me company as I toiled in the bellows of the forges, singing along to the rhythm of her father's everpresent hammer strikes. Her voice was more beautiful than the sirens'. My only friend.

Eventually, she became so much more to me. My first love.

Until I destroyed her.

We'd become one on the twelfth night of Bacchanalia, the one festival when Hephaestus let the forges go dark. All of Olympus celebrated with feast and drink, and she and I retreated to the bellows with a barrel of wine between us. I still remember the way the dwindling red of the embers glowed copper across her golden skin, her music-like cries as I entered her, our passions hotter than the dying forge.

Her body did not take to my seed. She had not been made for it. It soured in her womb, and the babe within her slowly killed her.

Neither she nor the baby survived.

I was banished to Tartarus for her murder. The gods' sentence was nothing compared to the shame and fury with which I punished myself. A thousand years I spent enduring tortures with Tantalus, Sisyphus, Prometheus… and in my mind, I was more deserving of Hades' cruelty than them all.

For none of them had destroyed a being so beautiful and lovely. One so kind as to offer kindness and companionship to someone as wretched as me.

A monster among the gods.

I'd thought that no one ever would again. Until…

"Wallowing again?"

I jumped, Iris's appearance as unexpected as it was unwelcome, breaking me from my reverie.

"*Fuck* the gods! Iris! What are you doing here?"

"I could ask *you* the same question! Don't you know there's farming to do? Wood to chop? Tractors to repair?"

She clapped her hands thrice in quick succession, waving at me to rise from the bed.

I reluctantly threw off the covers and sat up, muttering, "I wouldn't have to repair the tractor if *someone* hadn't broken it."

"What, no resistance this morning?" The goddess smirked, crossing her arms. "Family life suits you, Felix."

The hairs along my spine spiked in agitation and—*hope?* Did she mean that? Or was she mocking me?

Who was I kidding? I know the answer to that. Especially when it came from the mouth of a patronizing goddess. "What do you want, Iris?"

Despite my demeanor projecting more prickles than a porcupine, she gathered her draping skirts and sat beside me on the bed. "For once, I'm actually here to commend you, Felix. Hera is pleased with your progress."

"My progress?" The ember of hope flared once more…

"Yes! Yours and Apollo's. Betsy seems to have taken to your seed better than we could have hoped. In fact, Hera projects her supply may exceed even Apollo's needs before long. Which brings me to your next assignment."

…and snuffed out immediately. "Assignment?"

"Of course. You didn't think we'd just leave you alone, did you?"

I rose from the bed, creating some much needed space between me and the goddess. My insides twisted. "I'd *hoped.*"

"Oh, Felix," she sighed, and a pitying smile dimpled her cheeks. "This was just a trial run. And your and Betsy's results far exceeded expectations. We're ready to move on to phase two."

"Phase…two?"

"You think Betsy's the only human The Three have knocked up this year?" She laughed, and my stomach sank. "Or, well, I guess just the Two, I should say. Hades has always been a good boy. Although, with a wife like Persephone, who can blame him? The *ass* on that goddess–"

"Get to the point, Iris!" Clouds of steam puffed from my snout, growing larger the longer she babbled. Like always, the flippancy with which she and Hera toyed with my existence drove me to rage. Especially now that Betsy's name was getting thrown into their plans, I couldn't bear to listen to her ramble while she dangled my next punishment before me like a carrot on a string.

"All that to say, there's another batch of ladies on the way. Pregnant ones. Too many for Hera to keep track of, so we're just going to have you do it."

"*What?*"

"You know, prep their bodies for delivery. The same way

you did with Betsy and her milk. I have to say, that little felacio trick? Brilliant. I never even *considered* that swallowed essence would have the same effect as traditional delivery methods. This makes the whole operation even easier! I wonder if you can collect it in a cup and sneak it into their food somehow, if that would still work?" She tapped her finger to her chin, as if every word spewing from her mouth wasn't absolutely horrifying. "Oh! That reminds me. You're going to need a lot more food to feed all these extra bodies! And we'll need to set up some beds in the barn for now. You really can't procrastinate on fixing up that tractor anymo–*ah!*"

Her monologue cut off on a scream as I grabbed her about the waist and hauled her into the air. My fingers squeezed, thumbs practically touching as my hands encircled her, squeezing with far more intensity than I could restrain or control. My vision tinted red as I glared at her, preparing to bellow with all my–

"Felix! No!"

I released my grip as Betsy flew into the room, eyes sparkling with surprise as she took in the scene. Wait—it wasn't just her eyes that were sparkling. Her whole body was sprinkled with holographic flecks, a fact that distracted me for only a moment before I fully registered her expression.

Panic.

It was so close to the look of fear she'd given me when she arrived and saw me for the first time. Concern colored her wide, emerald eyes as her gaze darted from me to Iris and back again.

She hadn't looked at me like that in *weeks*. Seeing her eyes wide, her mouth agape, staring at me like a—a...

A monster.

I dropped the goddess immediately. She tumbled to the floor.

"What's going on here? Felix, what are you doing to Iris?"

"Betsy," I croaked. My pulse still reeled from rage even as the red in my vision receded and my brain cleared. "You don't understand, she was–"

"*Really*, Felix! You need to get that temper of yours under control! Especially once the rest of the girls get here."

"They're coming here?" Betsy blinked, her brow furrowing, as she offered Iris a hand to help her up from the heap she'd formed on the ground. The goddess took it, rubbing at her side tentatively.

"What are you talking about?" My neck was a swivel as I switched focus from Iris to Betsy and back again. "Why would you send anyone else here?"

"Because they're the mothers of the next generation of demigods! Felix, listen when I talk to you, for Pete's sake! I told you Zeus and Poseidon went on another bender to sow their wild oats."

Betsy's face paled. "Wait, Zeus did? Recently?"

Iris finished examining herself, appearing to discern no lasting injuries from her fall. She threw Betsy a disbelieving glance. "You're surprised?"

I gaped at the goddess's insensitivity. Betsy and Zeus's break-up was still fresh. She'd *just* had Apollo a month ago. Surely she realized that bringing multiple women he'd slept with here, to live with Betsy, was a terrible idea?

Then again, the gods had always been insensitive. Certainly with me. Perhaps it was seeing their callousness turned on Betsy that made my anger so acute. But that wasn't all that concerned me. "You said girls, *plural.* You can't mean children?"

"Of course not," the goddess scoffed. "You know what I mean. Human women."

"How many women did he impregnate?" I asked.

Betsy tilted her head at me, while Iris glared. I glared back.

"There's seven women total. And it wasn't *just* Zeus."

"*Seven* women? In two months?" Betsy went paler still, and started to sway. I lunged for her, wrapping an arm about her waist before she fainted.

She flinched. "I need to sit down."

Every muscle in my chest seized, but despite that, I helped her to the side of the bed. "Where's Apollo?" I murmured as I released her, hovering just in case she wavered again.

"He's in his chair; I moved it to the living room. Sesame Street is on."

The words came out in a monotone, so unlike the vibrant, whip-smart woman I'd come to care for so much in the past week. She didn't meet my eyes.

Something isn't right, my inner voice hissed. I wanted so badly to talk to her, to sooth her. This visit from Iris couldn't have come at a worse time. Betsy and I had just shared the most incredible night of my immortal life, and now...

She was leaning away from me, her body caving in on itself as she crossed her arms over her stomach. Her eyes glazed as she stared into the distance, seated on the bed, her thoughts seemingly a thousand miles away.

What was she thinking? What was making her shrink away like this?

"How long?" She asked, voice hollow.

Iris shifted, finally seeming to grasp that neither Betsy nor I were nearly as excited by her news as she had been to share it. Her lips pursed in consideration for a moment, before she puffed out with a sigh, "They're coming tomorrow."

"Tomorrow?" Betsy repeated, disbelieving, staring at her hands. My whole body went numb, as my heart seesawed between fury at Iris's absurd request and concern for Betsy.

"And you want Felix to… to give them the same thing he gave me?"

Oh no. *No.* That's what she was afraid of?

I so badly wanted to reach for her, touch her, hold her. *Comfort her.* Tell her there would never be another woman who I could give myself to like I had her.

I wanted to strangle Iris for even suggesting such a thing. Hera's plan was for me to give my seed to all of Zeus's exes so she didn't have to deal with them?

It wasn't just impractical. It was cruel. And not just to me, but to *them.*

All of the women who'd been used and abandoned by the Three. Including…

Betsy.

I'd given myself to Betsy, *all* of myself. My heart, my seed, my soul belonged to her and only her. I was a changed mino-taur. *She'd* changed me.

Surely Iris could see that?

I had to refuse. I had to declare, right here, right now: I would not give my seed to any woman other than Betsy.

"Well, of course. They'll die without it." Iris shrugged, delivering those words with as much nonchalance a knock-knock joke.

Betsy and I froze. I stared at her, pulse skyrocketing. Her face was a mask.

No. *No.* I had to say something. I had to fight this.

But… I couldn't.

Not when the gods still held me captive. Not when my entire existence was a punishment for my past crimes.

And so, I merely sat. Dumb. Unable to say or do anything to comfort the woman I loved.

Loved.

Oh gods. I loved her.

All that talk of not getting attached, of knowing what was

coming, and I couldn't even honor my own promise. And now, I would suffer the consequences.

Iris opened her mouth. "Think of the positives here, you two. Won't it be nice to have more women around, Betsy? Other young mothers like you, who–"

"Not like you."

I found my voice. Both Iris and Betsy snapped their heads toward me at my interruption, but I only had eyes for my roommate. I willed every ounce of my meaning into my gaze, praying to whichever god would listen that she might know the truth of my words.

"Betsy, there is no woman like you. Could never be. To me, you are…"

Unique? Special? Perfect?

Mine?

But any words I might have chosen died on my tongue as the woman I loved closed her eyes and shook her head. When she opened them again, tears glistened in a sheen across her lenses, and she was purposefully avoiding my gaze. Staring determinedly, instead, at Iris.

"I should leave," she said quietly.

"What?" Iris and I shouted in unison.

"Betsy, no." Iris put a hand on her shoulder. "That's ridiculous. Apollo still needs you. The women will need you too, to help them adjust to life here as well as you have."

Only then did Betsy look at me, as those words hung like the blade of a guillotine between us.

Adjust to life here as well as you have.

No woman could possibly take the place in my life that Betsy created. Betsy wasn't just a roommate to me, nor was Apollo merely Zeus's bastard son. In four short weeks, the two of them had become my entire *world.* No other person could fill that place in my heart, no matter how much *adjusting* they did. I wouldn't allow it.

"Absolutely not," I growled, rising to my feet. *Fuck the gods.* "I will not give my seed to another woman, Iris. I refuse."

"Felix." Betsy shook her head, and the sad, quiet voice with which she spoke was like a knife to my chest. Her tears spilled from her lashes, running in shining streaks down her jaw. "I'm angry, too. But think of what you're saying. These women need help. Just like I did."

"*No*, Betsy." I reached for her, but once again, she twisted away from my grasp. "*Please*. You're *different*. You can't expect me to just…"

I couldn't say it. My mouth wouldn't form the words.

She couldn't think I'd *fuck* another woman?

After last night?

"You didn't want to help me, either, right?" She laughed the saddest, most humorless laugh I'd ever heard. Everything about it singed my skin with a sense of wrongness. And her expression, so distant, so *resigned*, it broke my very soul. "At first? You wouldn't even touch me. And look what ended up happening."

Dear gods. *No.*

I sank to the ground, covering her knee with my hands as I desperately tried to make eye contact. But she avoided my gaze. "Betsy, no. Listen to me. *Please*. You and Apollo—you and *I*—it's different. Don't tell me you honestly believe that I would give to a stranger what I've given you? After what you gave me?"

She wiped at her eyes, and I longed to cradle her face in my hands. Kiss her sadness away. But every part of her body language screamed at me to keep my distance. I withdrew my hand.

This was so much worse than I'd imagined. I knew she would leave eventually, but I thought it would be on her terms. I thought I would be the only one to suffer.

But this? Watching the joy leave her eyes as she was *replaced?*

As *I* was forced to replace her?

No. *No!* This wasn't fair! She didn't *deserve* this! Why did Betsy have to get hurt?

And why was it *me* that had to hurt her?

Rage and despair battled for supremacy inside my chest. This was all Iris's fault. How had she managed to destroy everything so irreparably in so short a span of time? It was like the tractor all over again.

I'd fallen asleep completely happy and content, having had the most amazing evening of my life with the woman I loved. She had to realize that the bond we'd forged was something wholly unique? Irreplaceable?

But when she spoke, it was as if I hadn't said anything at all. Instead, she directed her words solely to the goddess, ignoring my pleas entirely.

"I'll take Apollo with me. We'll figure out a way to send me off with enough of Felix's stuff to keep me producing, but I've been overfull for almost a week now. He's already growing so fast. Who knows? He could be weaned by the end of the month. I can pump, too—save up my extra milk in Mason jars and freeze it to use when my supply starts to dry up." She paused, finally meeting my eyes, which were wide with horror. For a moment, something flickered across her face, and I thought she'd come to her senses. Reconsidered, maybe.

Only for her to shake her head. She bit her lip, and blinked repeatedly to hold back tears. But I knew the look in her eyes.

Resolve. Determination.

It was so inherently *her*, that it tore my very soul.

"You knew this would happen," she whispered. "You told me not to get attached."

"Betsy," I croaked. My hands trembled with the effort it took to keep them on my lap, to resist the instinct to pull her into my arms. "You have to know I… That I didn't realize–"

"Petra needs me," she interrupted, louder than she'd been before. She twisted her hands in her lap, and her face scrunched with emotion. "And these women need you. More than I do."

Water began to well in my eyes, and I shook my head.

I hated this. *Hated. This.*

I'd been to Tartarus. I'd had my liver pecked out by crows with Prometheus.

This hurt worse.

"Betsy, this isn't negotiable," Iris scolded. "You're staying. Hera intends–"

"So you're keeping me here against my will, then?" Betsy rounded on Iris, anger finally cutting through her tears. She shoved a thumb in my direction. "Like *him*? You're punishing me?"

I flinched, her tone smacking me like a backhanded strike.

Iris gaped, the first time I'd ever seen her speechless, if only for a second. She recovered quickly, smoothing her already-smooth hair. "Of course not. You haven't done anything wrong."

And that, at least, I agreed with. Betsy was perfect. She'd done nothing to deserve this: living out here in the middle of nowhere with a murdering minotaur in exile.

She tilted her chin, resolute.

"Well, then. If it's up to me, I don't want to be here when a bunch of other women show up, lining up for Felix's seed. You say they arrive tomorrow?" She glared questioningly at Iris, who hesitated, then nodded. "Fine. I'll leave tonight."

She rose from the bed, and I almost fell back from the suddenness with which the scent of her hair invaded my senses. I inhaled deeply, wishing I could bottle it. Wishing I could bottle *her,* and keep her here forever.

But she was right. I'd known this day would come.

I just didn't think it would be today.

So I let her go. She was already crossing the room, was practically to the kitchen when Iris stopped her by grabbing her wrist.

"It's not just women, you know. It's their children. It's Apollo's siblings. His cousin."

Something in Betsy's posture changed at Iris's words. Her head snapped to the fingers on her wrist, her eyes seething. She tensed, and the air in the room froze. For a moment, Iris and I held our breath as we awaited Betsy's response.

"Cousin?" One sardonic laugh barked from her lips, cracking out like a whip. "Singular? Just one cousin. So the other six, they're all *Zeus's* kids?"

The goddess flinched, and the anger for the king of gods that always simmered in my belly roared to a boil. Six women.

He'd knocked up six women in a handful of months. Used, then discarded. Like humans didn't even matter to him.

Like Betsy hadn't mattered.

"I only mean," Iris stammered, "you'd be separating him from his family, Betsy! Think for a second, and you'll realize that you're being selfish. Think about Apollo, and his future–"

And that's when Betsy exploded.

"Did *Zeus* think about Apollo's future? Oh wait, that's right, *fuck no!* You say *I'm* being selfish, when *he* abandoned both of us, to die in childbirth, while he went and *knocked up six. Other. Women!"*

She yanked her arm out of the goddess's hold and

stormed into the kitchen, leaving the two of us staring after her, ears ringing.

The goddess turned on me, her finger waggling before I'd even had a chance to collect my thoughts.

"Fix this, Felix," she hissed, spittle splattering my face as she closed in. "I swear to Hera herself, if you let this woman get away—"

"From what?" I whisper-shouted back. "From a parade of Zeus's exes? From Hera's mysterious grand plan? From whatever ruination you have planned for her? From *me*?" I shook my head, resignation settling into my bones like a lead weight. Betsy's words, ringing in my head like a death knell.

You told me not to get attached.

I choose to leave tonight.

That phrasing, those words: they were for me. She *chose* this. I couldn't help but believe she'd picked those exact words to telegraph to me that this was what she wanted. Could I deny her that?

Not only the future she wanted, but the one she *deserved* —a life free of the gods' meddling influence?

Free from me?

Iris was trying to con her into the same fate as someone who'd literally been sentenced for murder. Guilt her into helping a handful of women—women her own ex-boyfriend had slept with—get filled up with my semen. All to save them from the horrible labor and post-partum difficulties she'd endured.

I was furious *for* her, as anyone would be.

Obviously, I was furious with the whole situation. I'd fight it with every fiber of my being if I could, but…

But I knew how this would end. Fighting the gods was a futile pursuit. Eventually, they always got their way.

At least, they had with me.

The longer Betsy stayed, the more likely I'd simply drag

her into my misery. My eternal punishment, the one I'd earned for myself when I'd killed Hephaestus's daughter.

The gods would never let me be happy. Which meant, if Betsy stuck around, she'd never be happy either.

And if anyone deserved a shot at happiness, she did.

It was better this way.

"You and your damned stubbornness," Iris muttered. She was rubbing at her temples with her slender fingers, but the frustration seeped out of her voice as she continued, switching to an emotion I couldn't quite identify in the flurry of everything else I was processing. "Once, just once, I wish you and the rest of these mortals *trusted* us. Saw Hera the way I do. The way everyone used to, before… *ugh*. It doesn't matter. What matters is that you don't let yourself fuck up Betsy's life the way you've fucked up your own."

"Which is exactly why we're letting her go."

We glared at each other, neither one of us willing to budge. Eventually, she gave in, throwing up her hands with a sound that was something between a huff and a scream, before shouting, "I'll be back, dammit!" and poofing out of existence in a cloud of glitter.

Her and her fucking glitter.

CHAPTER 36

I finally pulled off Felix's robe for the last time and got dressed as best I could in jeans and an oversized t-shirt. I put the rest of my clothes in my backpack, and walked into the kitchen to finish packing up the rest of our things in the small suitcase I'd brought with me. Apollo's toys, baby stuff, and remaining diapers I squeezed into the main pocket, stuffed haphazardly around several mason jars of frozen breast milk and one (rather embarrassing) jar of Felix's *seed*, which I'd wrapped up in my flannel to keep separate from the rest of the whitish liquids.

He'd resisted the idea of jerking me off a doggy bag of baby batter when I'd first suggested it, but I wasn't about to let my boobs dry up in the next couple weeks after everything I'd been through. He'd spent most of the day in the barn, while I'd cleaned every trace of Apollo's and my existence from the farmhouse. I'd found the jar of semen in the freezer waiting for me with the rest of my breast milk after I'd finished packing up the bedroom.

I guess I'd be putting it on pancakes after all.

We didn't have our usual lunchtime quickie. I couldn't

bear it. Not after how perfect last night had been. Not when I knew it would be the last time.

I couldn't stand the idea of how much I'd grown to care for Felix in such a short amount of time. How much I'd miss him and the farm. How much it killed me to leave.

He'd told me not to get attached, and now I understood why. But *fuck.* I hadn't realized it would end like this.

Seven other women.

I was being replaced. Again.

Felix could say I was irreplaceable all he wanted. It didn't change the facts.

He and I stayed apart all afternoon. Even though it hurt, I knew it was for the best. Saying goodbye after all everything we'd been through? After everything we knew was coming next?

It was too painful to even think about.

Which is why I was so surprised to see Felix waiting for me in the living room when I gathered up Apollo to leave.

"Felix," I gasped, like I'd seen a ghost. And truthfully, I wasn't convinced I hadn't.

He looked awful. Somehow pale, his rich, reddish-brown fur looked almost gray, and he had bags under his eyes bigger than my suitcase. I hardly recognized him as he stared at the braided rug with his elbows on his knees, seated on the vintage couch. He turned to me, deep brown eyes shining as he took the two of us in.

"I couldn't let you leave without saying goodbye."

I hated goodbyes.

I'd had my fair share of them: from group homes to foster families. So many lives I'd walked away from.

But this one…

I shifted, the weight of my son already heavy in my arms. Carrying him up the driveway was going to be a nightmare. But I'd do it a million times to save him the heartbreak of losing his place here to a bunch of newer, younger demigod babies. I would never let him suffer like I had.

He'd gotten so much bigger than when we'd arrived. He wasn't walking yet, but he had grown another six inches and his weight had filled out, too. All that milk had been good for him. Whereas a week ago, he'd been the size of a human toddler, he could almost pass for a four year-old now.

You know. If human four year-olds had horns, snouts, hooves, and a prehensile tail.

Said tail poked out from the hole in Apollo's pull-up and whipped back and forth when he saw Felix.

"Make it quick. I've got a bus to catch."

His eyebrows scrunched, and the look of confusion on his face caused a physical ache in my heart.

"The nearest bus stop is miles away, Betsy."

"All the more reason to leave as soon as possible," I quipped, using every ounce of strength I had to keep the emotion out of my voice.

I missed him. Gods, I hadn't even left yet and I *missed* him. So much.

My arms grew heavy, so I set Apollo down and shrugged out of my backpack, grabbed the remote and turned on the TV. My son clapped as the first few notes of the Sesame Street theme rang out of the big, blocky speakers, and plopped his not-so-little butt down on the rug to watch The Muppets teach him about the letter of the day. "You've got until the promo break."

Felix sighed and stood. He held his hands out to his sides, opening his chest in a sad, vulnerable pose. "Don't leave."

I gaped at him. While Apollo giggled at Elmo's antics, I took in Felix in all his misery, completely at a loss for words.

"That's it? *That's* your big speech to convince me to stay? 'Don't leave'?"

He shrugged. "I don't know how long until the promo break."

"For *fuck's* sake, Felix, it's eleven minutes! Ten, now."

"Oh." His eyes darted to the screen, then back to me, and before I realized what was happening he'd closed the space between us and gathered me into his chest. I gasped as he squeezed the breath from my lungs. "The truth is, Betsy, I've spent all day agonizing over what to say, because I don't want to be selfish. I don't want to force you to do anything you don't want to do. I don't deserve you, I never have, and *you* don't deserve to be trapped here against your will. But I..."

He paused, long enough that I could extricate myself from his strong arms. Tears filled his eyes, and even though I knew it was cruel, even though I hated myself for doing it, I stuck to my guns.

Because as much as I hated hurting him, I couldn't stay. I couldn't let Apollo get replaced. I couldn't abandon Petra. I couldn't stand idly by as the gods forced Felix to endure punishment after punishment, using him to fix whatever problem Zeus and his brothers caused next.

Watching him and Apollo suffer for the rest of my life would be too much.

So I pushed him away. Physically, and with my words. Even though it killed me to do it.

"You *are* being selfish. We don't need you anymore, Felix. We don't belong here. It's time to let us go."

"*Please*, Betsy," he said, voice straining with emotion. "I love–"

Fuck. I couldn't let him finish that sentence.

So I interrupted before he could. "This was the plan, wasn't it? Didn't you say that you wanted Apollo to grow up without the gods meddling in his life the way they had yours? Well, Felix, it's clear that the gods will never stop meddling. They've got their plans for you, and it looks like you're going to be sowing your seed in a whole host of human women."

He flinched. "You *have* to know I don't want that. That I would never–"

"Never what? Fuck another woman?" I wiped at the tears springing to my own eyes.

I wished this whole day had gone differently. I wished Iris had never shown up, never given me Petra's letter. Most of all, I wished she and Hera had never decided to bring a bunch of Zeus's other exes here. Never reminded me how much it hurt to be swapped out for a new model. How much it stung to lose yet *another* family.

In one day, my whole world had been chewed up and spat back out in my face, along with any dreams I'd had of a future here with Felix.

Fucking *Iris.*

The thought of her reminded me of our conversation in the kitchen that morning. She'd said something about Felix. Something that had confused me in the moment, and came back to me now.

The woman he'd hurt. She'd made allusions to a past love of his, and even implied that he'd been physically abusive. It didn't make sense.

For all the reasons that I knew I couldn't stay, his temperament wasn't one of them. I *knew* Felix. He'd never hurt a woman he loved.

Not physically, anyway.

"I know I'm not the only woman you've slept with, Felix. What's six more?"

"It doesn't work like that with me, Betsy. I'm not like Zeus or Poseidon. I don't fuck random women."

"But I'm not the only one you've fucked, am I?" *Gods*, I was the worst. Why was I being so mean? Why was I blaming him for what the gods were doing to him? "There has to have been someone else."

A shadow crossed over Felix's face, a familiar one. And that's when it hit me.

Oh.

That pain, that sadness in his eyes—I'd seen it before. Back when I'd first seduced Felix, what felt like lifetimes ago. He'd been resistant to having sex with me—moreso than a mere grudge against the gods would make him.

No, there was a reason he hadn't wanted to be intimate with me. Something had happened. Something bad.

Let's just say, he doesn't have the best track record with physical relationships.

But *what*? What could Felix have possibly done that not only hurt his partner, but left a scar on his own psyche like that? It was the one secret he hadn't told me, the one mystery Iris hadn't explained away.

And this could be my only chance to find out.

I'd learned to never dig into people's pasts, to never pry when the people you lived with didn't want to open up. But things were different between Felix and me. There were no walls between us.

And even if there were, what did it matter now? I was leaving anyway. I couldn't fear him kicking me out if I already had one foot out the door.

I pressed harder, testing my theory. "You didn't just fuck her. You *loved* her, didn't you? And something happened. Something bad."

"Don't do this. Please. It was a long time ago, Betsy, over a hundred human lifetimes. You're different, I'm different— what we have, it's nothing like what Celedonia and I had. I know that now."

"Celedonia…" I crossed the living room and sat down on

the couch. Signaling that I was going to stay until we finished this conversation. "That's a pretty name. Was she a goddess?"

He closed his eyes, face scrunching in agony, before softening into resignation. A minotaur defeated. He sank into the cushion beside me. "Yes. Hephaestus's daughter."

A bell rang in the back of my mind at that name. *Hephaestus, Hephaestus...* one of the gods, obviously, but which one?

"I wronged Hephaestus, the blacksmith god."

Oh fuck. *Fuck.*

This wasn't just some ex he'd hurt. This wasn't a drunken fuck or a bad breakup. This was a whole other story—a Big-With-A-Capital-B story.

The story of what got him exiled from Olympus.

My throat went dry. But despite me knowing I was stepping on a hornet's nest, I had to ask. "What happened?"

"We got drunk together, during Bachanalia. We made love. And then..." he sighed, burying his face in his hands. "Please, don't make me say it, Betsy. Hephaestus never forgave me. I still haven't forgiven myself."

"Whatever it is can't be worse than whatever I'm imagining, Felix! Please, just tell me."

"Why should I?"

"Because I *care!*" I was shouting now, furious at the cryptic run-around. What was it with these Olympians? Why can't they just answer a fucking question? "This is the thing, isn't it? The thing that got you exiled?"

"Yes!"

"Then *this* is the reason we can't be together. The reason you'll never be out from under the gods' thumbs. I *deserve* to know." On the TV, an animated short played about the number three. The stark contrast between what Apollo was watching and what Felix and I were discussing was dizzying. I put a hand on Felix's knee, the first time I'd offered him comfort since Iris's stupid visit. I spoke again more calmly, trying to get him to understand where I was coming from.

"I'm exhausted, Felix. For almost a year, I've been lost in some kind of turf war among the gods that I didn't even know I was signing up for. Between Zeus and Hera, you and Petra... my human life and my minotaur life, I just feel like I'm getting pulled in every direction without a single sign-post pointing the way."

"I never meant to deceive you," he said, voice pained.

"I know you didn't." And I did. More than anyone, Felix had done everything he could to lessen the weight on my shoulders. He was so *good.*

I sighed. "Just be honest with me. Please. I don't under-stand. How could you have done something so deserving of this long of a punishment? I mean, you're *you.* You're Felix. Just last night, you changed my whole world. You're my–"

I snapped my mouth shut. *My soulmate,* I almost said. But that was crazy. His soul belonged to the gods. It *couldn't* belong to me.

I massaged my temples. I was getting lost in my thoughts again. Time for a new tactic. "Look. You're asking me to stay. But how can I even consider staying, if I don't know *why* you can't leave?"

He stared at me, brows twitching, as his entire face seemed to shutter closed in slow motion. The anguish he'd been over-flowing with seconds ago disappeared behind a stoic mask, and it made him look like a completely different person.

I didn't know who Felix was without his emotions. I'd thought I could read him like a book. Isn't that what I'd been doing this whole time? Gauging his body language, his facial expressions, everything he'd left unsaid?

I'd become so good at reading people. At anticipating their reactions. It was a survival mechanism, from living in so many different homes. I'd always thought, if I could figure out what someone wanted before they wanted it, and adjust to fit into their world, become the thing they didn't even know they were looking for, then maybe they'd realize that the thing they were looking for was *me*.

All I wanted was a family. And for most of my life, it hadn't even mattered who it was. They just needed to want *me*, and that would be good enough. Even if I had to change myself to become the thing they wanted.

But it never worked. Not with my foster parents, not with my ex-boyfriends, not with Zeus. No matter how much I changed, I could never be the person they wanted.

The crazy thing was, though, I hadn't really changed myself at all for Felix. I'd wanted to make him happy, sure—and at first, I'd wanted to earn his affection like I'd tried with every other person I'd been foisted on. I thought, if I could prove my worth, if I could earn my keep, if I could satisfy him sexually, he'd forget that Apollo and I were an unwelcome burden.

Little did I know, that never would have worked with Felix. He'd rejected the very idea that I'd needed to earn my keep. Whenever he *had* asked something of me, it was always clear that it was my choice to accept or deny, and he'd never expected me to give in order to receive. He just... took care of me. Cared *for* me.

The only other person in my life who'd ever come close to that was Petra.

Petra.

She needed me. And I'd abandoned her. Even now, I was putting off coming to her aid to hear Felix out.

I sighed.

While he sat here, beating around the bush and obfuscating his past, Petra suffered.

I was about to throw in the towel, grab Apollo and head back to Minneapolis, when at last he spoke.

"She got pregnant."

Any traces of feeling were gone from his voice. Every word was flat. "Her body rejected my seed, but not before it destroyed her. She died. The life inside her snuffed hers out, before it was even born."

What?

That was the Capital-B-Big-Bad that had gotten Felix exiled from Olympus? He knocked up his girlfriend, and she died from complications?

Something about that didn't add up. A goddess, dying from pregnancy? Really?

I wasn't exactly an expert in Olympian biology, but I *was* pretty well-versed in god-fucking and minotaur semen, and it was my experience that the gods could well handle just about any freaky shit the perverts could dream up. Sure, *humans* might get fucked up by fucking with an immortal. But a goddess?

Besides, Felix's cum was far from poison. If anything, it was kind of magic.

"Come on," I said, shaking my head. "That can't be the whole story."

He shrugged, leaning his elbows on his knees and hanging his head. "My seed killed her."

"There's no way." I put a finger under his chin, tilting his head to look at me. "Hephaestus's daughter? She was a *goddess,* Felix. I'm a human, and according to Iris, even I would be able to carry your offspring just fine as long as we stayed together. The only reason I almost died in labor with Apollo was because Zeus *stopped* having sex with me.

"Is that what happened? You knocked her up and then dumped her?"

"No!" Felix shot up from the couch like he'd been blasted

out of a cannon. "How can you say that? I loved her, Betsy, as surely as I love you. I never would have abandoned her."

"Then how would she–"

A loud *pop* cracked through the living room, and Iris slid into the room on a rainbow slide that had appeared out of nowhere.

"Betsy! You're still here! Fantastic. I just came to tell you both that–"

"Hold it right there, sister!" I growled, turning on her with my finger out and waggling with a vengeance. "You've got some 'splainin' to do!"

The goddess blinked. "Excuse me?"

"You told me Felix had a history of hurting his partners." I crossed my arms, raising an eyebrow and giving her what I hoped was the stankiest of stank-eyes. "But you conveniently left out the fact that the partner in question was Hephaestus's daughter. And that he didn't actually hurt her at all! It wasn't his fault she died in *childbirth*."

My stank-eye apparently needed some work, because Iris was unphased. She crossed her arms right back and arched her perfectly-shaped eyebrow right back at me. "Just as you would have, had Hera and I not intervened. Wouldn't you define *that* tragedy as Zeus's fault?"

"Of course it was," Felix snapped. "He never should have abandoned you."

"But that's the thing!" I shouted, furious that, in a room full of powerful immortals, I seemed to be the only one with brain cells. "Felix *didn't* abandon Celedonia. So why did she die?"

For a moment, neither Felix nor Iris said a word. I watched in real-time as my words sunk into my big, sweet minotaur's brain, and he tilted his head.

"You're saying that she… shouldn't have died. Not as long as I provided her with my seed," he slowly worked through the logic as I had. "Her body should have changed with my seed. With the baby."

"Yes! Exactly. That's what all this has been about, isn't it? Why I'm here? Why Iris is bringing a bunch of other women here?"

Felix chewed on that a moment. "Then… what caused her to perish?"

We both looked at Iris then, as Big Bird chatted and Apollo babbled in the background.

She twisted her hands, looking uncomfortable for the first time I'd seen. Then she plopped onto the couch, rubbing her hands over her face.

"Alright," she muttered, before glancing up at the two of us with an annoyed expression. "Clearly you two need to work this out before we can move on, so I guess we're doing this. Right before the girls arrive."

Felix and I exchanged a glance, before centering right back on her.

She inhaled. "Felix, Celedonia was not a goddess."

She paused, as if that should have been enough explanation.

"Neither am I," I said. "So what?"

"She was Hephaestus's daughter. So she was clearly more physically robust than Betsy, right?" Felix added, to me, "no offense."

"None taken."

The two of us faced off with Iris, both of us standing while she squirmed on the couch. She hesitated.

"She *was* Hephaestus's daughter in a manner of speaking. He brought her into the world, and he loved her more than anything he'd ever made," Iris explained. "But she was not his biological daughter. She wasn't biological at all."

Felix and I shared another glance. This one full of question marks.

"I don't get it," he said at last.

The goddess looked as if she'd rather be anywhere but here. But she reluctantly clarified.

"Celedonia was the first automaton. And arguably, one of the most sophisticated. But after her tragic end, Hera, Athena, and Hephaestus had to go back to the drawing board to rework the design."

"Wait wait wait," I cut in, my brain twisting itself into knots. "Are you saying that Felix's ex was a *robot*?"

"The most advanced and magical robot ever forged by Olympian hands, capable of sapient thought and near-godly emotion? Sure, why not. It's as good a word as any. Other than *automaton*, of course, which is the word I used because it is *the correct one*." She huffed at me, but I didn't back down. I crossed my arms, tapping my foot as I raised an eyebrow, waiting for her to continue. She rolled her eyes. "*Robots* are built by humans. Automatons are more complex than anything you mortals could dream up."

I didn't know about that. I mean, sure, the thing that drove me here was pretty cool, but it's not like it could hold a conversation. I opened my mouth to argue, but one look at Felix shut me right up.

He'd collapsed onto the couch, head in his hands, once again as pale as he'd been when I'd first walked into the living room twenty minutes ago. His hands were shaking, his horns tilting back and forth as he shook his head.

"Felix?" I asked. "You alright, big guy?"

"No," he whispered, barely audible above the TV. "Everything I know is a lie."

"Oh, stop being so dramatic. It wasn't a *lie*. You did kill her. She was never meant to handle procreation. And yet, with the amount of magic that Hephaestus had poured into her forging, she wasn't quite *not* meant for it, either. It surprised us as much as it did you, when she died. When she got pregnant at all, really. There was nothing we could do."

My face grew hot, and my hands clenched into fists at my sides. Fury rose like a tidal wave that I only barely contained. "Then why was Felix punished? It wasn't his fault!"

He was still silent, head in his hands and elbows on knees, as he processed this information. Iris answered, her tone sympathetic but matter-of-fact.

"He was punished because he *had* to be. Celedonia's death had the potential to throw Hera's entire plan into chaos. Goddesses don't just *die;* it's the kind of thing that catches the attention of the Three. And Zeus could *not* find out about Hera's automatons."

"*Why?*"

"Because it's how she keeps track of all his affairs!" Iris shouted, throwing her hands up and gesturing toward Apollo. "Do you think she has the time to watch over all of earth and keep tabs on every human her cheating husband has sex with? Of course not! So, she, Athena, and Hephaestus came up with a solution. An army of automatons that could infiltrate earth and keep track of all the Brothers' descendants. To keep humanity safe. Celedonia was the prototype. The proof of concept."

I blinked at her. There was a whole army of robots for keeping track of Zeus's bastard children? That was how Hera had known about me? How she'd found out about all the other women that were coming here?

Dear gods. He didn't just put *me* in a tough situation. He's been ruining lives left and right for thousands of years.

Including Felix's.

"So when she died, it had to look natural. And I took the fall," Felix murmured, knocking me out of my own thoughts. "Hera punished me as a cover story."

For the first time, Iris looked almost contrite. "If it's any consolation, she didn't want to do it. She's felt bad about it ever since."

"Oh, how *sad* for her!" I rubbed at my eyes, if only to keep lasers from shooting out of them. I was so angry, I wouldn't be surprised if they did. "Felix, meanwhile, was sent to Hades to suffer with Sisyphus! And Promenade and Tarantula!"

"Prometheus and Tantalus," he corrected. Despite the seriousness of the conversation, I could've sworn I saw a smirk buried in the corner of his mouth.

"Whatever! The point is, it isn't fair!" I turned back on the goddess, wagging a finger in her face. "She *owes* him, Iris! You all do! For making him suffer all these years. These *millenia*."

"You're one to talk," Iris snapped at me, contrition gone. "You're making him suffer right now! The first woman he's loved in almost three thousand years, and you're leaving him because you're jealous of a couple of Zeus's other exes staying in the barn."

"That's…" I began, before my righteous indignation died on my tongue.

I was furious with her. With Hera. Zeus. The whole lot of them, honestly, for treating Felix so poorly. For punishing him for something that wasn't his fault.

But at the same time, she had a point.

I was leaving him. Not because he'd done anything wrong, but because I felt guilty about losing touch with Petra, and too hurt to shack up with a bunch of my ex's exes.

And too afraid that one of them might replace me in Felix's heart.

"Don't bring Betsy into this, Iris," Felix said. "She's just as much a victim of the gods' cruelty as I am. She's facing an impossible decision."

"What's impossible about it? She loves you, for Eros's sake! Anyone with eyes can see it!"

Heat rose to my face again, but not because of anger.

She'd just blurted out the thing I'd been trying to deny this whole time. The feelings I'd pushed down deep, under so much hurt and baggage that it had started to fester. The real reason I had to leave, why I couldn't be here when the other women arrived.

Returning to Petra, who I loved dearly, wasn't my main reason for leaving. I missed her, of course, but if I was being honest, the real thing that was pushing me out the door was…

I couldn't bear to watch Felix replace me with another woman. I didn't want them sleeping in *our* barn. I didn't want to see him cooking breakfast for them, or building cribs for their babies. Most importantly: I didn't want any of them finding out just how wonderful a partner this hunky minotaur in the middle of nowhere, Minnesota could be.

Because if they did? If they learned what a catch Felix was?

They'd stay forever. They'd find a way to make him love them, the thing I could never figure out how to do, and they'd take their place by his side. Become his happy little family.

And once again, I'd be all alone.

And I couldn't bear to see him playing stepfather with anyone other than me and Apollo. I'd survived it in the past, I knew, but this time was different. This time would break me.

Because I love him.

"Betsy?" Felix gazed at me, his eyes shining. I swallowed the lump in my throat. "Is that true?"

"*Yes*, you idiot!" Tears streamed from my eyes as I burst into tears, devolving into a slippery, snotty mess. "Who wouldn't fall in love with you? You're amazing! You build cribs and high chairs, you plant food and make me breakfast every morning. You listen to my talk about my day and your face lights up whenever I compliment your cooking. You're generous, and sweet, and *so* fucking sexy, and you make the best fucking pancakes I've ever had in my life. What's not to love?"

"But if that's the case, then…" he tilted his head, that little line of confusion denting his forehead. "Why won't you stay?"

"I've been rejected so many times, Felix, and with how our relationship started, I…" I sighed. This was it. I was about to admit how pathetic I really was.

"I didn't want to let myself fall for you if you weren't going to catch me in the end. When I heard that all these other women were coming here, that you would need to sleep with them, too… that fear came back. With a vengeance. That once you had other options, you wouldn't want me anymore."

Tears obscured my vision, making me rub my eyes—so I missed it when Felix got up off the couch and lumbered toward me. But I didn't need to see it, because I felt his big, peach-fuzzy arms wrap around me and crush me into his chest. I breathed in his comforting scent, that warm musky sunshine smell, squeezing him right back.

"Betsy, if you stay," he spoke into my hair, and I felt his words buzz from the crown of my head to the tips of my toes. "I promise, I will *never* let you fall. I will always be here to catch you. You and–"

"Apollo!"

As if on cue, Felix and I broke apart at Iris's cry, just in time to see Apollo walking toward us.

Walking.

Walking! My baby was taking his first steps!

As I gaped at him, taking in this pivotal moment, his tiny hoof caught the edge of the braided rug and he stumbled. My heart stopped.

In a flash, Felix dove into a crouch and cushioned his fall

with his large, strong hands. He scooped him up and lifted him into the air between us.

"See?" He smiled at me, nuzzling his cheek to my baby's, making their horns clack together. "I'll never let you fall. Neither of you."

"Dee!" Apollo said, mimicking the letter of the day from the episode of Sesame Street that was just wrapping up on the TV. "Deedeeedeeee…da dah!"

"Dada?" I echoed, chest filling up like a balloon. "Apollo, did you just say *dada?*"

"Da-da!" He babbled again, slapping Felix's chest with his palm. "Dadadadada…"

The sallow pallor that had colored Felix's cheeks all day disappeared in a flush of pink. His eyes blew open so wide I could see the teeny crescent of white at the edges, as we both stared, slackjawed, from Apollo to each other.

"Well, would you look at that?" Iris crossed her arms again, but this time a smile crossed her lips. "I think Betsy's not the only one in this house who thinks you're worth loving. Looks to me like you've attracted quite the little family here, Felix."

He looked to me then, his big, brown eyes as deep and earnest as I'd ever seen them. "You're only family if you stay."

I gazed right back at the minotaur holding my child (my *walking, talking* child!), and my heart felt so full it could burst. How could I say no to both of them?

"Okay," I conceded, and a huge smile split his face. "I'll stay."

He leaned in to kiss me, squeezing me close, but I stopped him with a finger.

I gave Iris a pointed look. "But if I'm staying, then there's going to need to be some *big* changes around here."

I held the small, walking, *talking* young minotaur in my arms, his big, wide eyes darting animatedly between Iris, his mother, and me.

Me.

The monster that I was fairly certain he'd just called *dada.*

"Well, would you look at that?" Iris observed, an uncharacteristic smile spreading her thin lips. "I think Betsy's not the only one in this house who thinks you're worth loving. Looks to me like you've attracted quite the little family here, Felix."

Family.

It was the thing I'd been afraid to admit that I wanted, ever since Betsy and Apollo had wormed their way into my heart. But it was true. I had begun to think of the two of them as my family, no matter who the little one's father was.

Except…

My eyes met Betsy's, her gaze wide with shock and—*dare I think it?*—love, as she took in the sight of her baby in my arms.

"You're only family if you stay," I murmured.

Her face scrunched as she chewed her lip. This beautiful woman, the most incredible human I'd ever had the fortune of meeting, who somehow believed that there was another person in this world who might entice me to leave her?

The very thought was *laughable.*

I could no sooner betray her than I could rip off my own tail. When I imagined a future for myself, one of my own making, she was the guiding force that led me forward. I was incapable of rejecting her.

Which was why the next three words out of her mouth made me the happiest minotaur on Earth.

"Okay. I'll stay."

"I CAN'T GUARANTEE that Hera will be on board with this," Iris warned, tapping her infernal clipboard. On it was scrawled a list of demands, practical and personal, that Betsy and I required in exchange for warding Zeus's exes here at the farm.

It was still sinking in: I was not guilty.

While I had every right to be bitter about my unfair imprisonment and exile the past few millennia, I couldn't bring myself to be anything but euphoric.

Betsy was staying. Betsy was *mine.*

She'd taken Apollo back into the bedroom for a feeding and his afternoon nap, while I walked the goddess out to the front porch. The giddiness that had overtaken me earlier ebbed slightly in her absence, and I was able to address Iris more seriously as I sent her on her way.

"She doesn't have a choice. Either she agrees to Betsy's and my terms, or she loses my loyalty." My stomach twisted at the idea of pledging loyalty to *any* of the Thirteen, but in the building tensions between Hera and Zeus, I knew I could never side with the god who'd so callously abandoned my Betsy.

Saving her from death had been a wise move on Hera's part. If nothing else, it had earned the goddess a second chance to gain my trust.

Iris raised an eyebrow. "Your loyalty?"

"What else would you call it?" I grumbled. "Before, I served because it was my punishment. Because I believed I deserved my punishment for my part in Celedonia's death. But now that I know the truth…" I sighed, dragging a hand through my hair. "I will not continue to be complicit in my own punishment. Not only because it is unjust, but because…"

I trailed off, trying to piece my nebulous thoughts into something coherent.

"You have something to live for now," Iris said.

Her clear, blue eyes met mine, and for once, I saw something other than cool calculation there. It calmed something in me, making silent a drone of tension and anger between us that always simmered in the background.

"Yes," I agreed. "I do."

She held my gaze a moment longer, then nodded, her eyes falling back to the clipboard in her hand. "Well, the expansions on your home will take time. Certainly they won't be complete by the time the ladies arrive in the morning."

"Why do you say that?" I smirked. "Don't Hera and Hephaestus have an entire army of automatons at their disposal to serve as a construction crew? They could certainly raise another barn in a day, if nothing else."

"What's wrong with your *current* barn, again?"

My mind raced to the milking bench I'd just finished installing the day before.

I coughed. "It's filled with equipment. Daisy's in there now, and the tractor," righteous indignation replaced my embarrassment as I poked her sternum, "which *you* damaged, might I add!"

"Fine, fine." She waved a hand, clearly convinced, if a bit tired of the explanation. "I'll plead your case. Regardless, I'll return in the morning."

Another wave, and a giant, arcing rainbow appeared, stretching all the way into the clouds. I turned back to the front door, shaking my head.

"Good night, Iris."

"Good night. And Felix?"

I glanced over my shoulder, surprised to see that odd look on her face once more. It almost resembled...

No, it couldn't be. Not Iris.

"What?"

"Congratulations. On your new family."

When a dimple dented her cheek, I knew for certain that I hadn't been mistaken. What I'd seen in her eyes was genuine *kindness.*

"Thank you, Iris."

"Who knows?" She added, ascending up the colorful slide in reverse. "Fatherhood might be in the cards for you yet."

ONE YEAR LATER

I whisked like a mad woman, the giant, minotaur-sized utensil looking ridiculous swirling around the normal-sized bowl of batter.

Yep. I'd finally learned how to cook for myself. Or, truthfully, I'd learned how to cook for an entire village. What had started out as a group of eight women: the six exes of Zeus, the one of Poseidon's, and Petra, soon grew to include five more of The Three's rejected one-night stands. Three of them were still nursing, and I was whipping them up a batch of crepes by hand while Petra mixed a much larger bowl of pancakes in the Kitchenaid mixer on the counter.

The mixer was just one of several changes we'd seen around the farm in the past year.

"Don't forget the secret ingredient!"

I gladly held out the bowl, giving my wrist a rest while Petra proceeded to pour an entire Mason jar's worth of milk into the batter. But not just any milk.

Breast milk. *My* breast milk.

It had been weird at first, sure, but when the alternative was feeding a handful of strangers my boyfriend's jizz to keep their demigod fetuses from ripping them apart?

Sorry, I'm getting ahead of myself. Let me back up a little bit.

A year ago, when I'd confronted Iris about the impetus for Felix's eternal punishment that he'd "earned" by "killing" Hephaestus's "daughter," and she'd come clean about the *real* reason he'd been thrown in Hades, Felix and I declared that there would be a new status quo between him and Hera.

He wasn't going to be a pawn in her game any longer. If she wanted his cooperation in keeping her automaton army secret from Zeus and the Three, as well as taking care of all of the mothers of the Three's bastard children, then she'd have to *earn* his support. And mine.

Which meant no more busting into Felix's farmhouse and making demands. Especially not now that Apollo and I were living with him.

Of course, neither Felix nor I wanted a bunch of single mothers to die because Zeus and Poseidon had abandoned them. What kind of hypocrite would I be if I refused to help other women in my position?

My requests were simple: don't make Felix fuck anymore of Zeus's (or Poseidon's) exes, and let Petra come live on the farm. Iris agreed to those without much fuss, claiming that I'd proven that humans didn't have to *sleep* with Olympians to get the benefits of their *seed*.

The "blowjob loophole," she'd called it.

But that wasn't exactly good enough for me. Felix and I were on the same page: we were an item now, and that meant that *I* was the only one that got to drink his minotaur milk straight from the tap. And vice versa.

Iris had suggested sneaking some semen into their food,

but that also didn't sit right with me. Sure, Felix's cum was sweet and creamy to the taste, but that didn't mean I was excited to serve it up to all of Zeus's exes with their breakfast. The gods might have been okay with blurred lines regarding consent, but I wasn't. And I knew the idea made Felix uncomfortable, too.

I'd been warring with that dilemma while Felix and Iris had gone over his own set of requests he wanted addressed prior to the baby mamas moving in. He'd handed me Apollo, who'd immediately wanted back down onto the carpet so he could watch reruns of Mr. Rogers Neighborhood.

It was as I'd watched my son *walk* back to the TV that I got an idea.

The next morning, Petra had shown up on our doorstep along with the seven pregnant demigod mamas. Felix and I served them all breakfast, alright, but it wasn't made with *his* milk.

It was spiked with *mine*.

I figured, if my milk was good enough for Apollo—who'd grown exponentially since I'd started breastfeeding him with my super-milk—then maybe it was good enough to help these women grow their own little Apollos, too?

Seven months later, we had our answer.

Hera herself came down for the first delivery; she, Iris, and Asclepius all arrived to assist with Jessica (one of the mom)'s labor. I was biting my nails the whole time, more grateful than ever that I'd insisted Petra come live with us— as I'd needed her support to get me through Jessica's delivery even more than I'd needed her with mine. While the other moms helped out by boiling water, getting ice chips, and cleaning towels, *I'd* been pacing a hole through the floor of the living room.

When the sound of little demigod cries filled the farmhouse, and Iris slid downstairs on her rainbow to let me know that Jessica was happily nursing her healthy Olympian baby, I exhaled the biggest sigh of relief I'd ever breathed.

My hypothesis was sound. My breastmilk had the power to nourish the mothers of the gods. Apparently, as long as I was still getting *my* daily dose of magic minotaur seed, my milk would retain enough godly juice to give a growing family everything they needed to keep up with the demands of a young Olympian.

And Felix had no issues providing me with that. Nor did he mind assisting me with the milking.

Felix's stipulations for Hera, though, were a little more involved.

The farmhouse was small. Too small for so many people. And since the barn had become our "milking" space, Felix didn't feel comfortable having a bunch of women sleep there every night, as Iris had suggested. Especially with the increased demands on the two of us to provide enough magic milk for all of them.

In general, the whole idea of keeping The Three's exes in the barn left a lot to be desired, so he'd demanded that some of Hera's automatons come down to Minnesota to build out the property a little more. In a shorter timeline than any human construction crew I'd witnessed, Iris directed an entire platoon of those sapient robots in building a gigantic addition onto the farmhouse. What started as little more than a three-room cabin ballooned into a three-story estate, complete with an east *and* west wing, more than twenty bedrooms, and an enormous kitchen-slash-dining room that was large enough to seat the entire mixed family of moms, demigods, minotaurs, and (in Petra's case) friends.

The Kitchenaid had been a housewarming present. And you know, it came in handy when you had almost thirty mouths to feed. This morning, Petra and I were on breakfast duty, and I couldn't deny that the task was a lot more overwhelming now than it had been back in our tiny apartment in Minneapolis.

The two of us had come a long way since then.

"Mom, where's the orange juice?"

Apollo walked in, a little gangly and awkward still, with his furry, calf-like legs and skinny arms. In human years, I'd put him around sixteen—a truly mind-blowing transformation in the course of just thirteen months. He'd just endured another massive growth spurt, rocketing up from 4'8" to 5'11' in the span of a couple weeks. If it weren't for his tail swishing back and forth behind him, he'd likely lose his balance every time he took a step.

His forest green eyes bulged with panic when he saw me whisking, bounding over like a young foal and snatching the bowl out of my hands. "Mom! You're supposed to be taking it easy!"

"It's pancakes, Lo, not hay bales! I can handle it."

He shook his head, giving me the kind of skeptical eyebrow lift that would make his stepfather proud. "Nuh-uh, little lady." He'd started calling me that as soon as he'd surpassed me in height. Felix and Petra both thought it was hilarious. "You sit yourself down. Me and Aunt Petra can take care of this."

"Aunt Petra and *I*," my best friend corrected, nudging him with her elbow and making him grab the oven door handle with his tail to steady himself. "If you want to pass your GED, young man, you're going to need to work on your grammar."

"Come *on*! You're always talking about those weird human exams. You know none of us can take them!"

"No, but you *can* take the practice exam. And I'm not giving you your farm school diploma until you prove to me you're ready for the real world. Which means you'll be writing essays on *The Great Gatsby* for the rest of your immortal life!"

I held back a snicker as I watched the two of them argue and pour batter into pans. Petra had always been good in school. When she learned that living with me again meant also living with a whole hoard of young demigods, she'd decided she'd pull her weight by helping teach them all to read. It was amazing how quickly they caught on, too. These kids grew intellectually almost as quickly as they did physically.

It was a lot for me to process. Hearing Apollo and Petra discuss the finer points of Shakespeare and Mark Twain was pretty daunting when I'd been changing his diapers eleven months ago.

Some of the other mothers had worked as teachers, too, before they'd met Zeus. Between Petra with English, Zoe with math, and Heather with science, our upcoming class of immortals was getting a surprisingly well-rounded education.

The nice thing about living with so many people was that everyone had something to contribute. Katie and Jen were both nurses. Danielle was a therapist. And let me tell you: we'd all benefitted from a little group therapy processing our feelings of being unwanted and used by the gods. Even Felix had worked through some of his more traumatic experiences from his time in Olympus and Hades. I'd been a little jealous with him spending so much time with Danielle at first, but when he'd mentioned how nice it was just to have someone listen without judgment, I'd realized we all could benefit from that kind of treatment.

I'd let go of a lot of the jealousy I'd been holding onto. I'd been so insecure at first. About competing for Felix's affection, about whether or not I was as good a mom as the other ladies. But Felix assured me that I was the only woman he had eyes for. And as the farm grew, the extra hands ended up being much more of a blessing than a curse.

I learned to share the rewards and responsibilities of the farm with all of them. After all, with so many of us in the house, no one woman had to do it all.

Jessica was a great cook, so she'd taken over dinner duty from Felix most nights. Cassidy made the best apple pie; Jordan told the best bedtime stories. Erika built amazing pillow forts, and always helped the kids get their wiggles out. Jo knit and crocheted. And Annette had brought her sewing machine with her when she'd arrived at the farm. The two of them had begun showing a few of us how to alter the kids' clothes to make them more accommodating for tails, hooves, and even wings.

Oh, right. See, not all of the young demigods were minotaurs. In fact, only three of Apollo's brothers looked like him and Felix. The rest were a mix. We had three young girls who were almost nymph-like, one of whom had fairy-like translucent wings, a couple centaurs, a satyr, two cherubic twins, a gargoyle, and the second oldest child after Apollo, Griffin, was...well, a gryphon.

When they all gathered around the table for breakfast, it could absolutely feel like a zoo.

But it also felt like home.

As the tantalizing scent of syrup and flapjacks filled the air, the entire family filtered in. Phoenix, Cassidy's minotaur son, located the orange juice in the fridge, grabbing it and putting it in the middle of the table while his younger half-sisters set the plates and silverware. I leaned back in my chair, letting the rest of them worry about glasses and butter and all the other breakfast accoutrements while I rested my hands on my stomach.

"Good morning," Felix called as he entered the room last, taking a wide sweep of the chaos before his eyes settled on me. My heart glowed in response to the sparkle in his eyes. Somehow, even among all these moms, aunts, and kiddos, he still managed to make me feel like the only woman in the room. He smiled wide, making a beeline for my chair as he came around and hugged me from behind. "How's my mama feeling this morning?"

"Good! How's the corn maze coming along?"

Felix grinned. "Fantastic. By August, we'll have quite the labyrinth on our hands."

Petra shook her head. "I still can't believe Danielle suggested you put that together. Isn't it, I don't know, a little traumatic?"

"I have control over this one. It's on my land, for my family, and most importantly, I designed it," Felix explained. "It doesn't need to be my prison. It can be my safe space."

I nuzzled into him, kissing the fuzzy skin of his arm. "I'm proud of you."

"I'm proud of you, too, Bets. Glad to see you off your feet, *for once.*"

He gave me a pointed stare as he elbowed into the chair beside me. I rolled my eyes.

"Jeez, I don't know who's worse with the fussing, you or Apollo!"

"You better get used to fussing," Annette chimed from the fridge. She grabbed a pitcher of cow's milk and carried it over to the table, filling up my glass first. "After all you and Felix have done to take care of us? We're *all* invested in keeping you healthy."

A bunch of the other moms nodded in agreement. I grinned and leaned my head on Felix's arm, breathing in his sunshine-and-sawdust smell as the others doted on me. Wait. Sawdust?

"Felix. What have you been building?"

"Another crib."

"Another one?" I twisted my head to give him a look. "What's wrong with Felix's old one?"

"The twins are still using it," Erika said. The thin, golden-haired woman was the mother of the twin cherubs, two blonde boys who Iris assured us would eventually grow out of their baby phase, even if it took them a bit longer than their half-siblings. That was a thing with cherubs, apparently: even when they were fully grown, they'd still be child-like in some ways. They were six months old and, unlike the others, seemed it.

"We're rotating through them," Felix said softly, a mischievous gleam in his eyes. "But I don't mind. You know I like the chance to work with my hands."

He looked me up and down, and our latest session out in the barn flashed through my mind. I blushed.

"Honey," I muttered. "Not in front of the kids."

Only the moms and Petra knew about "how the milk got made." The most any of the kids knew about any of that was that nursing mothers got extra *supplementation* at meal time. Once, when Apollo had gotten curious and asked why, Heather had helpfully explained that they needed "extra protein" to help with the demands on their bodies. Thankfully, that had been enough to satisfy him. Despite the fact that he seemed like a teenager in most all ways that mattered, my baby was still just barely a year old. I wasn't ready to have the birds-and-the-bees talk with him quite yet.

Maybe in the next millennium.

"Pancakes are on!" Petra called, serving three stacks to the newest moms while Apollo placed two towering serving plates to the center of the table for everyone else. "Now, eat up! We're plotting out the fall vegetables today for the side garden, which means everyone who's walking gets a job outside. Except for you four," she added, pointing to the nursing mamas and me. "You all get to rest with the babies."

"Oh come on, I don't want to miss the planting!" I whined.

I'd been looking forward to it ever since harvest. I still remembered last year, when I'd walked out to find Felix and Apollo digging tiny wells for each seed, and my sweet little baby waving around his tiny trowel.

Happy tears sprung to my eyes as I watched my now not-so-little baby take his seat across from me at the table, shoveling four big pancakes onto his plate and topping them with a heaping spoonful of blueberry jam. Jam made from berries he and Felix and I had picked ourselves last summer, when he'd only been half as tall as he was now.

Felix leaned into me, taking his own seat to my left. "I know. They grow up so fast."

I nodded. "I'm afraid if I blink, I'll miss it."

He kissed my temple, reaching over and tangling his fingers with mine, still resting atop the swell of my belly. "Don't worry, Betsy. He's not going anywhere, and neither am I."

I smiled, feeling the love from every corner of the room as I took in the merry mayhem of our blended family. Beneath our hands, I felt a kick.

"And in a couple months, we get to do it all over again."

THE END.

BONUS EPILOGUE

FELIX

A COUPLE MONTHS AFTER THAT...

"*Oh, fuck*, Felix—yes, yes, *yes!*"

Betsy howled as I thrust into her. My hands gripped her wide hips, fingers digging into the soft flesh as she squeezed my cock with her fluttering core. She was bent over the milking bench, her forearms braced against the place her shins would normally occupy, allowing her to rest her head on the stomach support while her teats swung freely beneath her.

I could hear their weight smack the swell of her stomach in concert with the lewd sounds of our thighs crashing against each other in a hot, steady rhythm.

Since she'd grown larger with our child, our normal mating and milking positions had gone by the wayside. We'd gotten more creative, relying more on my upper body strength to provide support when more rigid structures became uncomfortable for her.

This position was one of my favorites, as it allowed me to

rut into her with abandon while also giving her growing body plenty of wiggle room.

And oh, how I *loved* to watch her wiggle.

I curled around her, belting my forearm beneath her hips so I could bury my fingers in her curls and flick at her sensitive nub, as my orgasm built with pulsing urgency. My entire lower body went tight, my legs quaking with anticipation, as my cock pumped inside her again and again.

A delightful squeak filled the air as I rubbed her sweet button, followed by a gasp. I could just picture the pink flush of her cheeks, the plush pout of her lips, as I zeroed in on her pleasure centers with my fingers and my cock. Before long, a low moan began to build in her throat, and it was all I could do to hold on to my control.

"That's it, sweet girl. *Moo* for me. Give me your cream as you come on my cock."

Her mouth opened wider, the moan increasing in volume, hitching with every thrust.

"Oh Felix, I'm gonna come–"

I couldn't help myself. I wanted to touch every part of her delicious body. I wanted to watch her precious face as she fell apart in my arms.

Quickly, I adjusted my grip on Betsy's hips, bending my legs to lift her flush against me. She yelped as I spun around and fell back against the center of the bench, twisting her body so that she faced me as I sat her soaking cunt around my cock. Our heels met on the leg supports at either side of our bodies, hers providing leverage as she rocked into me, mine holding us steady as my hooves dug into the soft leather.

Her torso fell forward as she grabbed the support bar above our heads, placing her nipples exactly where I wanted them.

Directly above my mouth.

"Oh, *yes,* Betsy," I growled, tilting my head to suckle one glorious, leaking tip against my tongue. "Please squirt your release all over me."

"Oh!" She screamed as I pushed my hips up, digging my hooves into the leather as her heels slid off the bench.

But as she fell, her delicious weight sinking down onto my face, I caught her hips with my hands, using the momentum to grind my cockhead into that perfect, intimate spot deep within her core.

Just as I'd promised all those months ago: I would never let her fall.

Unless, of course, it was falling off the edge of pleasure into pure bliss.

She keened above me as I felt her orgasm crash through her, a hot burst of flavorful milk flooding my mouth at the same time as her pussy spasmed uncontrollably around my cock, and it wasn't long before I, too, was coating her insides with my release. But as my shaft twitched and sprayed within her, I felt something… new.

"Felix–*Felix!*" Her tone shifted—subtly, but noticeably—even as her body still shivered with aftershocks. "I think I—ah!"

The full weight of her torso pressed into me as her arms snapped to her stomach. Immediately, I pushed our hips apart, sitting up and rearranging her in my lap without penetrating her.

"What is wrong? Are you alright?"

Her face twisted, breath coming out in laboured huffs.

Laboured…

Labor!

"I think—*ah,*" she gasped as her eyes squinted shut, and that was when I noticed there was a puddle of liquid beneath us. And it wasn't the usual ones. "I think my water just broke."

"I believe you're right." I cradled her to my chest, rising off the bench and practically galloping to the barn entrance. "Here, cover yourself with this."

I snatched her—formerly my—robe off the hook by the door, draping it haphazardly across her chest before stomping across the threshold and back to the farmhouse.

"Petra!" I shouted as I burst into the kitchen. Despite the expansive additions made to the original farmhouse, I always gravitated toward this room first. Thankfully, there was usually someone in here for one reason or another, and I was grateful to see that today was no exception. Jen, one of the mothers, was currently helping two of the children with their science homework at the table, and her eyes widened to the size of dinner plates as she took in our harried (and naked) appearance.

She recovered quickly when she took in Betsy's face, which was still twisted in discomfort.

"Is it time?" She asked me, rising from her chair. I nodded, and she turned to the two children. "Bella, go get Aunt Petra and Mama Katie. Philip, send Iris a dove."

My pulse beat in my neck like a battle drum. "Where do I take her?"

"East wing, fourth bedroom. Turn on the kettle when you get there. I'll grab towels."

The walls blurred past as I thundered through the hallways and up the stairs to the fourth bedroom of the east wing. This was Jen and Katie's domain: the two women had been nurses before coming here to carry their own demigod children to term. They'd helped over a dozen women give birth to Zeus's and Poseidon's children, saving them from the fate Betsy would have faced if Hera and Iris hadn't intervened over a year ago.

"Easy there, big guy, I'm not dying," Betsy huffed in my

arms. She clutched the robe close to her body, the tails of fabric threatening to flap away as the air rushed past us.

"I will not have you in pain." I shoved my shoulder into the fourth door on the right of the second floor hallway, stooping to flick the lightswitch on with my horn. My partner snickered as I thundered toward the bed, only to blink at the white comforter in distress.

"I've got towels!" Katie announced, running into the room and spreading them across the blankets. Carefully, I lowered Betsy down into the fluff, adjusting the robe across her naked body once again.

Her eyes darted down to my crotch, where my erection had long since shrunk back into its furry pocket. I saw relief in her eyes before they squinted with another contraction.

"How far apart are they, do you know?"

Both Jen and Katie were present now, stacking towels, linens, and removing a few tables and bowls from the closet in the corner. Another one of the mothers arrived, heading straight for the electric kettle on the bedstand and crossing to the bathroom to fill it with water.

"Betsy!" A frenzied voice (*finally*, another who seemed as concerned for her safety as I!) sounded from the doorway. In a moment, Petra appeared, curly hair springing from the two symmetrical poofs atop her head. "How ya doin', girl? Better or worse than the last time?"

"Better, no question," the patient grunted. Jen propped a few pillows under her knees, and she relaxed into the new position, eyes closing in relief as her contraction passed. "The horns are still a sonofabitch, but my whole pelvis seems wide enough to handle it this time."

A fire of pride spread through my chest. *I'd* helped make that happen. Prepare her body for the birth of a minotaur child.

Our child.

"What are you doing all the way over there, Daddy? Get over here and squeeze your wifey's hand!" Petra's bright eyes narrowed as she huffed at me.

Betsy's brow gave an uncertain wiggle. "Maybe after he puts some pants on?"

"You are more important than pants," I said, wedging myself in between Petra and the nightstand and wiping a few sweaty wisps of chestnut-colored strands from Betsy's forehead. Jen and Katie shared a look, but Petra spoke up before either of them could protest.

"That's right. Pretty sure all of us here have seen a penis before. Lord knows we've changed enough diapers by now."

My face heated. "My penis is a great deal larger than any of the ones you've seen *in diapers.*"

Katie covered her mouth, pink blooming across her cheekbones as she appeared to hold in laughter. Betsy reached across her chest to pat my hand. "We know, Felix."

"Who's got the timer?"

"Me!" Apollo rushed in, practically tripping over his long, skinny legs, waving a stopwatch as he answered Jen. "How long ago was the last one?"

"Lo!" Betsy frantically pushed the silky pink fabric covering her torso down between her legs, which, at their current angle, were granting anyone who entered the room an unencumbered view of her lower lips. "Get out of here!"

"What? Philip said my little sister was on the way!" The young male looked affronted. While, physically and cognitively, he was about the equivalent of seventeen in human years, he was still much like a child socially. It would still be several years before he was through puberty, and a decade or more before he was fully mature. The gap between his cognitive capability and his emotional maturity, or any of the other demigods inhabiting the house, was a bit of a minefield for us adults. We were still figuring out how best to navigate it. "I'm not going to peek or anything! I'm helping!"

A high-pitched *beep* punctuated his statement as he started the stopwatch. His mother dragged her hand from my grip and covered her face.

"Lo, grab your mother's other hand." I tilted my horns toward the opposite side of the bed. "And Petra, will you get her something thicker to cover herself?"

"On it!"

"*Felix*," Betsy hissed. "I don't want him in here while I'm pushing! He's too young to see this!"

"Mom, I helped with two other labors this summer! Didn't I, Mama Jen?"

We all stared at the blonde-haired nurse expectantly.

"Um. He did get me more towels when I asked."

"See? I helped!"

"Lo, I'm about to be in a lot of pain. I'd rather you not be here when I star—*ohfuckingchristonagoddamncrackerrrrr—*"

His eyes widened as she squeezed my hand, the curses fading on a long exhale as Katie caught Betsy's eye and breathed with her.

Hee hee hoooo, he he hoo.

I squeezed back, matching her rhythm, and placed my other hand on her thigh.

Gods, she was incredible.

I'd purposely avoided assisting in any of the other deliveries that had taken place since Hera had declared my farm to be the official birthing center and daycare for the gods' half-humanoid offspring. In truth, other than managing the farm and watching after Betsy and Apollo, I'd tried to keep a respectful distance from the other mothers and their children. While at first I'd done it to be respectful of Betsy's and my relationship, the situation had evolved until I was something closer to an uncle to the other young demigods. The mixed family dynamics had been rocky at first, but the mothers eventually came to appreciate my reserve, as none of their children had ever confused me for their father.

Apollo, however…

When the three of us were by ourselves, Betsy and I would let him call me "Dad." It was a term I'd come to adore. But among the other kids, we'd been careful to make sure he called me by my name so as not to make the others jealous.

It was when Apollo had been old enough to understand the difference, around four months or so, that Betsy and I decided to try for a child who would have no reason not to call me father. Now that all the young demigods were mature enough to appreciate my relationship with Apollo and his mother, we could finally begin our own family without fear of alienating the rest of our family-by-happenstance.

Katie peeked her head from the sheet that Petra had acquired to afford my love a little more modesty. "Girl, you're already at five centimeters. How did you not notice this sooner? By my estimates, you've probably been dilating for two hours already!"

Betsy and I met eyes, before quickly looking away. I'd taken her in the barn for milking close to three hours ago, and one thing had led to another…

"Oh gods," Jen winced. "No wonder things are moving so quick. You already stretched her out."

My mind raced, darting back to the moment I'd spilled myself inside her, pushing deep to feel an odd sensation at the peak of her channel. Almost like a ring that had kissed the crown of my flared head and…

Hades' beard. Had that been her cervix? Her… *dilating* cervix?

My cheeks burned. Betsy closed her eyes and sighed.

"Can we *not* discuss this in front of my son, please?"

"Discuss what? You dilating? Mama Jen covered that in

biology! That's when your pelvis opens up to let the baby through, right? I think it's great that Dad could help!" Apollo, technically correct but completely oblivious, smiled at me. "How do you even stretch a pelvis? Is it like some kind of special yoga?"

"We'll have time for the birds and the bees later," Katie waved, cutting him off. "Apollo, give Aunt Petra the timer and go down to the big kitchen to get ice chips from the fridge. We need a whole bowl of them."

He glanced between his mother and the rest of us, hesitating. "Um... okay... but don't have my sister without me!"

"Lo—" I started to growl, but he tossed the timer to Petra and darted out of the room before I could discipline him any further.

I shook my head. "Someone shut the door, please."

SEVERAL HOURS LATER, after the four of us had taken turns cleaning up Betsy and the delivery room, we let Apollo back in to meet his little sister.

"That wasn't very nice—" he began, only for his frustration to disappear the second he laid eyes on the tiny minotaur in his mother's arms. "Is that her?"

"Apollo, this is Cora," she said, tilting her arms forward so he could get a clearer view of her peaceful, sleeping face.

He stepped forward, silent for once, as he took in the little life. It had been all I could do to relinquish my own hold of her when it'd been time for her first feeding, and I'd fallen in love with Betsy all over again as she'd nursed our perfect, beautiful baby girl.

Cora. I reached out my fingers as carefully as I dared, barely tickling the gossamer-fine curls between the tiny nubs on her head. A little hoof poked out of the crocheted blanket Mama Jo had crafted for her.

"Would you like to hold her?" Betsy asked, voice slightly hoarse from the hours of pushing.

He nodded, and as I watched her carefully place the tiny bundle into his arms, I felt a hand on my shoulder.

"We'll give the four of you a moment," Jen whispered. "Just let us know if she needs anything, yeah?"

"Yes, thank you," I said, hoping that my eyes communicated exactly just how grateful I was.

Watching a human woman—but especially *Betsy*—give birth, was one of the most terrifying experiences of my life. Though I knew that all of the women in the room had been through over a dozen Olympian births in the past year alone, the horrors of watching the face of the most precious person in my life twist in pain because of something *I'd* put inside her had just about torn me apart from the inside out. Every physical pain she felt had echoed in my very soul. All I could do was endure her unbelievably strong squeezes as she curled her fingers around mine, wipe the sweat from her brow, and scratch my claws gently into her scalp to sooth away whatever stress I could.

After, when Jen had brought the babe to me—a writhing, screaming, red-faced little thing, my eyes had been so thoroughly obscured by tears I could barely make out her precious snout.

As I'd blinked my vision clear, her perfect face stared back up at me. My *daughter*.

I was a father.

Betsy had made me a father.

Then it had been my turn to squeeze, as I'd laced my furry fingers in between Betsy's soft ones, and knelt beside the bed to admire our child together.

"Congratulations, Daddy," she'd whispered, and my vision had swum once again. I'd closed my eyes, tilted my head into hers and twisted to press my lips to her forehead.

"You are incredible," I'd breathed, the words woefully inadequate. "Look at the miracle you made."

"*We* made."

Despite the exhaustion painted in every line of her face, she'd lifted her arm and laid it over mine, stroking her hand over Cora's beautifully soft head. And the three of us snuggled like that for minutes, the outside world fading away until the urgent knocking at the door had broken us out of our happy bubble.

"That'll be your older brother, Cora," Betsy had whispered, waggling the baby's fist that was wrapped around her finger. "What do you say you meet the whole family?"

Family.

As Apollo cradled his little sister, and Betsy leaned into my side as I rubbed her shoulders, my heart swelled with love and gratitude.

And for the first time in millennia, I thanked the gods.

WHERE CAN I READ MORE?!

If you loved this story, and you're wondering: when will the rest of the series be out?? You should sign up for my newsletter!

Any updates about future releases, special editions, book boxes, and more will be sent out weekly to everyone who gives me their email at www.cassandramedcalf.com/subscribe . It's the best way to keep in touch.

And there's always more spice, bonus scenes, new stories, and NSFW art on my Patreon! Get new chapters weekly, plus my ebooks & audiobooks for free when you subscribe at www.patreon.com/cassandramedcalf .

ACKNOWLEDGMENTS

There is no way I would be able to do what I do without the endless support of my partner, Andy. Herner, you are the absolute light of my life. My biggest cheerleader, my support system, and my best friend. And now, also, my *editor?!* I love you and the puppies more than I will ever be able to put into words (and considering I'm a romance author, that's saying something!). Thank you for putting up with my early mornings and late nights as I claw my way into a *hopefully* successful author career.

I am so fortunate to have a supportive family, even if I'm never letting them read this book. Mom, Dad, Kelley, and yes, you too, Sue (since I APPARENTLY HAVE TO CALL YOU OUT BY NAME NOW)—you all have always been my biggest fans, and I am so grateful for you.

So many authors are an inspiration to me (you can check out the list in Kraken's Castaway for more), but I would be remiss if I didn't mention Kathryn Moon and the worlds she creates. They are my happy place, and I love disappearing there.

I'm also lucky to be part of an amazingly supportive writer's group called The Bi+ Book Gang, led by the incredible Bailey Merlin. Y'all kept me writing through some of my toughest times this year, and the book wouldn't have gotten done without you. Thank you so much!

And finally, my readers! A few of you go above and beyond to support me on Patreon, and I cannot tell you how grateful I am. This year has been a tight one for me, and there have been months where Patreon has kept the puppies fed. So thank you. Thank you, thank you, thank you SO much for supporting me and reading along as I write my monster smut:

Danielle S

Judy

Bryce N

Jess T

Kitt3n Bree

Terri V

Cyrus

And my beta readers, without whom I would not have been able to release this book:

B.M. Light

Kaiidth

THANK YOU SO MUCH!

ABOUT THE AUTHOR

Cassandra Medcalf is a writer, narrator, audio engineer, food enthusiast, wine taster, do-it-yourselfer, and an amateur film critic (despite barely having seen any movies). She lives in Duluth, MN with her adorable husband and their even more adorable dogs. You can follow her and her family's hare-brained schemes and lofty pursuits on her website, cassandramedcalf.com (or, if you're just here for the smut, on Instagram @CassandraMedcalfVO).

ALSO BY CASSANDRA MEDCALF

STAND-ALONES

Fowl Play, A Small Town Sports Romance

FIXER UPPER SERIES - LGBT SMALL TOWN ROMANCE

Betting on the House

Betting on the Bird

Hot Rod Hookups

Here Comes the Bride

FOR THE LOVE OF TITANS SERIES - LGBT PARANORMAL ROMANCE

The Kraken's Castaway

Bride of the Kraken

www.ingramcontent.com/pod-product-compliance
Lightning Source LLC
Chambersburg PA
CBHW020907060726
47591CB00004B/1129